Praise for

Rising to the level of literary excellence... Donald Lystra's genuine flair for creating memorable characters and a distinctive, narrative-driven storytelling style that quickly engages the reader's total attention from start to finish.

— *Midwest Book Review*

Searching for Van Gogh is a captivating book about pain and healing, about the search for personal identity and meaning in the face of loss....Lystra masterfully blends personal and social aspects, constructing a story that remains vivid in the reader's memory long after finishing.... Inspired and deeply satisfying.

— *Historical Fiction Company* review

I was swept up in it from the first page and never doubted that I was in the hands of a master storyteller.

— Jerry Dennis, author of best-selling *The Living Great Lakes*, and many other works

I got as invested in these characters as I would in real people. Audrey is an especially rich character—absolutely convincing, multi-faceted, with a core of mystery. Highly recommended!

— ANDY MOZINA, AUTHOR OF CRITICALLY-ACCLAIMED NOVEL *TANDEM* AND OTHER WORKS OF FICTION

This is fine writing of the highest caliber. My very highest recommendation.

— TIM BAZZETT, AUTHOR OF *SOLDIER BOY* AND FOUR OTHER TITLES

Superbly told coming-of-age story. Magically, the author transforms Audrey Brubaker, with all her eccentricities and flaws, into the ideal mentor for Nate Walker (the narrator)....An excellent book.

— DENNIS TURNER, AUTHOR OF BESTSELLING *WHAT DID YOU DO DURING THE WAR, SISTER*

Searching for Van Gogh by Donald Lystra is an immensely enjoyable read and one that will stay with you long after you have turned the last page. I highly recommend.

— MARY ANNE YARDE, THE COFFEE POT BOOK CLUB

Well-crafted, thought-provoking, coming-of-age novel ... rewarding readers with its reveal of emotions, secrets, and innuendos throughout.

— *BLUEINK* REVIEW

Praise for Donald Lystra's Previous Works

Rich and wise and beautifully written....this novel again and again reminded me of why I fell in love with writing....the sudden but hard-won insights seem intensely real and right.

— Ellen Akins, *Minneapolis Star Tribune*

Lystra's graceful prose is evocative of place and time....This is a rich and satisfying read.

— Donna Marchetti, The *Cleveland Plain Dealer*

...luminous....a stellar collection of masterfully crafted gems.

— *BOOKLIST*, American Library Association

Lystra draws the bleak, beautiful landscape of the Great Lakes region in quick, sharp strokes, and brings its inhabitants to life with compassion and tenderness.

— *Kansas City Star*, Christine Pivovar

There's a transcendency (in the book) common to all good coming-of-age novels.

— *Time Out Chicago* magazine

There is a kind of innocence....that has not been so effectively portrayed since Salinger created Holden Caulfield. Lystra's style is spare and direct and yet profoundly evocative....An absolutely stunning debut.

— BIG RAPIDS (MI) *PIONEER*

(The final story) illuminates the themes and patterns that precede it and in so doing illuminates life....I won't forget this beautiful piece and what Lystra accomplishes in it and in this wise book.

— *MINNEAPOLIS STAR TRIBUNE*, ANTHONY BUKOSKI

Of the several dozen books I have reviewed for publication...few have given me the pleasure I find in Lystra's *Something that Feels like Truth*. In these stories, Lystra explores with intelligence and empathy those moments, often very quiet, when people make the decisions that will change their lives.....I can't recommend *Something That Feels Like Truth* highly enough.

— KEITH TAYLOR, POET AND AUTHOR; DIRECTOR, UNIVERSITY OF MICHIGAN BEAR RIVER WRITERS' CONFERENCE

What makes these 16 stories work is their portrayal of life in the Great Lakes region. They swell with empathy and a knowledge of the land and of the people who populate it.

— *CLEVELAND PLAIN DEALER*, VIDAS TURAKHIA

Searching for Van Gogh

A Novel

Donald Lystra

Copyright © 2024 by Donald Lystra

ISBN (ebook): 979-8-9897724-1-4
ISBN (Paperback): 979-8-9897724-0-7
ISBN (Hardback): 979-8-9897724-2-1

Cover Design by Sandy Robson

Title Production by The Bookwhisperer

Published by Omena Hills Press, Traverse City, Michigan.

All rights reserved.

No part of this book may be reproduced in any form or by any electronic or mechanical means, including information storage and retrieval systems, without written permission from the author, except for the use of brief quotations in a book review.

"If you hear a voice within you say you cannot paint, then by all means paint."

— Vincent Van Gogh

Chapter One

Audrey Brubaker said it was completely innocent. She wanted to be perfectly clear on that point. She had gotten the idea, she said, from that movie with Audrey Hepburn, *Breakfast at Tiffany's*, where a young woman in New York City hangs out with rich businessmen and gets paid for going out to dinner and being nice to them, and she believed the similarities—having the same first name and being a country girl trying to make it in a big city—was a sort of providential message. What she would do, she said, was to go in the afternoon to the lobby of one of the big hotels—the Saxony or the Cosmopolitan or the Pantlind—and strike up a conversation with a man who looked like a successful businessman. After making small talk for a while, which she was good at, she would ask him if he'd like to take a walking tour of downtown Grand Rapids. Almost always the businessman would say yes. And then she would take him for a walk around the city, explaining the history and pointing out the important buildings and who the streets were named for and what the statues were about. When the walking tour was over the man would give her ten or twenty dollars, and often he would ask her to have dinner with him.

"And that's my livelihood," Audrey said. "That and the Rexall lunch counter."

"What if the men, you know, get fresh?"

She gave me a crafty smile, as if she was going to tell me something interesting that I would like to know about.

"They almost never do," she said. "Businessmen are lonely, more than anything else. They just want someone to listen to their jokes or sit with them on a park bench while they brag about their kids or pour out their tales of woe."

"But what if they *do* get fresh?"

"There are ways to handle it," she said. "A hug or a kiss on the cheek will go a long way." She looked at me with a knowing expression, as if she were letting me in on a secret only a few people understood. "In my opinion, sex is oversold."

We were sitting in the Starlight Lounge after one of Audrey's clients—a Mr. Smollett of the North American Ball Bearing Company—had walked out. I sat back in the booth with Smollett's drink in my hand and I thought about what Audrey had said and whether I could believe her. I tried to picture her hugging Mr. Smollett and whether that would work. Whether that would be enough.

"I saw that movie with Audrey Hepburn," I said. "I saw it last year with my girlfriend. And I remember the girl went out to dinner with rich businessmen. But I don't remember her giving tours."

"I added that part," Audrey said. "I think it's an improvement, frankly. It's like I'm doing them—the men—a little favor, like Dale Carnegie says you're supposed to do."

That was another one of her peculiarities, a passion for Dale Carnegie and how he could teach you how to win friends and influence people so you could have a better life. But I'm getting ahead of myself. I should probably say how I met Audrey in the first place because that explains a lot about what came later, like the time we broke into Audrey's parent's house, and our trip to northern Michigan to bring my brother's body home. That would be the logical place to start, which is something, logic, I think I'm pretty good at.

Chapter Two

I had seen her for three days in a row. She would come walking along the sidewalk in the late afternoon, just above the spot where I had set up my easel along the riverbank, and she would stop and watch me paint, leaning forward with her forearms resting on the rusted iron railing, and with the tall downtown buildings rising up behind, and with the breeze from the river blowing out her long dark hair and making the white cotton dress flutter around her legs.

At first we didn't talk. But on the second day I turned and nodded slightly and she smiled and nodded back. But I didn't say anything. Not a single word. It wasn't shyness because I had a girlfriend the year before and we had been in love and I had learned about girls in that way, learned that they are not the strange exotic creatures I'd thought them to be, but just another type of human being. It was more about my painting; I'd only started doing it a few weeks earlier and I was still self-conscious, part of me unsure whether it was genuine or just an effort to give some meaning to my life.

This was in the fall of 1963, when I was seventeen and working in a factory and trying to be an artist. In June I'd graduated from high school in a suburb of Detroit but instead of going off to study electrical engineering at a university, as I'd always planned, I had argued with my father about the cost of college and the argument had ended, finally, with my decision to find a job so I could support myself. Pay my own way in the world. Have the freedom of that.

So I was working in a car factory in Grand Rapids, helping the electricians who wired the giant machines that made parts for Oldsmobiles and Buicks. I rented a sleeping room in the house of a retired couple on Fulton Street, just across from the park and the zoo, and I'd bought a '48 Pontiac Star Chief to get around in. Most days, after getting off work at the car factory, I would drive to a place along the river and take my artist gear and find a spot to paint. The spot where I was working then was on a walking path just a couple of feet above the water; it gave a view out onto the wide river with its ripples and cascades, and the abandoned furniture factories lined up along the far shore, and downstream to the Sixth Street Bridge with its complicated iron work and with the cars going over, the sunlight flashing off the glass and metal like little explosions. I felt, in the artistic way I was trying to think about the world, that that combination of things—the turbulent water and the sad decaying factories and the complicated iron bridge—said something about the world that was true and important, if I could just get it down on canvas.

On the third day the girl called out, "You're using the wrong color."

I turned and saw her standing up above me on the sidewalk. My first instinct was to ignore her, because I was deep into my painting and I didn't want to break my concentration. But then my better manners broke through.

"What color are you talking about?" I had to raise my voice so it'd carry up to her.

"The color of that old factory." She pointed across the river.

"That one over there." She wiggled her finger to emphasize where she was pointing.

I knew exactly what she meant because it was something I had thought about, the proper color of the factory in my painting, and I had decided finally to show it as red, or deep red, which I thought would suggest rust and decay and deterioration, and deepen the experience of looking at my painting.

"What it is in real life doesn't matter," I said. I paused, wondering if I should say more. "It's an artistic decision," I added, though immediately I regretted saying those words because they sounded pompous and false. Something I hadn't yet earned the right to say.

"Can I come down and show you?" Without waiting for an answer the girl ducked under the iron railing and came down the dirt path that angled back and forth across the slope, her shoes slipping a little on the steep ground so that she had to grab branches and pieces of shrubbery to keep from falling.

"You see," she said. She was a little breathless from coming down the bank. "I'm talking about that factory right there. The brown one with all the broken windows." She pointed to the factory, then turned to my painting and gestured to where I'd shown it on the canvas. "You've made it red."

"Like I said, it doesn't matter that it's different from real life. I'm trying to interpret it artistically, not reproduce it exactly the same."

The girl looked at me, raising one hand to shield her eyes from the low setting sun, which was behind my back and shining on her face. She looked at me for a long time, then she smiled.

"Orange will work better," she said, "because it's a complimentary color to the blue." She pointed to the blue water in my painting. "They're complimentary colors, orange and blue are. They'll make your statement bolder."

I didn't know what to say then. I had thought the girl was

speaking from ignorance but her comment about complimentary colors made me think she knew something about painting, and perhaps more than me. Which wouldn't have been hard because I'd only started doing it that summer and had no training. But I had studied mechanical drafting in high school and from that I'd learned about perspective and how objects look when you see them from different directions, and I had read the *Time-Life* series about the great painters of Europe, and I had read the letters from Vincent Van Gogh to his brother, Theo, where he spoke about the passion he brought to his work and how he was guided by that passion to make great paintings. With only that much preparation I thought I could make worthwhile paintings myself if I could find the right attitude to do it with, the correct passion, you might say, for being an artist.

"You need to know about color theory," the girl said now. "It tells you what colors go together and which ones don't. If you're going to be any good as an artist that's something you need to know."

"I guess you must be an artist yourself."

She laughed. "I suppose I'm as much an artist as you are." But right away I saw her face show regret for being so blunt and she tried to correct herself. "Though you do have some talent. I'll give you that." She gestured toward the painting. "The way you've shown the bridge with all those wavy lines is very interesting. Like it's not completely solid but has an unsteady quality like the flowing water." She looked at me. "Like it's as temporary as the water, which, in a way, it is." She shrugged. "Anyway, that's what I get out of it."

I had been looking at the girl while she said these things. She seemed a little older than me, though I couldn't tell you exactly why, with dark eyes and a small mouth tinged with bright red lipstick. She had a face that you could look at for a long time and not feel uncomfortable, and I thought she was pretty, too, though in a way some people might not see or understand.

"Maybe I'll study it," I said. "The color theory."

We were silent then for a while, neither of us knowing what to say next, perhaps, now that the subject of the factory color had been exhausted. Out on the river the last rays of sun were touching the crests of the turbulent water, and the factories were covered now in deep shadows.

"How does it happen that you know so much about painting?" I asked, which was a way I was trying to talk then. I mean saying "how does it happen" and phrases such as that.

"I sit in on classes at the Kendall Design School," she said. She turned away and looked out onto the water, as if something there had suddenly caught her eye. "But I'm not exactly a student because I can't afford the tuition." She kept looking out at the water. "I'm learning about furniture design, which is what I plan to do some day. Kendall's where all the famous furniture designers teach. Eero Saarinen is one. Charlie Eames is another. I suppose you've heard of them."

The names meant nothing to me, but I didn't say it. Instead I said: "I didn't know you could sit in on classes if you weren't enrolled."

"Officially you're not supposed to. But some of the professors, if you're nice to them, will let you do it. And sometimes..." she moved her gaze away from the river and back onto my face. "Sometimes I just sit in the hall outside the classroom and listen through the door." She shrugged, as if what she'd said was of no importance.

"That's interesting," I said, although the thought of her sitting in a hallway listening to a lecture through the door seemed very odd.

"I work, too," she said. "I work at the lunch counter at the Rexall drug store on Leonard Street. And I do other things, too, here and there." She made a lopsided grin. "A girl has to do what she has to do to get by."

She turned then and walked over to the edge of the river, as if she'd suddenly lost interest in our conversation. She leaned down and picked up a rock and threw it out into the water, reaching back like a baseball player and sending it far out from shore.

"And what about you?" she asked. She was looking at the splash her rock had made. "What brings you here. A young boy painting in the jungle along a river."

"I'm not so young," I said. "And this isn't exactly a jungle." I gestured up toward the tall downtown buildings.

"Okay," she said. "Those are good points." She turned around and looked at me. "But my question still stands."

At first I thought I should say something about my brother Gary, because I knew my painting had something to do with him. But I didn't have the words to explain that yet—or to talk about it in any way—and so I said nothing.

"All right," the girl said, "have it your way." She walked up close and stared into my face. "The witness has chosen not to answer, your honor," she said. "We'll note that in the record. But it'll be held against him." She started to walk away. "Adios, amigo," she said.

"I thought I could learn something from it," I blurted out before she'd reached the path. She stopped and turned around. "Painting. I thought it could—you know—let me see more deeply into life."

She looked at me, waiting for me to say more.

"In school I took the math and science courses," I said. "But those things never seem to take you anywhere. Anywhere that's important about your life." I stopped talking and glanced from side to side, as if I was hoping someone would emerge from the bushes to make sense of what I was trying to say. "I've done some reading about painters," I continued. "They seem to get something out of it. More than just what their pictures are about; something about what's below the surface of what they paint. What's really true." I raised my hand to make a gesture

9

but stopped halfway because no further words came to mind. No words to use the gesture for.

"Anyway," I said, and I let my arm fall back down to my side. "I thought I'd try to do it."

The girl looked at me, her eyes narrowed, as if I were a puzzle she was trying to understand. Then she said: "Well, hurray for you. The witness is trying to understand the world, your honor. Let's wish him good luck." She turned and started toward the path.

"Wait a minute," I said. She stopped and looked back. "I think I'm finished for today. The light's no good now." I gestured out across the river at the shadowed factories and at the water, dull now and unsparkling. "Do you want to go somewhere and talk? Maybe you can tell me more about color theory."

"I can't," the girl said. "I have an engagement at seven."

"Can I see you again."

She smiled. "I suppose that'd be acceptable. Just call the Arlington Hotel and ask for Audrey Brubaker in room 334. And bring your latest painting. I'd like to see how you're progressing on that front."

"Okay," I said, though I was surprised to learn she lived in a hotel. "And next time I'll know about the color theory."

"Okay," she said. "It's a deal then."

She took another step in the direction of the bank, but again she stopped and turned back.

"You wouldn't happen to own a car, would you?" she asked.

"I do. It's not much but it runs."

"Maybe you can do me a favor sometime. I have a secret mission that'll require a car. That could be your payback for me telling you about color theory."

I laughed. "What's the secret mission?"

"If I told you it wouldn't be a secret, would it."

"I'll need to know where we're going if you expect me to supply the transportation."

"That's true," she said. She stopped and cast her gaze off to the side. "But you don't need to know about it ahead of time." She pointed a finger at me. "I'll tell you what. I'll let you know just before we leave on the mission. Then you can decide if you want to do it." She looked at me, her eyes squinted down to narrow slits. "Though if you decline I'm afraid I'll have to kill you." She made a motion of holding a revolver and shooting me, her hand jerking as she fired off each imaginary shot. Then she turned and started up the dirt path, reaching forward to grab branches and sometimes placing her hand flat against the hard bare ground.

Chapter Three

When I got back to the house on Fulton Street it was already getting dark. The streetlights were coming on, casting shadows of tree branches onto the empty pavement. I parked in the alley behind the house and walked around to the front door. As I came up the steps onto the porch I saw the orange glow of a cigarette in the corner. When I looked closer, I saw it was my mother. She was sitting on the glider, rocking slightly.

"Hello, Nathan," she said from out of the darkness.

"This is a surprise," I said.

I went over and bent down and kissed her on the cheek. She was dressed in clothes I had never seen her wear before: blue jeans and a heavy gray sweater and scuffed white tennis shoes. Her hair was different too: parted in the middle and pulled back along both sides and held in clumps with rubber bands.

"What are you doing here?" I asked.

She smiled, holding the cigarette awkwardly to one side. "I drove over this afternoon to see you. I have an adventure to propose. A mother and son adventure." She paused to take a quick puff from her cigarette. Then she smiled again.

"I'm going to drive to Camp Carlisle and make arrangements to bring your brother home. I'd like you to come along. For company. And to teach you something about family obligations."

I picked up a metal lawn chair and brought it over and sat down beside her.

"Don't you think that would be a good idea?" she said. "For you to come along with your poor old mother?"

"You're not old," I said. "And you and Dad aren't poor."

This was true. My father was the son of a bus driver but he'd worked as a salesman for the National Cash Register Company and had made his way up through the ranks to become an executive at the central offices in Detroit. During the time he was getting his promotions our family had moved from one sales territory to another, never staying long enough to feel like we belonged. I still felt that way, like an outsider, always ignorant about the local rules that show you're in a place where you fit in.

My mother squinted through the roiling cloud of smoke she had just exhaled. "Okay," she said. "I take it back about being poor."

I looked at her, wondering if she was serious. Gary had been killed in March in a shooting range accident at Camp Carlisle in northern Michigan while taking basic training in the Army. My parents had been in Italy at the time, on vacation with a tour group from the Elks Club, and I'd been off on a camping trip in the Manistee Forest. The Army people couldn't locate any family members to tell them what to do with Gary's body so they'd buried him in the cemetery at Camp Carlisle. With full honors and a 21-gun salute, they'd said, as if that would make us feel better about Gary being dead. But my mother wasn't satisfied with her first son being in a military cemetery in northern Michigan and she'd tried to get my father to bring Gary home. Gary wasn't a soldier, she'd said. He was a talented pianist who had no business being in the Army. But my father had resisted. He'd fought with Patton up through the boot of Italy and he believed in military service. It had been his idea for Gary to enlist; the Army would make a better man of him, he'd said. Put some steel into his spine, which he badly needed. Now Gary would rest among his Army comrades. Not the worst thing that could happen to a person in this world.

"Well?" my mother said to me now. "What's the verdict?"

"I've got commitments here," I said. "I can't just drop everything in a moment's notice."

"Like what?" she said. "Tell me about your commitments."

I looked at her. I wasn't used to hearing her speak in such a blunt way.

"Well, there's my job for one thing."

"Don't try to kid me," my mother said. "It's not a serious job. I daresay they have other workers who can help the electricians wire the machines. Or whatever it is they have you doing there." She raised her cigarette but stopped before it reached her lips. "Though I don't mean to denigrate your hard work, Nathan," she said. "Or to suggest that you're not well versed in electricity."

"Okay," I said. "Maybe it isn't such a great job. But what about my painting? I'm learning things that are making me a better painter."

"That's a valid point," my mother said, and she nodded in a slow thoughtful way. "I know painting's important to you now. Though I can't say I know exactly why. I always thought you were cut more from the cloth of an Einstein than a Rembrandt." She was silent for a moment, staring out toward the street where cars were going by. "But you can bring your....equipment....or whatever you call it. Your brushes and tubes of paint and whatnot, and we can stop every day for a session of painting. An hour or two, would that be about right?"

"What about Dad?" I asked. "What does he say about this?"

My mother looked away. I saw her face harden. "He doesn't know about it yet," she said. "He doesn't even know I've come over here this afternoon." She looked back out onto Fulton Street where a car was trailing black smoke from its exhaust. She followed the car with her gaze until it went out of sight around the corner, then she turned back to me and smiled. "But it doesn't matter. This isn't his project. It's mine."

"All right," I said. "But there's another matter."

My mother inhaled from her cigarette and blew the smoke out fast, so that it made a sound coming through her lips. I think she was trying to show exasperation with my objections.

"I've met a girl," I said. "I'm just getting to know her."

"Oh my," my mother said with a teasing smile. "Romance has entered the picture."

"Not romance," I said. "Just an interesting girl I've met."

"What does she do? This interesting girl."

"She's a student at the Kendall School. She studies furniture design. And she works in a drug store to earn money."

"I see," my mother said, and she repeated the words "furniture design" as if there was a hidden meaning there. Then she said: "She could come along. If she was willing to miss a few days of classes she could come along."

"It's not that simple," I said. "I've promised her I'd help with something. A project. Some sort of project."

"My, my," my mother said. "You are in great demand for favors from helpless women."

This time it was my turn to show exasperation. I got up and walked across the porch, standing with my hands in my back pockets and looking over at the zoo where there was a pond with ducks and swans and peacocks strutting on the banks. I stared for a long time without saying anything. Then, still looking across at the pond, I said: "Why are you doing this,

Mom? Gary's been dead for five months. Why are you doing this now?"

And that was when she started to cry. She tossed the burning cigarette over the porch railing and started to cry. I moved over to comfort her, but she raised a hand to stop me. So I was left standing there, feeling awkward and stupid and useless.

Chapter Four

When I saw that my mother didn't want my help, I left to take a walk to give her time to settle down. When I got back, Mrs. Thatcher came out onto the porch as I was coming up the front steps. "Your mother's inside," she said. "I had her lie down in the bedroom in back. The poor woman was quite distraught."

"That was very nice of you," I said.

"Maybe she should spend the night here."

"Thank you. I'll go up and tell her."

My mother was lying on the bed asleep. Her eyes were red and swollen but otherwise she seemed to be all right. She lay on her back with one arm angled across her stomach and the other lying at her side. Her mouth was slightly open. I could hear the faint sound of her breathing.

I went over and untied the tennis shoes and slipped them off her feet. Then I put my hand on her shoulder and looked down into her face until she opened her eyes.

"Oh, hello Nathan," she said in a drowsy voice. "I must have fallen asleep."

"That's all right," I said. "Mrs. Thatcher says you can stay here tonight."

She smiled and raised her arm and touched my face, cupping her hand so it fit against my cheek. "This isn't the way it's supposed to work," she said. "I'm your mother. I'm supposed to take care of you, not the other way around." She turned her face away and looked off to the side. "Though I didn't do such a good job with your brother, did I?"

"That didn't have anything to do with you, Mom," I said. "It was an accident."

"I don't mean the shooting. I mean that he was there at all. In the Army. I should have stopped it."

There was a folded blanket on a side chair and I went over and shook it out and covered my mother with it. She rolled onto her side and pulled the blanket up under her chin. "I'll see you in the morning then," she said.

"Right," I said. "I'll see you in the morning."

I left the bedroom, drawing the door closed behind me, and went downstairs to where there was a phone on a side table in the dining room. I dialed the number of our house in the Detroit suburb. My father answered after two rings. I could hear some desperation in the way he spoke.

"It's me," I said. "I thought you should know that Mom's here. At the house where I stay in Grand Rapids."

"Grand Rapids," he said. "What in the world is she doing there? I was ready to call the police."

"It's okay," I said. "Everything's fine. She upstairs asleep now. She was tired and now she's asleep."

"Listen, Nate," my father said. "I'll be there in three hours. I'll drive over tonight and bring her back."

"That's not necessary," I said. "She's fine now. There's no emergency. She can drive herself home tomorrow."

"Nate, I'm coming over."

There was a long silence while neither of us spoke. I thought about the arguments we'd had last spring and I had a momentary urge to tell him to go to hell, but that wasn't something I could say to him. During all our arguments, I had never raised my voice or been insulting. When I decided to take the job at the car factory in Grand Rapids I simply told him my decision and walked away. I wanted to make it clear that he had no say in the matter if I was willing to pay for everything myself.

"Don't you want to know why she drove over here?" I asked.

He didn't answer.

"She wants to go to Camp Carlisle and make arrangements to bring Gary home. And she wanted me to go with her."

"Christ," he muttered.

"Maybe it's a good idea, Dad. I can see how it'd be nice to have Gary back where we are. I was thinking of going with her."

"Listen, Nate. It's not a good idea. Bringing Gary home would only open wounds that are just starting to heal. Gary's dead. It's a great tragedy but your mother has to learn to live with it."

I stood holding the phone. And suddenly I realized that calling my father was not just a simple thing that I had done but a sort of betrayal of my mother. And I felt the sudden weight of it, the weight of it on my conscience, I guess.

"Losing a son is a terrible thing for a mother," my father continued. "And Gary was so special to her. I suppose you know that better than anyone."

"Why don't you let me drive her home tomorrow, Dad? We can leave early and be there before noon." I was thinking that driving back tomorrow would give me time to talk with her and make it seem better. Not so much of a betrayal.

There was a pause before my father spoke. "I'll be there as soon as I can make it, Nate. I'll meet you outside the house."

I said okay and hung up the phone.

19

I HAD three hours to kill before my father would arrive so I decided to walk over to the zoo. I had found a way to get inside after they closed the gates at eight—an opening in the chain link fence behind the Monkey Island—and I liked to go there after dark and walk among the animals. Most of the time you couldn't see the animals because they were in their dens asleep, but it was exciting, still, to walk and feel the wildness around you. I liked to go there during the day, too, because I'd found it was a place where you could sometimes meet a girl. In a zoo there is always something to talk about—something having to do with the animals that are nearby—so if you met a girl you were never at a loss for something to say, and sometimes, if the talking was going well, you could take a girl's hand, just casually, as if you hadn't really thought about it, and you could walk together for a while and feel there was a bond between you. Almost always a girl would let you hold her hand, and sometimes a girl might let you kiss her, affectionately or even with a bit of passion. I was seventeen and living alone and working in a factory and it was nice to walk in the afternoon with a girl and to have her care a little bit about me, even though it wasn't a serious caring and I would probably never see her again.

After a while I left the zoo and walked back to the house on Fulton Street. I sat on the glider on the front porch and waited for my father. It was very late, one or two o'clock, and I was very tired. For a while I tried to stay awake by thinking about the girl I'd been in love with the year before—Diane was her name—and to remember some particular thing that we had done together, the exact words we had spoken back and forth, and how she had been dressed, and how her face looked when she had something interesting to say or a joke to tell. I tried not to think about the ending, when she told me she'd fallen in love with someone else, and how she was sorry but that was how things sometimes happened. And then, quite suddenly, my thoughts veered off in a different direction, to Audrey Brubaker, and I wondered if I could have her for a girlfriend. She was older than me, which seemed to be a barrier, and she was not particularly pretty, although she was pretty enough in a way that I liked, with dark intelligent eyes that seemed to gather you in, and with a tall slender body that looked strong. And then without warning my thoughts changed again, in the direction of my brother, which I did not want to happen. We had never gotten along, not in the way brothers are supposed to, and I regretted that now and wished it had been different. Gary was always the star of the family, a budding musical genius, and I was—just a regular boy, I guess—a regular boy who liked mathematics and electricity and other things most people don't care about. I remembered Gary practicing for endless hours at the shiny grand piano my parents had bought for him, his eyes half closed, his body leaning slightly forward, as if he could actually force the music directly from his fingers into the giant instrument. And then I remembered my father getting the telephone call from someone at the Army base, the day after he and my mother had returned from Italy, and how he had called us into the living room and had us sit together on the sofa while he stood and told us the terrible news, doing it in a slow and careful way, as if he were explaining something complicated that he wanted us to thoroughly understand. There had been a terrible accident at the Army base, he explained, it was nobody's fault but it had happened, and Gary had been killed. When he spoke that word my mother gasped and put a hand up to her mouth, and when he finished his careful explanation he hugged my mother for a long silent moment. And then she left the room and walked slowly up the staircase, holding tightly to the banister, to her bedroom, where she stayed alone for the rest of that day.

When I'd finished with that memory I was tired of thinking

but I couldn't stop. Even though I wanted it to stop, the thoughts kept coming: about working in a factory instead of being at a university, and about Diane leaving me for another boy, and about my brother being dead for no good reason. And then I think I began to cry a little—anyway I could feel tears on my face—and after that I finally fell asleep.

Chapter Five

When my father's car arrived the brilliant sweeping headlights shined into my eyes and woke me. In the half-light from the streetlamps I watched him get out of the car and come up onto the porch and stand uncertainly at the front door. When I spoke to him from out of the shadows he jumped a little.

"There you are," he said. "I didn't see you."

He stood by the door and I came over and stood beside him.

"Well, I guess you better take me to your mother," he said.

I led him through the front door and up the staircase and into the back bedroom where my mother was asleep. I stood in the doorway and my father went up and sat on the edge of the bed and shook my mother awake. He spoke her name in a soft voice and shook her gently so she would not be startled, and I remember thinking that it was a considerate thing to do: to wake a person in a gentle way so they would not be confused or frightened, the way you can sometimes be when you're brought awake suddenly by a bright light or a loud noise or something happening in a dream. I have probably not brought out clearly enough that my father could be gentle. I mean there was a gentle side to him; he was not always stern, although he was stern much of the time.

After a moment my mother came awake. She looked up at my father and smiled in a drowsy way. "Oh, hello, Jim," she said. "What are you doing here?"

"I've come to get you, Anne," he said. "We're going home. I'm going to drive you home now. You can sleep in the car."

"No," she said. "I'm going with Nathan to Camp Carlisle. We're going to bring Gary home. We're leaving in the morning. Where is Nathan?" She sat up and looked around and saw me standing in the shadows by the door. "Oh, there you are. Tell your father we're going to drive to Camp Carlisle and get your brother."

"No, Anne," my father said again. "I'm going to take you home. This business about Gary; it's not a good idea. We'll talk about it tomorrow."

My father stood and put his hand under my mother's arm and lifted slightly. And I saw her pull back. But it was only for an instant. And then she did what my father wanted and they stood and left the room together. Though as they passed me in the doorway she stopped for a moment and looked at me, not with anger or disappointment or regret but with a kind of weary sadness. And that's when I felt the betrayal again, and I said, "Maybe we can do it later, Mom. Take that trip to Camp Carlisle." And I smiled to try to make it seem all right, to make it seem like it was just a natural outcome of what had started four hours earlier on the front porch, when she had greeted me coming home from work, and not so much of a betrayal.

Chapter Six

The next day at the car factory I worked with one of the electricians—Tommy Lankinaw was his name—to install switches on a giant metal stamping machine. The switches had little fingers that were pushed when a sheet of steel was in the right position in the machine, completing an electrical circuit that would let the machine operate and bend the steel into the shape of the right front fender of the Oldsmobile Rocket Eighty-Eight. It was a kind of work I liked to do because it was so logical; each switch was like a question and all the answers had to be exactly right before the machine would work.

While we worked Tommy talked to me about bowling. I wanted to think about Audrey Brubaker and how I could get to know her better, but Tommy kept talking about bowling. He had made a study of the game, he said, and had learned in a scientific way how to make the ball move and strike the pins you were after. His team had won the league championship the year before and he had been given a special trophy for being the best player. And I remember thinking that if the world was organized around bowling then Tommy would be near the top, the governor of a state, maybe, or the head of a big corporation.

It was an odd thought but it was the thought I had while listening to Tommy.

After work I drove to my painting spot along the river and set up my easel and started to paint. I kept looking back over my shoulder for Audrey Brubaker and at five she appeared, just as she had before, standing above me on the sidewalk. I called up and she smiled and raised a hand. Then I packed up my painting things and scrambled up the bank.

"I changed the color of the factory." I held out my painting.

"Cool," she said. "Now you know one more thing than you knew before."

"Can we go someplace and talk?" I asked. "Maybe you can tell me some other things about painting."

Audrey was leaning back against the rusted iron railing. Her legs were crossed and the wind was blowing out her hair so strands of it danced around her head. The sun behind her showed the outline of her legs through the gauzy fabric of her dress. She held a book in her left hand.

"I'm afraid I have another engagement," she said. She reached up and moved a strand of hair that had blown across her face, pinning it behind her ear. "But you can walk to the hotel with me. I think that would be acceptable."

"Okay," I said. "Great."

Audrey began to walk along the street that ran beside the river and I fell in step beside her. We passed the Civic Auditorium, grey and grim-looking like a fortress, the space around it an expanse of empty asphalt. The city seemed subdued and empty. There were tall buildings and wide streets but not many people and only a few cars. It reminded me of the ending of a movie I had seen the year before, where radiation from an atomic war wipes out all the people but leaves the buildings. I told this to Audrey and asked if she thought we would have an atomic war.

"I used to think we would," she said. "That we'd all be blown to smithereens in one giant explosion. But now I don't. I think the President will keep us out of one." She turned to me and shrugged. "Anyway, mass extermination isn't a subject I like to think about."

I regretted bringing up atomic war because I suddenly realized some people might find it depressing. Though it had almost happened the year before so it was something that was on my mind. I remembered standing in line at the school cafeteria last October when I heard the news about the Russian and American ships coming together off the coast of Cuba, intending to fight it out, and I remember trying to decide if the atomic bomb that would be dropped on Detroit would wipe out our suburb too. And I remember deciding that it would.

"What do you do beside sitting in on art lessons?" I asked next, to change the subject.

"I live and breathe," Audrey said, and she laughed. Then she said: "I work at the lunch counter at the Rexall Drug Store on Leonard Street. I believe I told you that yesterday. I make sandwiches and ice cream sundaes and French-fried potatoes, etcetera, etcetera, etcetera." She cocked her head and looked over at me. "I'll make you a malted milk for free if you come by and visit me sometime." She put her hand on my arm and looked away and batted her eyes, as if the prospect of me visiting her at the Rexall Drug Store filled her with great pleasure, and I laughed.

"What about you?" she asked. "What do you do when you're not being an artist?"

"I work at the car factory on 36th Street," I said. "I work with the electricians."

I thought about telling her more about my job; how I was interested in electricity and had studied it on my own, and how I'd taken the mathematics courses that tell you how it works, and how I'd built an electric circuit that made the dots and dashes you use in Morse Code. But I had tried to do that before

—talk to people about electricity—and it had never worked out very well. What I mean to say is that they were not particularly interested. So I said something else.

"What's the book?"

She held it up so I could see the title: *How to Win Friends and Influence People*, by Dale Carnegie.

"It tells you what rules you should follow to get people to like you," Audrey said. "So they'll respect you and listen to what you have to say." She looked at me. "Like how I told you yesterday about color theory. Helping people is one of the rules, as long as it's something easy for you to do. Another rule is using a person's name a lot when you talk to them. Dale Carnegie says that for most people their name is the most beautiful sound in the world."

"Why do you want people to listen to you, Audrey?"

She laughed a little at my faint attempt at humor and then her face grew serious. "It helps you have a successful life. To be successful in your career. Like getting people to buy your furniture, which is the line of work I plan to do some day." She looked at me with a quizzical expression. "Don't you want to be a success in life?"

"I don't know," I said. "I haven't thought about it."

"Well, you should," she said. "It's a cruel world if you don't have money."

We started to cross the long Pearl Street bridge. I was trying to decide if I'd made another mistake by saying I didn't know if I wanted to be a success, and whether I should try to change it. When we got to the center of the bridge, Audrey stopped and leaned over the railing and let a ball of spit drop from her mouth into the river. Then we stood there for a while, side by side, looking out onto the water. It was a nice fall evening and the colors of the setting sun—the oranges and the pinks and the yellows—were lighting up the buildings along the riverbank, covering them in brilliant hues that I had never seen before.

When I turned toward Audrey I saw the beautiful colors reflected on her face. And suddenly I started to feel a little bit romantic, and I slid my hand over hers where she had placed it on the railing and she let it stay there. After a moment of standing quietly, I put my arm around her shoulder.

She stiffened and pulled away. "What are you doing?" she said.

"I was going to kiss you. I thought it would be all right."

"Well it isn't," she said. "You can't just kiss a girl whenever you want to. Her opinion counts for something too."

"I'm sorry," I said, and I realized I had made another mistake. "You're right. I shouldn't have done it." I removed my arm from being around her shoulder, and then I said: "But you see I had a girlfriend last year and she ditched me for another boy. She broke my heart. I'm still getting over that."

Audrey made a face. "Don't talk nonsense," she said. "You don't have to talk nonsense to me. Just say what's on your mind and we'll get along all right."

We started walking again. I tried to think of something to say to undo the damage I had done by trying to kiss her and by saying I didn't know if I wanted to be a success. But before I could think of anything Audrey began to speak. She talked about the history of Grand Rapids, how it had been settled as a logging center and then changed to making furniture. Then she talked about the furniture workers' strike of 1911 which had ended in disaster for the workers. By then we'd gotten to Division Street and she stopped and turned in my direction. "That's my abode up ahead," she said. She pointed to a tall building at the end of the block.

I looked at the building. It was old and run down. Some of the windows were covered with plywood, and the awning over the entrance was torn so that a piece hung down and flapped lazily in the breeze.

"I'll walk up to the door," I said.

"No you won't," she said. "If you recall, I told you I have an engagement. It'd be rude if my engagement saw me walking up with someone else."

"Okay," I said, though I was disappointed to learn that her engagement was actually a date. I turned and faced her. She had been acting a little strange, with all that talk about the history of the city, but in spite of that I liked her and I wanted her to know, so I placed a hand lightly on her shoulder.

"Are you going to try to kiss me again?" she asked.

"No," I said, grinning. "I've learned my lesson. But I want to because you're so pretty."

"Oh, I'm pretty you say." She spoke the words in a teasing way. "Well, that's an entirely different matter. If you say I'm pretty." And then she leaned forward and closed her eyes and kissed me, but only for a brief moment and with one hand held flat against my chest.

"There" she said. She whispered in my ear with her face up close to mine. "Maybe that'll help you forget about being jilted by your old girlfriend." She smiled and turned away.

I began to walk back in the direction we had come from, but as soon as Audrey was out of sight around the corner I stopped and followed her. I walked up and looked around the edge of the building. Audrey was near the hotel entrance, walking toward a man who wore a suit and a colorful tie and shiny oxford shoes. They greeted each other with smiles, and then they started walking back along Division Street, in the direction where I was standing in my hiding place, and I had to run away so they wouldn't see me.

Chapter Seven

The next day at the factory the foreman met me at the time clock as I was coming in. He pulled me off to the side before I could punch my timecard and told me he had to let me go.

"Someone filed a grievance about you," he said. "That you're taking a union job."

"But I can't join the union until I've worked here for six months," I said. "When you're under eighteen you have to wait longer. That's the rule."

"I know that. I'm aware of that. Do you think I'm stupid?"

I looked at him but he shifted his gaze instead of looking back. I could tell he felt guilty about the unfairness of what he was doing. Firing me for no good reason.

"I need this job," I said. "I'm saving money for college."

He looked at me for a moment, then he took my arm and pulled me over to the side, away from the men who were standing in line for the time clock.

"I have an idea," he said. "I don't know if it'll work but maybe it will. If it doesn't work we'll both be in trouble." He came up close and lowered his voice.

"I'm going to put you in the tool crib until you get to six months," he said. "The tool crib is where the journeymen come to get their special tools. It's sort of like a lending library. You give them the tool and they sign a card that says they have it and will bring it back." He looked at me. "It's an unusual job so it's not listed in the union contract. Anybody can do it."

He took hold of my arm and led me out of the time clock area. We passed rows of welding machines that were throwing sparks up into the air and then the production lines where workers pushed sheets of steel into giant machines that shaped them into car parts. We walked through the tool-and-die shop where six gigantic milling machines were shaping giant blocks of steel and then to a caged-in area that had a counter across the front and shelves behind filled with tools.

A short, gray-haired man was standing behind the counter. "This is Jimmy Palmer," the foreman said. I reached out to shake his hand but then I realized he didn't have one. His right arm ended just below the elbow and his shirt was folded over and pinned so that you couldn't see the stump. "Jimmy," the foreman said, "Nate here needs a job so I'm giving him to you. He can sharpen the drill bits when they come back and calibrate the electric meters so they're reading right. He's got a particular interest in electricity so that'll be something good for him to learn about." He turned to me and grinned and swatted me on the arm to show that things were okay between us again. Then he turned and walked away.

"Come on in, kid," Jimmy said, and with his good arm he lifted up a section of the counter and I stepped through. "I'll give you the cook's tour."

"Most of the journeymen own the tools they use every day" he said, "your wrenches and your pliers and your screwdrivers and such as like that, but sometimes they need a special tool they don't have. Here, I'll show you." He took hold of my arm with his good hand and began to steer me down one of the aisles, naming the tools that we passed: "Here's your torque wrenches, and your tapping kits, and your high range micrometers, your spanner wrenches, trolly jacks, nut snuggers, gear pullers, hydraulic jacks...." When we came to the end of the aisle we stopped. "Next aisle over is the tools for the electricians, and next after that for the millwrights and pipefitters. You can go through those by yourself. Just learn the name of the tool and where it's at."

We walked back to the counter area. "Tools are important," he said. "So you've got to keep them in good condition. That'll be your job." He looked at me. "And some of the cutting tools get dull so you've got to sharpen them from time to time. You'll get the hang of it pretty quick," he said. "It's not hard if you've got half a brain."

After that we stood together at the counter and I watched him hand out tools to the men. He showed me the card system and how you filled out the information—the name and the date and the badge number of the man who took the tool—and the little box you checked when the tool came back.

When he was finished telling me about the card system he turned in my direction. I had been looking at his right arm while he was speaking and he noticed.

"What do you think about my wing?" he said. He raised his right arm so it stuck out like the wing of a giant bird.

"It's okay," I said. "It's fine."

"There's a good lesson here," he said. "A good lesson for a boy like you to learn. It's about paying attention when a machine is running. Like you shouldn't make a gesture when you're standing next to a running band saw."

I looked at him. I didn't know what he was talking about so I said nothing.

"I didn't know the lesson and so I did it," he continued. "Made a big sweeping motion with my arm when I was talking to a guy. I was trying to tell him where he could find a vending machine that had cigarettes. Just trying to be helpful to a friend. Anyway, when I reached out to point him in the right direction my arm swept through where the blade was turning."

"I'm sorry," I said, because that was all I could think of to say.

"The funny thing is that I never felt it. There was just a little tug on my right side and when I looked I saw that part of my arm was missing. My first thought was that I was dreaming or had lost my mind. But then I saw the part that was lying on the floor and I saw the running saw blade and it all came together. Then I passed out."

"I'm sorry about that," I said for a second time.

"It's not so bad. You learn to adjust. They took care of me, the company did. Put me here in the tool crib where you don't need two good arms."

❧

WHEN THE LUNCH break came I went to one of the pay phones outside the workers' cafeteria and I called my mother. I wanted to call her during the day when my father wouldn't be home. At first we made small talk about the weather and how my job was going and what late-fall flowers were blooming in her garden. And then I started to apologize again about not going with her to Camp Carlisle and I said that maybe we could do it at some later time.

"Don't worry about that, Nate," she said. "It wasn't a good idea. Your mother let herself get carried away by her emotions. I see that now. I understand that. So don't give it a thought."

I was relieved to hear this because it made what I had done—calling my father—seem like the right thing, nothing to feel bad about or to have regret for. But hearing my mother speak—the words she used and the way her voice sounded, so calm and cool and in control, so different from the urgency I had heard two nights earlier on the porch—made me feel sad in a peculiar way.

"Maybe we can make arrangements with the Army people," I said. "There's probably a way to get Gary back if we pay them some money. Pay them for the trouble of digging up his casket and sending it home on a train or a truck. I could check that out if you want me to."

There was a pause, and it went on for a long time, and I began to think my time had run out on the pay phone and we had been disconnected. But then my mother spoke, and I could tell from her voice that she had been collecting herself from some strong emotion.

"No, that's all right, Nate. We'll leave Gary where he is. It's fine. Your father's right. The Army people know the best way to handle these things."

After that we didn't say too much. I told her about my new work assignment and how I was getting to know some of the factory workers. But it was only talk to fill up time, to keep our connection going for a while in a polite and pleasing way. Though I couldn't help thinking there were other things we should be saying to each other, important things that might affect her life or mine, and make a difference in how things went forward in the future. And then I realized that after that night at the house on Fulton Street we had lost something, some invisible bond between a mother and her son, and then I wondered if that was just the way life is when you were setting out to be an adult, that you leave things behind because you have to deal with other things, new things that are important and demand your full attention.

"Okay," I said to my mother after the pleasant talking had gone on for a while. "I guess I should be going. My break's almost over and I should be getting back."

"Of course. You have responsibilities. Have a good day, Nathan. I love you."

"Yes. I know. Of course. I love you too, Mom."

Chapter Eight

Over the next few weeks I kept working in my painting spot by the river. I'd found there were many pictures you could paint from the same spot depending on which way you looked, or what subject you choose, or how the light fell on a certain day. I had seen Monet's paintings of haystacks in the Time-Life series, where he showed the same scene in different seasons and in different weather, and I thought that I would try to do that with the river and the factories and the bridges.

Though the real reason I stayed there, probably, was because it was along the walking route that Audrey took each afternoon. It got to be a routine. She would come walking by my painting spot along the river and make her way down the steep slope and we would talk for a while. Usually, she would give me ideas that would help with my painting, like the colors to use for different objects, and how to arrange things on the canvas, or how to use light and shadows to make an object seem solid even though it's painted on a flat surface. She carried a little sketchbook and sometimes she would sit on a fallen log that was nearby and sketch out ideas for pieces of furniture: chairs and tables and beds and cabinets and armchairs; all the things you put into a house to make it possible to live there.

"There are different styles of furniture," she said, "but you've got to develop your own style if you want to amount to anything. You can copy something without knowing it because it's so common you think it's the only way it can be done." She stopped sketching and looked at me. "The same thing goes for painting, by the way."

"I understand," I said.

Sometimes she would talk about designing other things than furniture—the common objects you find in a house—like pots and pans and ashtrays and letter openers and lamps and ball point pens. "It's called industrial design," she said. "And it's where the future is. Ordinary things that are made in a factory but you still want them to be beautiful." She looked up at me. "Just because a thing is common doesn't mean it can't be beautiful." A moment later she added: "That's my fallback position vis-a-vis getting a job, in case you'd like to know. If I can't get one designing furniture I figure I can get one designing ashtrays and ball point pens."

Sometimes I would stop my painting and sit next to Audrey on the fallen log and we would talk about other things than art. She was interested in politics and what was happening in the world, like the Negroes' problems in the South, and the space race with the Russians, and whether Kennedy could make things better for the poor countries of the world. She said she was going to vote for Kennedy in the next election because she believed he was doing the right things and if we could just be patient a lot of the problems would get solved and the world would be a better place.

I told her I'd watched Kennedy's inauguration on a TV that had been set up in the school auditorium, and later I had sent away for the special edition of *Life* magazine that celebrated his inauguration, and I had memorized the speech he gave that day, and later other speeches, the brave and beautiful parts of them, about going to the moon, and how the treatment of the Black race was not fair, and why the steel companies should not raise their prices after they had promised not to. I told her I had memorized the speeches and would recite them in my head while walking home from school or lying in bed at night or sitting in a theater waiting for a movie to begin.

"That's crazy," she said, laughing. "I don't believe you."

"Okay," I said. "Watch."

I stood and assumed the attitude of an orator, my feet apart, my head thrown back, one arm raised toward the sky.

"The torch has been passed to a new generation of Americans...." I intoned, trying to mimic Kennedy's strange Boston accent, "....born in this century, tempered by war, disciplined by a hard and bitter peace, proud of our ancient heritage, and unwilling to witness or permit the slow undoing of those human rights to which this nation has always been committed, and to which we are committed to today, at home and around the world."

I finished with a deep bow.

When I looked at Audrey she was shaking her head, as if she found the spectacle difficult to believe, but she was smiling too.

"Is that enough?" I said. "Because I've got a lot more."

"No," she said, laughing. "I believe you now. But I still think you're crazy."

Sometimes, sitting on the fallen log with Audrey with the sun going down and thoughts of art in my head, I would start to feel a little bit romantic, like I had felt that day on the Pearl Street bridge. But I didn't try to kiss her again, or be affectionate in any other way. After seeing her go off that first night walking with the businessman, I understood that I was not the kind of boyfriend she wanted. It was obvious she was looking for someone who was established in life and had shown himself to be a success, which I had not yet done.

And there was a second reason I didn't try to be romantic with Audrey and it's harder to explain. I noticed it first on a day in late October, after the leaves had fallen and the bright fall colors had been replaced by the somber shades of winter. I had started a new painting and was trying to capture this change, like Monet had done with his haystacks, when I suddenly realized that Audrey was not around. I set down my palette and my brush and followed the path along the river. After I'd gone a short distance, I found her standing along the shore, staring out onto the water with a fixed expression. When I came up close I saw tears on her face. She turned toward me and tried to smile.

"What's wrong, Audrey?"

"Nothing."

"You're crying."

"Am I?" She rubbed beneath her eyes to wipe the tears away.

"What's the matter?"

"It's nothing."

"It must be something."

"No, I'm fine."

She tried again to give a brave smile, but failed, which made her look even sadder.

"It's nothing you need to know about."

"Tell me."

"Well then, if you must know it's the trees." She waved her hand across the sky. "They're bare now. Just black ugly branches with a dull grey sky behind. It makes you feel different, don't you think? All that emptiness. Like you're unprotected."

"Unprotected from what?"

"From the bad things that can happen to you."

I stepped forward intending to comfort her in some way, but before I could do anything she reached and took my hand and led me back along the river path to my painting spot, hand in hand together, and of course I was reminded of the girls I'd walked with in the zoo, except with Audrey it was different, because it was not affection I felt but something deeper, something darker, something I didn't have a name for.

Chapter Nine

One day in early November my father called and said he was going to be in Grand Rapids the next day on business and he wanted to have dinner with me.

"Is this about anything in particular?" I said, because he had never asked me out to dinner before. We had eaten together in restaurants when we'd traveled on hunting and fishing trips, but we had never done it for no reason.

"No," he said. "I'm just going to be in town and thought it would be nice to have dinner with my son."

I was standing in the hallway outside the bedroom I rented from Mr. and Mrs. Thatcher, where the phone was on a stand. I'd been getting ready for bed when the phone rang, and I was dressed in my pajama bottoms. I could see Mrs. Thatcher peering at me through a narrow opening in their bedroom door. I knew she didn't like seeing me without a shirt.

"Just a minute," I said to my father. I set the phone down and went back into my bedroom and put on a tee shirt.

"Is it anything special we need to talk about?" I asked when I came back.

My father laughed. "You asked me that already, bub," he said.

"It's just to have dinner together. To talk a few things over. That's all."

"Okay," I said. "I'd like that."

"Great. Why don't you meet me in the lobby of the Pantlind Hotel at six. We'll put on the feed bag together."

"Okay," I said.

The next day I walked to the Pantlind Hotel from my painting spot along the river. I was a little late. I'd had an idea about how to paint the Sixth Street Bridge like Van Gogh might do it and I had lost track of time. When I came into the big high-ceilinged lobby I spotted my father standing near the newsstand reading a newspaper. When he saw me walking up a surprised look came onto his face.

"Well, I guess we won't be eating in the Timber Barons' Room," he said. He was looking at my clothes, which were the khaki clothes I wore to work.

"I'm sorry," I said. "I didn't think about my clothes."

He grinned and then reached out and we shook hands.

"That's okay," he said. "We'll go to Kewpee Hamburgers instead. We'll be more comfortable there. That's more our cup of tea, anyway."

We left the Pantlind Hotel and started to walk to Kewpee Hamburgers, which was only a couple of blocks away. It was beginning to get dark, and store lights were coming on, throwing yellow light out through the windows onto the people passing by. Earlier it had rained and the streetlights and the traffic lights reflected off the wet sidewalks in colorful moving patterns. It occurred to me that it was something I should remember and use sometime in a painting.

"Anyway, we wouldn't be fooling anybody by eating in the Timber Barons' Room," my father said, and he laughed a little. And I thought he meant that neither of us really belonged in a fancy restaurant like the Timber Barons' Room, even though he was wearing a suit and a tie and would seem to fit right in. He could be that way sometimes, as if the success he'd had in his career had been an accident, and he was fooling people by being in places where he didn't belong.

At Kewpee Hamburgers we gave our order at the counter and then found a booth in back. And at first we didn't talk. We hadn't really talked in any important way since the day I'd told him I was going to take a factory job in Grand Rapids. And I knew that was still a thing between us.

"Your mother's better," he said, finally. He laced his fingers together and put his hands on the table. "I think she's finally coming to terms with Gary's death." He looked down at the tabletop and shook his head. "Losing Gary. It was a terrible thing. No mother should have to go through that." He raised his gaze and looked across at me. "He was her favorite. I guess that's no surprise to you." He grimaced a little as if it was painful for him to tell me Gary was her favorite son, and he wanted me to know. "Of course she loves you just as much, Nate. Love is not the question. But his piano playing. It made him very special."

"I understand," I said. And I did, because it was something I had known and learned to live with.

"Anyway," he said, "that's not why I'm here. That's not what I want to talk to you about." He unlaced his fingers and leaned forward and placed his forearms on the table, as if he was getting to the important part of what he wanted to say and wanted to be close to me to say it. "You should be in college, Nate," he said. "You're a good student and you should be in college. I understand that now. I didn't at first but now I do. Your mother talked to me about it." He started to say more but just then the man behind the counter called out our number. I went up and got the tray of hamburgers and carried it back to our booth.

"I think I may have handled it badly," my father said, a moment later. He was holding a wrapped-up hamburger in one hand. "When we talked about college, I mean. Which maybe caused you to do something you shouldn't have. Working in a factory isn't what you should be doing right now." He stopped talking for a moment, as if he wanted me to think about what he'd just said. "So I wanted to tell you that," he went on. "And I wanted to say that we—your mother and I—could help you out. With the money part of college, I mean. We could help you out with that. Whatever course you'd like to study. Electricity or whatever."

He began to unwrap his hamburger from the waxed paper. He unwrapped it slowly, as if his thoughts were still on something else.

"Your mother helped me understand the situation better," he said. "She has a very strong opinion that you should be in college. And she argued with me about it. Argued more than I'm accustomed to." My father stopped talking for a moment and looked off to one side with a musing expression, as if he was recalling the argument with my mother and how unusual it had been.

"Anyway," he said, "she wanted me to tell you that. Tell you that she stood up for you. That she was on your side." There were some French fries in a plastic basket and he squeezed out some ketchup to dip them in. He took a bite of his hamburger and started to chew, keeping his eyes on me.

"Let me think about it," I said.

"I never went to college," my father said. "Things were different then. Only a few went. Regular people, I mean. So I don't know too much about it. Although I know enough to know you should be there. Your mother helped me understand." He smiled in a slightly guilty way, as if my going to college was something he should have known about himself.

I took a bite of my hamburger and chewed it. Then I set my hamburger down on the tabletop. I reached out and touched the ketchup bottle lightly with my fingertips. I don't know why I did that because I didn't want any ketchup. It was just something to do with my hand.

"I'm learning some things at the factory," I said. "It's not wasted time. I'm learning about tools and how to use them and how to take care of them. And about how you do a job. The steps you go through to do it right."

My father looked at me but said nothing.

"And I'm learning some things about electricity. Not the scientific principals but how you work with it in the real world. The switches and the wires and how to build the circuits."

I looked across at my father. He had a puzzled look on his face.

"And I'm beginning to like the men," I said. "I didn't at first, but now I do. Some of them are interesting in ways you wouldn't expect. One is a pretty famous bowler. And another lost his arm in a terrible accident but he learned to accept it and get on with his life."

My father's expression became more puzzled. Deep lines appeared in his forehead. And I realized I was not making myself clear about the factory, so I tried something else.

"And I'm painting," I said. "Maybe you don't know that."

"I do," my father said. "Your mother told me."

"It's interesting," I said. "It makes you look at things in a different way. Like trying to see beneath the surface. Beneath the way things seem to be on top."

My father looked at me with a curious expression, and I thought he did not understand what I'd just said about painting —that I had still not made myself clear—so I began to add more details, to talk about the abandoned furniture factories and how I'd shown one of them as dark red but changed it to orange to make my statement bolder, and about how Van Gogh had distorted the color and shape of things to create a certain impression, and how I was trying to do that in my paintings too. Then I said: "I like it, painting, and I guess I'd like to keep doing it for a while." I looked at my father but my gaze slipped off. "Maybe not go to college. Not right now."

My father set his hamburger down.

"I think that would be a mistake," he said. "These days you need college if you want to amount to something."

My father turned his head and looked at the booth across the aisle where a man and a woman were holding hands across the table. The man brought the woman's hand up and kissed the back of it.

"I guess you know that if you're not in college you'll be drafted into the Army," he said. "If you're not in college where you can get a deferment."

"I know," I said. "I'll deal with that when it happens."

"It'd be fine with me if you went," he said. "You know how I feel about service in the military. You could go into the Army now and go to college after. But it'd be hard on your mother. She wouldn't like it. Not after what happened to Gary. It'd set her back in her recovery."

"Don't worry," I said. "I won't be drafted."

"I hope you're not thinking about doing something foolish."

"I haven't decided what I'll do. But I won't be drafted."

After that we ate our hamburgers in silence. I had said as much as I could say about my life in Grand Rapids and how it wasn't so bad. Not so bad as it might look to someone who wasn't living it. Then a big group of people came into the restaurant all at once and it got crowded and noisy. People stood in the aisle next to our booth.

I thought about the things I'd done with my father when I was growing up, the hunting and fishing trips we'd taken together, the baseball games at Briggs Stadium and the Soap Box Derby where I had built a derby car and raced it down a hill against other boys. I wanted to find another subject we could talk about. Something that would turn out better than college and the draft.

47

"Are you going deer hunting this year?" I asked, because that was something he loved to do and did every November with his friends.

"No," he said. "The men I work with in the central office aren't inclined that way. They favor different pursuits. Golf and tennis and sailing boats on Lake St. Clair is more to their liking."

"That's too bad," I said.

He stared at me for a moment before he spoke. "Hunting and fishing," he said. "They're a poor man's sports, Nate. That's something I've learned. Going off into the woods to shoot an animal or catch a fish. It's not the kind of thing a serious man should do."

His gaze drifted off to the side. I could tell he was thinking about something. Then his gaze came back and settled on me.

"Things change in your life, Nate," he said. "If you want to move up in the world you have to be willing to change. Let go of the things that don't fit in your life anymore."

He took a bite of his hamburger and finished chewing before he spoke again.

"Of course it's your decision. I'm talking about college now. I think you should go to college but it's your decision. But think about it carefully. How you feel today may not be how you'll feel forever."

He finished eating his hamburger and he balled up the wax paper and put it into the plastic basket. Then he stood. "I should be heading back," he said. "I've still got a couple of hours on the road."

He looked down at me and I could tell there was something more he wanted to say. Something that would maybe be hard for him to say and hard for me to hear. Something about Gary, maybe, or about my mother, or about how I was being foolish with my life. But the aisle was full of people now and it would've been hard for him to say anything important in the middle of all the noise.

"Take care of yourself, bub," he said. "And call your mother from time to time. She likes it when you do."

He put a hand on my shoulder and squeezed. Then he turned and made his way through the crowd and out the swinging door and into the night which had become full-dark now. And as the door came closed behind him, I sensed a feeling rising up, something unexpected, and I realized that we would probably never talk this way again, a father giving advice to his son about how to live his life, and in that particular way I was on my own now.

ॐ

LATER, walking back to my car, I thought about what my father had said about hunting and fishing, how they were a poor man's pastime, not things you should do if you were serious about life and wanted to move up in the world. And this surprised me, because I knew how much he had loved those things before— before he got his big promotion to the central offices in Detroit. Growing up, I remembered him telling me interesting facts about being outdoors, like when caddis flies would be hatching on a trout stream, or how to bring down a deer with a single rifle shot, or where pheasants could be found in a field of corn. He had learned those things growing up in western Pennsylvania during the Depression, when hunting and fishing were reasonable ways of putting food on the family table, and he'd kept loving those activities as an adult. Many weekends found him in the woods or fields with his friends, men like him who worked for a large corporation and who longed for a diversion, some taste of freedom, on their days off.

I remembered one autumn evening last year, after a sudden

rain shower, when I'd spotted him from my upstairs bedroom window, practicing fly-fishing casts in our back yard. Still wearing his crisp white shirt from work, he built huge figure-eights with his fly line in the sodden September air, dropping the nine-foot tapered leader at the edges of my mother's flower beds, delicate as a breath. Again and again the line floated down and came to rest against the shiny blades of grass, and each time he allowed it to rest there for a moment, an expectant look on his face, as if he actually believed he might coax a trout out from under the begonias. Finally, he reeled in the line and broke the bamboo rod down into sections and slipped them one by one into the aluminum carrying case. But then he continued to stand there, staring through the darkening twilight of our new suburban neighborhood, until at last all I could see was the bright smudge of his white shirt. And I remember wondering what he must be thinking, a man in a white dress shirt with a fly rod in his hand, looking out across the perfectly manicured landscape of his new back yard, all lushly green, trimmed, and tended, conforming perfectly with the obligations of his new successful life.

Chapter Ten

The next day I went to my painting spot along the river but Audrey did not come by. After a while I gathered up my gear and left. I walked down to the corner of Powell Street, walking slowly and examining the things I was passing—the buildings and the store signs and the people hurrying along the sidewalk—and I tried to imagine how those things would work in a painting. Van Gogh had changed the shape and color of the things to make a certain impression, and I tried to imagine how I would do that, change what I was seeing and what impression I would try to make. When I got to Brush Street I looked across and saw Audrey walking with a man. At first I thought he was the same man I'd seen her with that day outside her hotel, but when I looked closer I saw that he was different, short and heavy and with slicked-back hair. Just a regular-looking businessman but different from the other.

I called out and Audrey looked across and saw me. She turned to the man and said something that made him nod his head. I made my way across the street, dodging cars as I went.

"Hello, Nate," Audrey said. She took a sideways glance at the man and smiled. Just a quick smile that came and went.

"You didn't come by to see me," I said. "Are you trying to break my heart?" I said this as a joke. It wasn't something I would normally say, but it seemed like something an older man would say, and with the businessman standing there I wanted to seem older.

"No," Audrey said, "I'm not trying to break anyone's heart." She took another sideways glance in the direction of the man. "This is Robert Smollett. He can tell you everything you've ever wanted to know about ball bearings and he can sell you some if you're so inclined." She smiled again and looked at him. "Robert, this is Nate. He's an artist friend of mine."

Smollett stepped forward and we shook hands. I had to set my painting down to do it.

"We're headed to a watering hole I know about," Smollett said. "It's just down the street a ways." He looked at Audrey, then back at me. "Maybe you'd like to join us. You can show us that painting you've got there." He nodded toward the painting. "I'm actually a bit of an artist myself, though I favor the paint-by-numbers approach."

I looked at Audrey. She looked back at me and shrugged.

"Okay," I said.

We walked down Brush Street, Mr. Smollett on one side of Audrey and myself on the other. At first nobody talked but then Audrey began to name the buildings we were passing and saying how old they were and what famous architects had designed them. I found this strange but Smollett seemed to think it was all right. Anyway, he didn't say anything.

We stopped in front of a building that had a bright blue neon sign over the entrance showing a champagne glass with bubbles coming out. Below the neon sign were the words *Starlight Lounge*. "Well, here we are," Smollett said.

Inside, it was dark and gloomy. A long mahogany bar ran down the left side of the room, with sparkling bottles lined up on shelves behind. There were not too many people and I thought it was because it was too early. Too early to be drinking liquor in a bar.

Smollett led us to a booth near the back and we slid in, Audrey and Smollett sat on one side and I sat on the other.

"So let's see that painting of yours," Smollett said.

"Okay. But be careful. It's still wet."

I took the painting out of the wooden press I kept it in and brought it up onto the table and leaned it back against the wall. It was the same scene I had been painting before—the abandoned factories and the Sixth Street bridge and the flowing water—except I had done it differently, with swirly lines and blurry edges that made it hard to tell where one thing ended and another thing began. I thought painting it that way would show that everything in life is connected, part of the same great cosmic plan. I explained this to Audrey and Smollett, and about how I was trying to paint like Van Gogh.

"I'm afraid your art talk is too deep for me," Smollett said, when I finished. "I mean all of what you just said about art. I like art but I like to know what I'm looking at. Norman Rockwell's one of my favorites. Your painting there...." he nodded toward the painting. "....is nice but I think you've got more work to do."

I was looking at Audrey while Smollett said these things. She had a sort of congested expression on her face, as if it was painful to hear what Smollett was saying. When he finished talking she said, "I think it's a wonderful painting, Nate." She reached across the table and briefly touched my hand.

Just then the waiter came and took our order. He looked at me for a moment, and then he looked at Audrey. I could tell he knew we were too young to be there, too young to be drinking liquor in a bar, but he didn't say anything. Audrey ordered an Old Fashioned and Smollett ordered a neat bourbon. I asked for a Manhattan, which was a drink I'd seen Cary Grant order in a movie but had never drunk myself.

While we waited for our drinks we talked, though it was

Audrey who did most of it. She explained about how Grand Rapids was settled as a logging town and that was why it had become a center for making furniture, because the wood was already there. Then she talked about the furniture worker's strike of 1911, which I had heard from her before, and then about the senator from Grand Rapids who had gone over with the Democrats to set up the United Nations.

While Audrey was talking Smollett watched her with a little smile on his face. Once or twice he looked over at me and winked, and once he glanced down to where Audrey's lap was, though it was not a glance because he held it for too long.

"Well, that was certainly interesting," Smollett said when Audrey was finished. "I suppose we're all better people for knowing it." He reached up and touched Audrey on the shoulder, as if he was congratulating her for having done a good job. Then he turned to me and smiled. "What line of work are you in, Nate?" he said.

"I work at the car factory on 36th Street. I work in the tool crib where they keep the special tools."

"I'm sure that's fine work," Smollett said, "but you might want to think about doing something in sales. That's where I've made my career and it's been good to me."

His expression turned serious, as if what he was going to say next was very important and I should pay close attention. "Every business starts out with a sale, Nate. Think about that." He narrowed his eyes and looked at me and nodded. "Someone has to build a product and someone else has to keep track of the money, but the first thing that has to happen is that a salesman has to get someone to buy it."

"I guess that's true," I said. "I never thought of it that way."

"You guys can keep having your brilliant conversation," Audrey said, "but I'm going to the ladies room." She slid out of the booth, sort of bouncing over on the bench till she came to the edge where she could stand up. Smollett watched her walk away, watched down low where her hips were moving inside her dress. He turned back to me and smiled and said. "She's a nice piece, wouldn't you say? A little small in the chest but she has a pretty face."

I looked at Smollett. He had a grin on his face. "Maybe you'd like to join us after dinner when the fun begins?"

"What are you talking about?" I said.

"We're going to dinner. I'd ask you to come along but I'm afraid my expense account only goes so far. But after dinner you could join up with us back at the hotel." He smiled.

It took me a moment to figure out what he meant and when I did I reached across the table and grabbed his tie and pulled him hard in my direction. It was a stupid thing to do, something I probably wouldn't have done if I had stopped to think about it.

"Hey!" Smollett said. He leaned forward over the table where I had pulled him. His eyes were wide and his face was close to mine. I could smell his sour breath.

"Hey!" he said again. And I thought for a moment that I should probably hit him, that that would be the logical next thing to do. But I had never hit a man and I didn't know how to do it. What I mean to say is that I didn't know where to aim the blow or how hard I should make it.

"Get out of here," I said.

"What?" His voice was a little croaky because I was still holding his tie.

"Get the hell out of here or I'll smash your face."

I let go of Smollett's tie and he stood up. He pulled the sleeves of his jacket to smooth them out, first on one side and then on the other. Then he sort of stretched out his neck and centered his tie where I had pulled it loose.

"I guess you fancy the girl yourself," he said, smiling. "There's nothing wrong with that. But you could have just told me. There's no need to get unpleasant." And then he turned and walked out of the Starlight Lounge.

When Audrey came back the drinks were on the table. "Where's Robert?" she said. She scanned the bar as if she might see him in some other part.

"He had to leave," I said. "He remembered someplace else he was supposed to be."

Audrey looked at me with a kind of squinty expression. I could tell she didn't believe me, and I got ready to say a better lie.

"Oh, well," she said, before I could think of anything. "I guess it's no great loss." She smiled. "I don't think he was too interested in the history of Grand Rapids anyway. My talents were being wasted on him."

"I agree," I said, though I didn't understand what she meant about the history of Grand Rapids.

Audrey looked down at the drinks still sitting on the tabletop. "I guess we'll just have to have our own party, Nate." She picked up her Old Fashioned, and I picked up my Manhattan and we clinked our glasses together. Then we each took a swallow.

"What do you do with the cherry?" I asked. I fingered it in the Manhattan drink and lifted it out by the stem.

"You're supposed to save it to the end," she said. "But you don't have to. It's a free country, so I guess you can do whatever you want." She reached across and took the cherry from my hand and put it in her mouth. "There," she said, smiling, "now you don't have to worry. I've saved you from the agony of making a decision."

We sat and drank our drinks. I finished my Manhattan and then I started on the neat bourbon that Smollett had left behind. I was beginning to feel light-headed. The room began to feel blurry, like a photograph out of focus, so you didn't know where one thing ended and another thing began. I remembered that that was the effect I was trying to create in my painting—to show the universality of life—and I vaguely wondered if getting drunk would make me a better painter.

Audrey lifted her Old Fashioned and finished it with a single swallow, then she tilted back the glass so that a couple of ice cubes went into her mouth. She sucked on them for a while, looking off to one side as if she had something on her mind.

The waiter came back and we ordered more drinks. We were both getting a little drunk and we knew it, but we wanted to keep it going. At least I did. It seemed to be putting us in a different place where different things could happen.

When the waiter left I turned to Audrey. She turned too, just looking back at me and smiling.

"Yes?" she said, because she could tell I had something I wanted to say.

"Audrey," I said, "that time when I walked you back to your hotel. You met a man by the entrance."

"Yes."

"And you went off with him. Walking."

"And...." She spoke with her voice rising up, as if encouraging me to get to the point.

"And then tonight you were with another man. Mr. Smollett."

She started to poke her finger into the Old Fashioned.

"I just wondered who they were."

Audrey let a moment pass in silence and then she said: "Are you asking me if I'm a prostitute?" Her gaze came up and met mine. A tiny smile was on her face.

"No. Of course not. I just wondered who they were. The men."

Audrey looked back down into the Old Fashioned. She raised her finger and put it into her mouth to get the whisky off. Then she breathed in a large amount of air and let it out slowly, as if what she was going to say next would take a lot of effort. And then she told me about Audrey Hepburn and *Breakfast at*

Tiffany's and the walking tours and how that was how she supported herself.

When she was finished, I leaned back in the booth with the drink in my hand and I thought about what she had said and whether I could believe her. It seemed unlikely that a man would spend an evening with a young woman and then just shake her hand and go away. I looked across at her. She was gazing back at me with a pleasant smile.

Was it possible she was a prostitute? This girl I'd sat with on the riverbank on so many afternoons. Talking about art and furniture and politics and anything else that came into our heads. I had never known a prostitute or used one, so I didn't have much to go on, though I had seen them in movies, and once I'd been with some boys and we had talked about hiring one to teach us special things about fucking. But I knew that prostitutes were broken women who had failed at life and turned to doing sex in desperation, as the only way to hold their lives together. But Audrey wasn't broken and she didn't seem desperate. It was the opposite, in fact. She had a plan for her life and was studying things to make it happen. I mean Dale Carnegie and the lessons at the Kendall School.

"Audrey," I said, "I believe you."

"That's very generous of you." She spoke in a slightly sarcastic voice.

"But you shouldn't be doing it."

"Oh. You think so, do you?"

"Yes. Something's going to happen. You're going to get hurt."

"Well, so far it's worked out fine."

"Maybe," I said. "But that doesn't mean it'll always be fine. Men...." I tried to think of how to say what was in my mind but I couldn't find the right words. I looked at Audrey. "You've just got to stop, that's all."

Her expression was sharp now. I could tell she was getting angry.

"I'm not sure you're the best one to be giving me advice," she said with a stiff smile.

"Maybe not. But I know how men are." I looked at her. "Do you think they'd want to take one of your tours if you weren't a pretty young woman?"

Audrey looked at me for a moment and the moment seemed to last for a long time. I didn't know what was going to happen next, though I knew she was mad. Then she slid over to the edge of the booth and stood up. She was standing up above me now, looking down.

"Just try it some time," she said, in a voice tight with anger. "Stay in the house for months and months like a prisoner. After the person you loved has run away and left you all alone. And then you lose the only thing you care about. Just try it. And then tell me what you would and wouldn't do."

"What? What are you talking about?"

She looked at me with scorn. "Anyway, what do you know about men?" she said. She seemed to spit the words out. "You're just a boy who doesn't know if he's Thomas Edison or Pablo Picasso. I don't need advice from you."

She turned and started to walk away.

"Audrey," I called out.

I wanted her to come back so we could finish the conversation in a better way, but she just kept walking.

Chapter Eleven

After that afternoon in the Starlight Lounge, Audrey stopped coming to my painting spot along the river. At first I was disappointed but then I felt it was all right. I wasn't used to spending time with a girl who knew more than I did about so many things, and one I couldn't be romantic with. So I decided that having Audrey for a friend was keeping me from a normal life. I mean a normal life where girls are concerned.

And then one night when I was in bed and trying to fall asleep, I decided I needed to have sex with a woman to make further progress in my life, that not having sex left me at a disadvantage with my painting and with my life in general. I'd read in several places that a man doesn't really understand life until he's made love to a woman. Hemingway said if you did it right the earth would move, and Henry Miller said that the end of it was like seeing the Holy Trinity. I had been thinking about sex in a romantic way but I knew there was another way to think about it, and I should understand that way too.

I had missed a chance a few weeks earlier. The girl's name was Gloria and she worked at the factory on the production line that stamped out metal brake housings. I met her in the workers' cafeteria one day and we had talked and gotten along, and after lunch we had gone walking in a grassy area near the loading dock. When we got to a secluded place behind the crushing machine Gloria turned suddenly and kissed me fiercely on the mouth, and after a moment of fierce kissing she raised herself on tiptoes and whispered in my ear that I could fuck her if I paid ten dollars. There was a place she knew about, she said, where we could be alone and everything would be all right. But I didn't want to do that and I tried to explain it to her so she would understand. So I told her about Diane, the girl I'd been in love with the year before, and how we had done certain things together, sometimes with affection and sometimes with passion, and how because of that I knew the difference. And because I knew the difference, I wanted my first time with a girl to be about affection and not about money.

When I'd finished my explanation, Gloria looked at me with a surprised or possibly a puzzled expression, and then she broke out laughing. "You're a very unusual specimen," she said through the laughter, and I could tell from the way she spoke that it was not a compliment. Then she turned and walked briskly away, not looking back to see if I was following.

But that was then, and this was now, and now it was different.

THE NEXT DAY at work I walked through the factory looking for Gloria. I walked along all of the small-parts stamping lines but I couldn't find her. When I got back to the tool crib I asked Jimmy Palmer if he knew how I could find a girl.

"What do you mean, a girl?"

"A girl. A girl I could go to bed with."

Jimmy laughed out loud, which made me feel a little embarrassed, and then he turned and walked away, still laughing and shaking his head. But later in the day he handed me a slip of paper with a name written on it—Shirley—and a telephone number—GL3-8722. "Here," he said as he laid the slip of paper on the workbench. "She'll take care of you."

That day after work I called the number. I called from a telephone booth outside a gas station because I didn't want the Thatchers to hear me talking to a prostitute. After four or five rings a woman answered.

"Yeah," she said. "Is this Leonard?"

"No. I'm not Leonard. I'm someone else. I'm Nate."

"I was expecting a call from someone named Leonard."

"No, I'm Nate."

I heard a sigh, as if she was disappointed that I wasn't Leonard.

"Okay Nate," she said. "What do you want?"

I tried to think about what I should say and how I should say it—the exact words to use to hire her as a prostitute—and I suddenly realized I should have worked that out ahead of time because it was hard to think of the right words just in the moment. The right words to ask a woman to go to bed with me.

"Are you still there, Nate?" the woman asked, after the silence had gone on for a while.

"Yes." Then: "A friend of mine gave me your number. He said you have a sort of business and that I should call you about it."

"A business?"

"Like making dates with men. Going out on dates."

"Do you want to make a date with me, Nate? Is that what you want?"

"Yes. I guess so."

"Okay, where are you? What hotel?"

"I'm afraid I'm not staying in a hotel. I'm staying in a place that's restrictive about entertaining women."

"Are you at the YMCA or something?"

"Something like that."

"So you need to get a place."

"I guess so. Yes."

Shirley was silent for a moment, then she said: "Do you know the Wayfarers' Motel on US-37 near the Krogers. Just north of town?"

"I'm sure I can find it."

"Okay. Can you be there at eight? No, wait a minute."

I heard some papers rustling at her end.

"Nine," she said. "I mean nine. Can you make it at nine?"

"Yes."

"Get a room there. At the Wayfarers' Motel. Ask for room number twelve because that's the one they know about. I'll be there right after."

I thought of something.

"By the way, Shirley, how much will it cost, if you don't mind me asking?"

"Twenty-five for half an hour. If we go longer the rate goes down to twenty. But half an hour is usually enough."

"Okay. Thank you."

I went back to the house on Fulton Street and took a shower and changed out of my work clothes. I wanted to look nice for Shirley.

※

AT NINE O'CLOCK I was in room number twelve at the Wayfarers' Motel. Actually, I was there at quarter to nine because I was feeling a little nervous and I wanted a chance to calm down before Shirley showed up. There was a side chair in the corner of the room and I moved it over by the window. Then I sat down and leaned back and crossed my legs because I thought that would show Shirley how relaxed I was. Not nervous in any way.

Shirley showed up a few minutes after nine. She was older

than I thought she'd be—maybe in her forties—and she had on heavy make-up and bright red lipstick. Her blonde hair looked like it needed to be washed, but otherwise she was all right. She wore a long trench coat with a tightly cinched belt and she had on tennis shoes. When she took off the trench coat she only had a slip on underneath.

"Okay," she said. She turned to me, standing there in her slip.

"It's a pleasure to meet you, Shirley," I said. "I appreciate you coming on such short notice."

"Yeah, well that's what I do. Whyn't you get undressed?"

She moved over to a side chair and put her coat on it. "Do you have any special things?" she asked.

"I'm afraid I don't understand what you mean by that."

"Anything special that you like. Some guys have special things they like to do. I can usually accommodate them as long as it's not too crazy."

"No. I just want to do it in the regular way."

She looked at me and laughed. "The regular way. That's a funny way to say it. You're a real card."

She turned to me and put her arms out. "Do you want to undress me, or should I do it myself? Some guys like to undress me."

"No. Well, yes. Well, before we get to that can we talk for a while? I'd like to get to know a little bit about you. Can we do that? Can we talk?" She looked at me with a puzzled expression.

"I'll pay extra if talking isn't part of the normal deal," I said.

"Okay. I don't care. But you only get the half hour. A half hour for everything, the talking and whatever else we do. That's the rule. If we go over half an hour it'll cost you extra."

"I understand."

Shirley went over to her purse and took out a cigarette. She lit it with a match, cupping her hand around the flame so that it lit up her face in a dramatic way. Then she sat down in the chair near the window and crossed her legs.

"Shoot," she said.

"What?"

"Let's start talking. That's what you said you wanted."

"Okay." I thought for a minute. "Where do you live, Shirley?"

"Sorry. I don't give that information to my clients."

"I mean in a general sense. Not your exact address."

"I live in Summit Township."

"Okay. And do you have another job. I mean do you do anything besides..." I made a sweeping gesture of the room "....besides this."

Shirley took a deep drag from her cigarette and blew it out before she answered.

"I waitress some. But no more than I have to. It gets to my feet. Being on my feet all day."

"Okay. Well, I can understand that. I can certainly understand that." I nodded my head slowly to show I understood. "I work at the car factory on 36th Street and I'm on my feet all day and it can be hard. I work with special tools."

"Special tools. What're those?"

"They're the special tools the journeymen use. The skilled trades who do specialized work like the electricians and millwrights and pipefitters."

Shirley gave me a blank stare, as if she didn't understand what I'd just said but didn't care enough to ask me to explain. It was a look I'd seen before, when I'd tried to talk to a girl about electricity. So I tried to think of something else to talk about. Something better than where I worked. And I choose the first thing that came into my mind.

"What do you think about going into space, Shirley?" I said. "Do you have an opinion about that?"

"You mean the satellites?"

"Yes."

"Well, I didn't like it when the Russians sent up that monkey." She took a deep drag on her cigarette, then blew the smoke out through the corner of her mouth. "I thought it was cruel to send a monkey up to outer space when they knew he was going to run out of oxygen and die."

"I think it was a dog," I said.

"What?"

"I think it was a dog they sent up. The Russians did."

Shirley looked at me.

"The dog's name was Laika, if my memory serves me right."

Shirley stood up. "Look," she said. "Let's get this over with. I'm tired of yapping. Either we get started or I leave."

Shirley crushed out her cigarette in an ashtray on the bedside table. Then she came over and sat on my lap. It was unexpected and I think I showed it on my face. I could feel the slippery smoothness of her slip. She touched my cheek and then she brushed the hair back off my forehead. "You're kinda cute," she said. "Younger than I usually get."

"Thank you. You're very attractive yourself."

Then Shirley put her hand behind my head and kissed me, sort of pulling me against her mouth. And her mouth felt nice. I have to admit it felt nice. But not as nice as Diane's. That was the first crazy thought that came into my head: that Shirley's mouth felt nice but not as nice as Diane's. And then I opened my eyes, still kissing her, and I saw her hair up close, sort of stringy and needing to be washed.

I pushed her away, trying to do it gently.

"What?" she said.

I didn't want to give the real reason, so I said something else. "My knee hurts," I said. "I've got a bad knee and it hurts with you sitting on my lap like that."

Shirley jumped up. "Sorry. I didn't know."

"There was no way you could've known. I should've told you. Before you sat on my lap and everything."

Shirley stood in the middle of the room in her shiny white slip. I sat in the chair. And then I thought that I should begin to rub my knee to make it look like it really hurt, so I began to rub my knee.

"You poor guy," Shirley said. "Having a bum knee like that. And you so young."

I looked at Shirley. She grimaced, as if she was feeling the pain I had just told her about. Sharing the pain with me and wanting me to know she shared it. So I wouldn't feel so all alone in my suffering. And suddenly I started to feel differently about her, like I wanted to kiss her again, even with the stringy hair, and to go ahead with the other things I'd had in mind to do.

"It's better now," I said. I stood up and forced a smile. "Rubbing makes it feel better." I slapped my knee a couple of times to show it didn't hurt. "Do you want to go to bed now?" I said.

"No way," Shirley said. "I don't want to be responsible if your knee acts up again." She picked up her trench coat and started to put it on. "You should get a doctor to look at it. They can do wonderful things with joints now. My friend Sylvia had a hip that kept going out on her and they fixed it and now she's back to work."

Shirley walked over to the door and grasped the doorknob. But instead of opening the door she turned back and looked at me. "Seriously," she said. "You should see a doctor." She stood for a moment, staring off to the side.

"So I guess I won't charge you for anything," she said. "Technically, I should charge you for a half hour but I won't. Because it was only on account of your knee that we didn't do anything. And you couldn't help it about your knee so it wouldn't be fair to charge you." Shirley moved her gaze onto my face and smiled. "Promise me you'll see a doctor about your knee and I won't charge."

"Okay," I said. "I promise. Thanks. So maybe I'll see you again."

"Maybe," she said. "But only if you get your knee fixed." She looked at me with a stern expression, her eyes squinted down to narrow slits, like she was giving me an order. "Remember, that's our deal," she said. "First get your knee fixed and then you can call me."

Another smile came onto Shirley's face and then she turned and opened the door and left the room. And as the door came closed behind her I felt a loss. Even though she'd been in the room for only a short time I was already starting to miss her. Under the right circumstances I could see where we could be friends. If she wasn't a prostitute, we could be friends. Or maybe even though she was. Perhaps that didn't matter. A friend who tries to share your pain and gives you good advice and doesn't charge you when something's not your fault.

Chapter Twelve

A few days after seeing Shirley I decided I wanted to see Audrey again. Painting by myself in my spot along the river wasn't as much fun when she wasn't there to talk to. And I missed the things she told me about painting, the little bits of advice that made my painting better. And I missed our conversations too, even though she was smarter than me and knew more about the world and how to live in it. But if I wanted to see her again I knew I had to tell her I'd been wrong to say she should stop giving tours, because that was the point where our friendship fell apart. And after I'd thought about it for a while I realized she was right. After all, it was her business and not mine. And maybe it wasn't so bad. She took money from men for being nice to them, but was that really any different than a pretty salesclerk who smiles while selling you a necktie, or a waitress who jokes with you so you'll leave a bigger tip.

The next day in the afternoon I went to the Rexall Drug Store on Leonard Street. I stood for a while in the greeting-card section, partially hidden behind a rack of Hallmark cards, and I watched Audrey working behind the lunch counter. She wore a light blue dress with a tiny white collar and a frilly apron that had a deep pocket where she carried the order book. I watched from my hiding place as she made milkshakes and soda drinks and sandwiches and brought them to the customers seated on the stools. She looked completely different than when I'd seen her at my painting spot. What I mean to say is she looked diminished— that's the best word I can think of—like a smaller version of the person I'd seen before. For a while I thought about leaving without saying anything but then when her back was turned to make a malted milk I stepped quickly across the store and sat down on one of the stools. When she brought the malted milk to the man seated four seats to my left she saw me but didn't react in any way. She placed the malted milk in front of the man and asked if she could do anything else for him. He said no but that he'd call her if he thought of something. Then he smiled in a kind of lecherous way to show he didn't mean just the food. Audrey rolled her eyes and turned away. Then she came over to where I was.

"What do you want?" she said.

"I just came to say hello."

"I mean what do you want to order. This is a lunch counter. You've got to order something if you want to sit here."

"Okay," I said. "Bring me a Coke."

Audrey went and got a Coke and brought it back. She set it on the counter and then began to turn away.

"Wait a minute," I said.

"What?"

"I want to talk to you about the other day. Our conversation. When you told me about giving the walking tours to businessmen."

Audrey looked at me.

"I might've been out of line. Telling you what you should and shouldn't do. That's not my business. That's up to you."

Audrey kept looking at me.

"It's just that I feel very strongly that it could be dangerous for you. Going out with men you don't really know." I looked at her. "But it's your decision, not mine."

"So you're saying it's all right?" Audrey said.

"Well, no, not exactly. I still think you shouldn't be doing it. But, like I said, it's up to you."

Audrey stared at me with a blank expression. Then she leaned forward so her mouth was near my ear.

"Fuck you," she said in a whispery voice.

"What?"

"I said fuck you. That's another way of saying get out of here."

"You want me to leave?"

"Yes."

"But why?"

"Because you think you know what I should be doing better than I do myself. And I'm tired of that. I'm tired of people telling me how I should live my life." She started to turn away but then she stopped. "I went through all of that last year and I'm not going to do it again."

"What? What are you talking about? What happened last year?"

She stared at me for a long moment. Then she turned and walked away. I waited for a while. When I realized she wasn't coming back I left.

&.

A FEW DAYS later I had an idea of what I could do to make things better between Audrey and me. I had finished my latest painting of the abandoned furniture factories and the Sixth Street Bridge, and I had used Audrey's ideas to make it better. And I thought that I would give the painting to her. Giving it to her would be a way of saying how much I valued her advice and of showing that I'd *taken* her advice, that what she'd told me was important and I had used it.

So on the day I finished the painting I walked with it to the Arlington Hotel. I had memorized some things to say when I gave it to her, how I'd explain that it was both a gift and an apology, but when I got to the hotel she wasn't in so I decided to leave it at the front desk with a note attached. I took some time to write the note because I wanted it to be exactly right. When I was finished it said:

Audrey

This painting is for you because you helped to make it better. Better by a long shot. I hope what I said to you the other day has not ruined our friendship. It was a stupid thing to say. I miss you and would like to see you again.

Your friend, Nate.

"What's this?" the desk clerk said when I set my painting on the counter.

"I'd like you to give this to Audrey Brubaker when she comes in."

"We're not a delivery service."

I pushed the painting a few inches in his direction so he'd know I wasn't giving up.

"It's special," I said. "It's a special gift. Can't you do it this once."

"I don't make the rules," the man said.

I reached around and got my wallet from my back pocket. I took out a five-dollar bill and placed it on the counter. "Here," I said. "Will this help?"

The man glanced at the five-dollar bill, then he rotated the painting so he could read the note.

"That's a big mistake," he said, pointing to the note. "Apologizing to a woman like that. You want to keep the upper hand."

I said nothing.

The man looked down at the five-dollar bill again. Then he reached and took it off the counter and put it into his pocket.

"I guess breaking the rule just once will be okay," he said. He picked up the painting and put it behind the counter.

"Be careful with it," I said. "It's still a little wet."

THE NEXT DAY after work I did not go to my painting spot along the river or to any other painting spot. Instead I went to the library to look for a book about how to stay out of the Army draft. My father was right. In just two weeks I'd turn eighteen and have to register with the local draft board, and because of how things were going in Vietnam I was pretty sure that I'd be drafted. But I had thought it over and decided I didn't want to be a soldier. Part of the reason was because of what had happened to Gary, but a bigger part was that I didn't understand the need for fighting in Vietnam. In World War Two it had been simple—there had been a great evil in the world and it had to be destroyed—but in Vietnam it was more complicated. I had heard the argument, and it took several steps of reasoning, moving from one obscure point to the next, before you finally reached the conclusion that we had to go to war. I guess you could say I wasn't convinced. Not convinced that I should go and fight people I didn't know in a country I had never heard of.

So I had thought about the different ways of staying out of the Army, but none of them seemed exactly right for me: I didn't have a job that was important to the country's safety, and I didn't have a wife and a family to support, and I was not a homosexual, because the Army didn't want you if you were that way. For a while I thought about going to Canada and beginning a new life there, in Montreal or Nova Scotia or the Yukon, some exotic place that would teach me something different about the world and make my hiding out be worthwhile. And then I thought about finding a doctor who would say I had a medical problem that prevented me from being a soldier, like bone spurs or an enlarged spleen, even though I didn't know what those things were. And then I thought about going to a minister of some religion and telling him I didn't believe in violence, that any kind of violence was against my deepest principals, so he'd write a letter saying I was a conscientious objector.

And then I realized that the reason none of those ways seemed right was because they were all too easy. All you had to do was say a thing that wasn't true and they would take you off the list. They'd mark you down in a different category and you'd be free. But it seemed to me that avoiding the draft would be a turning point in my life and change the way I thought about my country and being a citizen in it. All the pledges of allegiance I'd recited at school and the national anthems I'd sung at baseball games and the famous men I'd learned about in history—the Presidents and the Generals and the founding fathers—would be wiped away. I mean they would *have* to be wiped away for me to feel okay about what I was doing. Not ashamed.

And so staying out of the Army should not be easy. That was my final conclusion. I should have to pay a price.

So I had gone to the library to find a book that would help me stay out of the draft. I was particularly interested in whether you could pretend to be a homosexual, because it seemed that having people think about you that way would be a sacrifice. But after I got to the library I realized I didn't know what words to use to look it up in the Dewey system, and none of the words I tried led to anything that seemed helpful.

So I left the library, feeling a little depressed that I hadn't found any help there. As I was coming down the wide front steps that brought you down to Bridge Street I saw Audrey walking along the sidewalk on the other side. She wore the white dress I'd seen her in on that first afternoon, the cotton dress that shifted in the wind, but her hair was done up in a ponytail instead of falling loose around her shoulders. She was alone.

I called out to her and she looked across and spotted me and smiled and waved. And that made me feel better, because it meant that she'd forgiven me.

"Did you get the painting I left for you?" I said, after I'd come across the street.

"Yes. It was sweet of you, but I'm going to give it back. It's too important. Because it's when you became a real artist."

"But I want you to have it. If I've become an artist then it's because of you."

She smiled. "That's nice of you to say. But let's table the subject for now and talk about it later." Then she said: "Speaking of that, why aren't you painting now?"

"I was in the library looking for a book about how to keep from getting drafted. But I couldn't find anything."

"I thought you were patriotic. Memorizing the President's speeches and such. Dodging the draft doesn't seem exactly patriotic."

"I am," I said. "Patriotic. At least I think I am. But the war that's starting in Vietnam is different. We shouldn't be there. I think Kennedy will see that pretty soon and get us out."

"You could run away to Canada," Audrey said. "I know boys who've done that. It's not far."

"It's not far but you can never come back." Then I said to her, just as a joke, "I think I'm going to do something to one of my fingers. Maybe smash one with a hammer. I don't think they'd want me in the Army if I had a messed-up finger because I couldn't hold a gun or shoot it."

Audrey took my hand and held it up and looked at it.

"Which finger would you do it to?"

"I hadn't gotten that far. They all seem important." I grinned to show that I was kidding.

"Why don't you smash a toe?" she said. "You don't need toes so much in regular life. Not as much as fingers. But in the Army you need toes for marching." She looked at me and I suddenly realized she was serious. "I think a smashed toe would keep you out," she added.

"I don't know if I could stand the pain."

"Get drunk. Getting drunk will help. You won't feel the pain so much."

"I can't buy liquor. I'm not old enough."

"I'll do it for you." She turned around and looked across the plaza to the stores along Bridge Street. "There's a party store over there. I can buy some liquor there. Then we can find a place to do it. An alley or that place along the river where you paint. Some out-of-the-way place where no one will hear you if you scream. We could do it with a rock."

"I don't know," I said, stalling for time. "Let me think about it."

"Don't think too much," Audrey said. "Sometimes thinking can get in the way of a good idea."

It was obvious now that Audrey was serious. But then I noticed my own thinking was beginning to change. Because suddenly Audrey's idea didn't seem so bad. Her enthusiasm had sort of captured me and won me over. And I liked that she would help me do it. Do something that would be important to my life and make a difference. And I realized, too, that smashing a toe—the pain it would cause and the damage it would do— would be a loss, a sacrifice big enough to earn the right to not become a soldier.

"Stay here," Audrey said, without giving me another chance to speak. "I'll be right back."

While she was gone, I thought about what was going to

happen and if I had nerve enough to let Audrey do it. I knew it would hurt but I believed Audrey about the liquor, that it would make it not so painful. Enough that I could stand it.

After a few minutes Audrey came walking back across the plaza. She smiled and waved a brown paper bag over her head.

"What kind did you get?" I asked, when she got close.

"Bourbon," she said. "That's the all-American liquor. It'll get you drunk fast." She looked around. "Let's go down to your painting place. We'll have some privacy there." She took my hand and began to lead me toward the river, turning back every once in a while and smiling in an encouraging way.

When we got to the river we went down the path to the painting spot, holding hands to keep our balance. "There," she said, when we got down to the walking path. "Sit there." She pointed to the fallen log. Then she twisted the cap off the bottle and handed it to me.

I started to drink the bourbon, looking out at the river and trying not to think about what was going to happen next. After I'd taken four or five swallows, I began to feel it working on me, a kind of lightness that started in my head and spread out to the rest of my body. Then I took a good deep swallow which took the bottle down to half and I felt it hit me harder, a kind of floating sensation, like I was losing my connection to the earth.

While I was drinking the liquor, Audrey had followed the path along the river. When she came back she was excited. I could see it in her face.

"There's a heron's nest down there." She pointed back along the path. "I think it's a blue heron. One of those big ones." She was excited and there was redness in her cheeks. "How're you coming with the liquor?" she asked.

"I think I'm a little drunk."

"A little drunk won't do it. Drink the rest." She pointed to the bottle that was still half full. I lifted it and tilted it back and let the rest run down my throat.

"Good boy," she said. She took the bottle from my hand and set it on the ground. "Now we get to the interesting part."

Audrey walked down to the edge of the river and searched until she found a stone she liked. She hefted it in her hand like she was gaging the weight of it. Then she came back up to me.

"What do you think?" she asked. She handed me the stone. "There's a place on one side where it bulges out. So I think I can smash the right toe without smashing any others."

I was feeling fully drunk now. I couldn't fix my gaze on anything without it slipping off and landing on something else. Audrey was still talking but she sounded far away, like her voice was coming through a tunnel. And I noticed there seemed to be little gaps in my awareness, like when the sprockets on a film projector begin to slip. Then, before I realized it, Audrey was kneeling on the ground. She took off the shoe and sock on my left foot and placed my foot against the trunk of a tree, just where the trunk came out of the ground.

"Okay," she said. "I'm going to do it to the middle one. Is that okay with you? Can I do the middle?"

I couldn't speak so I just nodded my head.

"Maybe you should look away," she said. "It'd be better if you don't know when it's coming."

"Wait a minute." I reached down and grabbed her arm. "I'm not sure I can do this."

"Sure you can. Be brave. Be brave for me." Then she said, "Here. I'll give you something to distract you."

Audrey stood and unbuttoned the white dress where it was buttoned down the front. She slipped her arms out and the dress fell loose around her waist. She stood there for a moment, like she was uncertain what she should do next. Then she shrugged and bent forward and reached around behind and undid her bra and let that fall too. "There," she said. "Now you've got something else to think about. Not just your poor old toe."

I stared at Audrey's breasts. And it was shocking—with me just sitting by the river on a nice fall afternoon—to see her like that. But I tried not to *look* shocked; I tried to look like seeing a girl's breasts was the sort of thing that happened to me all the time.

"Okay," she said. "That's enough." She knelt down and put my foot up against the tree trunk and spread my toes so the middle one was separated from the others. I kept trying to see her breasts, but I didn't have a good view. With her kneeling down it was sort of an angle view, with everything kind of overlapping and in the way.

Just then I heard a loud whirring noise and the blue heron that Audrey had talked about rose up out of the grass with its wide curved wings beating back the air and its long stick-like legs hanging back behind. And suddenly everything was wild, too wild for me to deal with, with the heron flying, and Audrey with her breasts bare, and the sunlight glinting off the water, and my foot against the tree trunk waiting to be smashed.

And then for a while there was nothing.

Chapter Thirteen

I was lying on the ground looking up into the deep blue sky. A hawk circled overhead, just gliding slowly through the currents of air. The ground felt damp beneath me. I turned my head. Audrey was sitting on a log near the river. She had a stick in her hand and she trailed it in the water so it made tiny ripples on the surface. Her dress was back together.

I sat up and shook my head to try to clear the confusion away. Audrey heard me and turned around. "There you are," she said. "You've come back." She came over and knelt where I was sitting on the ground.

"What happened?" I said.

"You conked out. I guess the excitement was too much for you."

"Did you smash my toe?" I moved the toes on my left foot but none of them seemed to hurt too bad. Not how you'd expect if one of them was smashed.

"No," Audrey said. "It seemed like it wouldn't be fair to smash it with you conked out."

She had a tiny smile on her face that made me think of something.

"Were you really going to do it?" I asked.

Her smile got bigger. "No," she said. "Of course not. I'm not an idiot." She smiled again. "I just wanted to see you drunk."

I laughed a little. Partly at Audrey's joke and partly in relief. "Thank you," I said. And then I said: "I just wanted to see your breasts."

She laughed again, but then her expression got serious. "But how're you going to stay out of the draft? You still haven't solved that problem."

"I don't know. Maybe I won't register."

"I don't think that'll work. They'll come and get you."

"Maybe. But first they'll have to find me."

Audrey smiled, as if she liked the idea of me not registering even though she thought it wouldn't work. Then she stood and reached down and took both my hands and helped me up, leaning back and pulling. I felt a little dizzy and she saw it; she stepped forward and put an arm around my waist.

"Sit on the log for a while," she said. "Wait until you're back to feeling normal."

Audrey led me over to the log and I sat down. After a minute she took off her shoes and knotted her dress on one side and went out to wade in the shallow water along the shore. Every once in a while she reached down and picked up something off the river bottom—a colorful stone or a piece of tree bark or the skeleton of a crayfish—and she would hold it overhead and wave her arm as if she'd discovered some great treasure. After a few minutes she came back on shore and sat next to me on the log. Her legs were dripping water on the ground.

"You told me to fuck myself," I said.

"What?"

"That's what you said when I came to see you at the Rexall the other day."

"Did I?" she said. "Well, that was certainly rude of me." She looked at me. "Sometimes I get carried away. You'll have to learn to ignore that part of me."

"Dale Carnegie probably wouldn't like it if he knew you told someone to get fucked."

She laughed. "No. I suppose not."

We sat for a while without talking.

"Do you ever wonder where it all comes from?" Audrey said, looking out at the river.

"What do you mean?"

"The water. It just keeps coming down the river. So much of it. You'd think it'd run out after a while."

I laughed. "It gets replaced. The water evaporates and then goes up in clouds and comes back down as rain."

"I've heard that," Audrey said. She had a serious expression on her face, her eyes squinted down to narrow slits. "About evaporation. But it doesn't make sense to me. Because there's too much of it. Too much water to go back in the air." She looked at me. "The air seems puny compared to all the water."

I thought about what she said. And I sort of understood her point. Because the water in the river was big and powerful and there was so much of it. It was hard to believe how so much water could go back in the air.

"I guess you just have to believe it even if you don't understand," I said.

"It's not that I don't understand," Audrey said, and there was some sharpness in her voice. "I'm not stupid. I just can't imagine it. I can't imagine all that water going back in the air. I can't picture it in my imagination."

I was about to say more, to explain about humidity and the dew point and how evaporation worked to bring back water to the river, but then I realized Audrey was saying something different; she was saying that there are things you can explain with words that you can't capture in your mind, can't make a picture of, incredible things that were still true. And then I wondered if there were other things like that, things I could explain in a scientific way but couldn't grasp in my imagination. But then my thinking broke down, and I couldn't carry the thought any further, could not bring it to a conclusion. But I made a point to remember to think about it later, because it seemed like an important thing to understand.

"Do you remember when I asked you about your car and about doing me a favor?" Audrey said next.

"Yes."

"What about tomorrow night? Are you available tomorrow?"

"I guess so. But you still haven't told me where we're going."

"It's my parent's house in Newaygo. There's something there I need to get. I have to do it at night, when they're asleep."

"What is it? The thing you need to get?"

Audrey looked at me for a minute as if she wasn't sure she wanted to answer my question. And then she said: "It's a baby's christening dress. Do you know what that is?"

"No."

"It's what a baby wears when he's getting baptized in a church. It's a special dress to show that the moment is important."

I turned and looked at Audrey. And I probably looked confused. Because I had never heard her talk about a baby. "Tell me about it," I said.

And then she did, explaining that she'd had a baby the year before when she'd been living with her parents in Newaygo. But she'd lost the baby after only a few days and now she wanted to get the christening dress. She had stitched it together herself, she said, using scraps of white satin she'd been given by the home economics teacher at the high school and for her it was a symbol of the pure soul her baby had when he came into the world, and that he still had when he left it.

"While I was pregnant they kept me in the house," Audrey said. "My parents did. They were afraid of what people would say about us in town and at the church, that they would get a bad impression about us. About our family. My dad runs the hardware store and he thought the town would turn against us and he'd lose his customers. So I was sort of a prisoner, just staying in the house all day and watching old black-and-white movies on TV and trying to figure out how I was going to be a mother. And I guess that gave me a low opinion of myself; that I was a person who couldn't go out into the world and be seen by normal people."

Audrey stopped talking. She sat for a moment just staring at the ground. Then she spoke again.

"And that wasn't all," she said. "My parents treated me different. That was probably the worst part. It was like I wasn't their daughter anymore, like I was just a stranger who happened to be living in their house. They hardly ever talked to me and when they did it was usually to remind me of what a terrible person I was."

Audrey's hands were folded on her lap and she was looking down at them. She stopped talking for a moment and I could tell she was remembering the time when those things happened, remembering how it had felt to be rejected by her family and to feel ashamed. "Anyway, my parents tried to deliver the baby at home, because they wanted to keep it a secret," she continued. "And it didn't go exactly right. The baby was turned around and they didn't know what to do. And there was a lot of blood and I passed out for a while. And then I sort of went delirious for several days; at least that's what they told me. When I finally came awake it was all over. The baby had died and they'd sent it away to be taken care of."

Audrey stopped talking but I knew she wasn't finished. She pushed the tip of the stick into the dirt and twisted it so that it made a little hole.

"After that I ran away," she said. "As soon as I was strong enough, I ran away. After everything that'd happened I wanted to start over. My old life had been ruined and I wanted to make a better one. Begin at ground zero." She turned and looked at me and shrugged, as if starting a new life was a simple thing to do. "That's when I got the idea about learning to design furniture," she said. "Grand Rapids is where they make a lot of it so I thought if I could design it I could find a job." She twisted the stick and started to make a second hole. "And there was another reason," she said. "I liked the idea of it—the idea of furniture—how you use it to make a house be a place you want to live in." She stopped talking and threw the stick in the direction of the river, but it didn't quite reach the water. "I never felt that way in my parents' house," she said. "But I was pretty sure it was possible to make a house feel like a place where you belonged. If you did it right, it was possible."

"Anyway," she said, after a pause, "I'd like to get that christening dress so I'll have one thing to remember my baby by. One thing to show that he was here."

It took Audrey several minutes to say all of these things and when she was done she was crying. She wasn't making crying noises but tears were in her eyes and on her face. And somehow the silent crying made it seem even sadder, as if the pain that caused it was always just below the surface and could break out at any time. At some point during the telling she had reached over and put her hand on top of mine, as if she wanted us to have a stronger connection than from the words she spoke, as if something could be conveyed by touch that couldn't be done with words.

I let a long moment pass before I asked the next question.

"What about the boy who got you pregnant."

Audrey looked at me and then she looked away. "He left," she said. "When he found out I was pregnant he left town. No one knew where he went. He just left." Her gaze came back to me and she winced, as if it hurt to say what she was saying and she wanted me to know it hurt. "Up until then we'd been planning to get married," she added, and she smiled in a kind of bitter way. "I really loved him. I thought he loved me."

Audrey drew her fists across her cheeks to wipe the tears away. She took another deep breath, as if to show that the sad part of the story was over and she was going on to a better part. "You won't have to do anything," she said. "Just drive. I'll go into the house and get the christening dress. All you'll have to do is wait outside." She turned and smiled at me. But it was not a normal smile; it was a smile that took some effort, as if she had to force it through some other feelings. "So will you do it?" she asked.

At first I didn't answer. I wanted to think before I gave an answer, so I stood up and walked down to the bank of the river and stared out onto the water. Somehow, looking out at the water helped me think. And what I thought is that we would be breaking into a house at night like burglars. And even though it was Audrey's parent' house, we'd be going in without them knowing, which would be a crime. I would be crossing a boundary, putting myself on a different side of regular life. And I wondered what that would mean, and whether I could ever come back and have a normal life again.

But then I thought about my life right now: how I was living on my own instead of being at a university, and how I was trying to be an artist even though I had no training, and how I was scheming to stay out of the draft and not be patriotic. And I realized those things were on the other side of normal life too. I'd put myself there already.

I turned around and looked at Audrey. "What time?" I asked.

"How about midnight? Can you manage midnight?"

Chapter Fourteen

The next day at midnight I drove to the Arlington Hotel. Audrey was waiting under the canvas awning that had the torn piece hanging down. She was dressed differently than when I had seen her on the street, in blue jeans and a sweatshirt and tennis shoes. A blue stocking cap was pulled low across her forehead.

She opened the door and scooted inside.

"You look like a burglar," I said, because I thought she did and I thought that saying it would be funny.

"What?" she said.

"You look like a burglar."

"That's stupid," she said, and there was some anger in her voice. "We're just going to get something that already belongs to me."

We drove out of town and then north on highway 37, past the fruit orchards and the old farmhouses with hulking barns that you could only see as shadows. We went through the little town of Grant, and then back out into the country again, only now it was different, not orchards and farmhouses and barns, but pine forests and low tangled swampland with water standing between mounds of grass.

We were mostly silent. I thought Audrey was probably thinking about what would happen once we got to her parents' house, making a plan about how she would get the christening dress without having to face her parents. I was thinking about what I would do if Audrey got discovered, how I would explain myself so I wouldn't get in trouble too.

At some point along the way I asked Audrey what a christening dress was for, and she told me it was the special clothes a baby wears when he's being baptized. "It's an important step, getting baptized, and you want to show it's important with what the baby wears because he's entering into the Kingdom of God. Anyway, that's the theory." She paused to wipe away some fog that had formed on the side window. "Though I'm not sure I believe all of that," she said. "About the Kingdom of God and such. Like why does God let so many bad things happen? Bad things that happen to people who don't deserve it, like those little Negro girls in Alabama who got blown up in church last Sunday. Why would God let that happen?"

"Or someone who's a great pianist and joins the Army and gets shot," I said.

Audrey looked at me with a puzzled expression. "What? What are you talking about?"

I was silent, thinking about whether I wanted to tell her about Gary, because it seemed to fit in with what she was saying about God not being fair. But I decided it was too big a subject to bring up in that moment, when we were on a mission to get Audrey's christening dress and needed to keep our minds set in that direction, and not get distracted.

"Nothing," I said. "It was just something I heard about."

After that Audrey was silent again and I thought she was probably thinking about God now, and whether what she'd said was right in terms of how she really felt. "But I like the idea of the christening dress," she said, all of a sudden. "I like the idea of a baby being pure in the beginning. I like that part of it. Starting out with no strikes against you. Before bad things begin to happen."

We were coming into Newaygo now, coming down the big hill that takes you into town, and then past the sand mold factory and then the downtown stores, closed now with just a few lights burning to keep the burglars away, and then past the theater with its marquee saying *The Birds* was playing and how much it would frighten you, and then past the village square with a Civil War soldier standing on a pedestal, and then over the bridge across the Muskegon River with the hydroelectric dam downstream and the roar of water crashing down and a mist drifting slowly through a spotlight beam.

"Keep going on this road," Audrey said. "I'll tell you where to turn off."

We left Newaygo and drove another mile or two along the highway. Audrey told me to turn onto a gravel road that angled off to the left and then onto a two-track drive that went back into the forest. "Turn off your headlights," Audrey said after we'd gone a short way on the two-track drive, and then we drove for a while with the headlights off, just guided by moonlight. After another minute we came up a small rise; when we reached the top I could see the dark shape of a house against the lighter background of the sky.

"Stop here," Audrey said.

We sat in the darkness, not talking, just looking at the black mass that was the house. I sensed that Audrey was still trying to decide what to do next, how she was going to get the christening dress out of the house without her parents knowing. And then I realized that she didn't really have a plan; she wanted to get the christening dress but she had not thought through all the

89

details of how to do it. She was still trying to figure that out, now, just before going inside to do it.

"What do we do now?" I said, after the silence had gone on for a while.

"I guess I'm going to go inside and get the dress," Audrey said. Though I could tell from the way her voice sounded that she was nervous. Nervous about waking up her parents, I suppose, and nervous that they would make her stay.

"Will your parents give you any trouble?" I asked.

"If I do it right they won't know. They'll stay asleep. I've got a key to get in the back door." She opened her hand and showed a silver key resting on her palm. "Once I get inside I'll do everything in the dark."

But I could tell from her voice and the expression on her face that it wasn't only fear that was holding her back; there was a sadness in her voice too, sadness because she couldn't return to the house that she'd grown up in, not return as a member of the family but only as an intruder, someone who doesn't belong there, and what a big loss that was.

"I'll go in," I said to Audrey. "Tell me where the dress is and I'll go in and get it."

At first Audrey didn't answer. She sat looking out at the house showing dark against the sky.

"Are you brave enough?" she asked me. "What if you get caught?"

"I'll tell them it was a mistake. I'll tell them I thought it was a friend's house I'd gone into. A friend I wanted to play a trick on." I looked at her. "Or I'll run away. I'll hear them coming and I'll run out of the house before they can see me."

"Okay," she said. "You've convinced me. You're smart. I'm sure that in the critical moment you'll think of something." And then she explained that the dress was in a closet in the room that'd been her bedroom, and how I could find my way there in the darkened house. "It's on the first floor. After you go through the living room you'll see a door on the left. That's it."

I sat for another moment gathering my thoughts. Or maybe I was gathering my courage, because I'd never broken into a house before, or done anything else that went against the law. Then I said, "Okay, here goes nothing," and I laughed a little to try to make it seem okay, something we were doing just for fun and not a serious thing like breaking into a place we had no right to be in.

And then I thought of something else: "Wait a minute," I said. "Let's turn the car around and keep the engine running. In case we have to make a quick escape."

I backed the car around so we were headed in the right direction on the two-track road. Then I stepped out and closed the door behind me, just pushing so it wouldn't make a slamming sound. Everything was quiet. The only sound was the far-off croaking of some frogs and the wind gently riffling through tree branches. I made my way up to the back door of the house, crouching low and moving quickly, trying to stay in shadows. The back door was locked, but I used the key that Audrey had given me and I turned the latch and pushed the door open and stepped inside. I was standing in a kitchen, and suddenly everything felt different, and I realized that by coming through the door I'd violated an important principal about where a person lives and the sacredness of that, a space that is your own and where you feel protected and where other people can't come in unless you ask them.

I stood for several minutes, letting my eyes adjust, straining to hear a noise, something that might show I'd been found out: the sound of a mattress being squeezed by someone getting out of bed, or footsteps on a stairway, or the squeak of a hinge on a door that's being opened. But there was nothing, only the sound of my breath coming in and out of my body, and the throb of my heart beating strongly in my chest.

Everything seemed bigger, all of my sensations.

But nothing happened, and after another moment I began to feel a little better, though I was still too frightened to move. So I decided to wait a little longer, just inside the door, wait until the space felt better, because I was in it now and wanted it to feel normal.

While I waited I looked around. Some plates were drying in a rack on the counter and there was a glass with ice cubes melting in the bottom. Some papers were held by magnets on the refrigerator door.

I stepped over so I could see the papers. I don't know why but I did. Maybe I hoped to learn something about Audrey's parents, whose house I had broken into and whose daughter I was helping. One of the papers was a bill from the Cherryland Electric Cooperative for $13.57, and one was a coupon from Kresge's for twenty-five cents off on a bottle of hair shampoo, and one was a letter from the St. Paul Home in Detroit saying that the baby was doing fine and would soon be placed in a nice Christian home.

I stood for a moment frozen, sort of dazed by what I'd read. And then I read the letter for a second time to make sure I'd gotten it right, and then I read it for a third time so I could fix the details of it in my brain. Finally, I placed it back onto the refrigerator door.

I began to move again, making my way through the house, taking small steps so I wouldn't trip on something and make a noise. And then I saw the door to Audrey's bedroom and I went across and pushed it open and stepped inside. The closet door was in the left-hand corner, just like Audrey had said. The christening dress was easy to spot, even in the dim light, because it was white and shiny, different from the other clothes that hung there, the blouses and the dresses and the petticoats. I slipped the christening dress off the hanger, being careful so the metal hangers didn't rattle, and I put it over my arm and closed the closet door. As I turned around, I spotted something shiny on a bureau against the wall. I went over and picked it up. It was a photograph in a silver frame of Audrey and a blond-haired boy standing in front of a lilac bush in bloom. They were dressed in formal clothes, as if they were about to leave for a high school prom. Audrey wore a bright yellow dress with a corsage pinned near the shoulder and the boy was in a white tuxedo with a colorful cummerbund. Audrey smiled radiantly and the boy stood close beside her with an arm around her waist and he was smiling too. I brought the photo up and looked closely at the boy, wondering if he was the one who'd gotten Audrey pregnant and then abandoned her. I examined his face, looking for some clue that might show he was unreliable or disloyal, but I couldn't find it. He looked like a normal boy, as far as I could tell.

I set the photograph down. A piece of paper lay off to one side and I picked it up. It was a letter from the Kendall School dated April 16th, 1961, saying the work examples Audrey had submitted were deemed to be of very high quality and the school would be pleased to enroll her as a student in the coming fall semester. Almost as an afterthought the letter noted that tuition would be three-hundred and forty-three dollars, due in full at the beginning of each term. A large red X had been drawn through the number and in the margin had been scrawled: "HA! HA! - Why not a million?"

I set the letter down and was about to leave the room when I heard a noise that wasn't clear to me, that didn't fit with anything I recognized, and then another sound, the snap of a switch, and then a sudden blinding brightness filled the room and Audrey's father was standing in the doorway with a pistol in his hand and it was pointed at my chest.

"What the hell is going on?" he said. "Who are you?"

I was blinded by the sudden light and blinking, trying to make sense of what was happening from the intermittent images that danced before my eyes, like one of those silent films where the movements don't quite flow together.

"That's a baby's dress you've got there," Audrey's father said. "Are you a pervert. One of those. That you like babies' clothes?"

I didn't know what to say. And suddenly I realized that although I had a plan for what to do if I was caught coming into the house, I didn't have a plan for what to do after I had the christening dress and was holding it in my hand. I hadn't thought things through that far, which was a weakness of my plan.

Audrey's father stepped over so we were almost touching. He put his face up close to mine. I could smell whisky on his breath and see the whiskers on his face. He put the barrel of the pistol under my jaw and pressed hard so I had to tilt my head back. And in that moment I believed he was going to shoot me, and I tried to get ready for that to happen, for the blackness that would follow a great explosion, and then nothing, just an emptiness, like being carried off by some fierce wind, and I began to cry.

But it didn't happen. Audrey's father didn't pull the trigger. And when I realized I wasn't going to die, that the blackness was not going to take me, that there would be other moments of being alive, I felt a great release and made another sound, a startled gasping sound like when you reach the surface after being under water, or wake from a bad dream and realize that things are going to be all right.

"Why you're just a boy," Audrey's father said, and some of the anger seemed to have gone out of his voice, like he could talk in the way a man would talk to any boy under normal circumstances, and not when the boy was stealing something from his house.

It was quiet for a while, perhaps several minutes, though it was hard to know because I'd lost a sense of time, was just experiencing things in a kind of timeless vacuum. And then Audrey's father said: "You know I could shoot you, don't you, son? You understand that, don't you? The risk you're taking. I could pull this trigger and no one would care or be on your side or stand up for you. Do you understand that? Or are you stupid?" And he spoke as if he were explaining something to me, something I should know about, a rule I should take with me into life to be a better person. And then I knew he wasn't going to shoot me, because rules don't matter if you're dead. What would be the point of that?

"Yes, sir," I said. "I know that." Then I said, "I'm sorry."

"So I'll ask you again. What are you doing here?" Audrey's father took the pistol away from my chin and waved it in a circle to show that he was talking about the house now, all of it, and not just Audrey's bedroom.

"I was getting this dress for Audrey," I said. "She wants it."

He stepped back. "You know Audrey?" he said.

"Yes, sir. A little."

"Where is she?"

At first I didn't say anything. But then I remembered the gun barrel held against my chin: "She's staying at the Arlington Hotel in Grand Rapids. She lives there now."

"And she wants this dress? Audrey wants the baby dress?"

"Yes, sir. That's what she said."

"And she sent you here to get it?"

"Yes, sir."

Audrey's father was quiet for a while, holding the gun at his side now and not on me, his gaze moving back and forth between me and the dress. "Well, you go ahead and take it to her," he said. "If she wants it that bad, tell her she can have it." Then he raised the gun and pointed it at my chest, but casually now, like he was using it to make a gesture and not to shoot me. "Now get out of here. Tell Audrey she can have the dress. But I'd advise you not to get mixed up with her. She's a different girl than she seems to be. Her mother and I know that about her. We know that now."

"All right," I said. "Thank you, sir."

I stepped past Audrey's father and walked back through the house, which was easier now because some light was spilling out from Audrey's bedroom. I opened the back door and went out into the cool night darkness, where I knew that Audrey was waiting for me in the running car.

Chapter Fifteen

I opened the car door and the dome light came on and I had a glimpse of Audrey's face, which was tense and drained of color. "Here," I said. I leaned in and reached across and handed her the christening dress. Then I slid in behind the steering wheel.

"You got it," she said, excitedly. She took the dress from me and sort of buried her face in it. And then she turned to me and smiled. But the smile quickly faded. And then I realized that tears were still on my face, the tears that had come when I had thought I was going to be shot, and I rubbed below my eyes to take them away.

"What's wrong?" Audrey said. "What happened in there?"

But I didn't say anything because I wanted to get away. That was the most important thing to do in that particular moment, so I put the car in gear and started down the two-track drive, going fast, much faster than when we had come, the headlights shining white against the tree trunks, casting giant sweeping shadows off into the forest, the tires spinning when we went through sand and then grabbing when we got on solid ground and then out onto the gravel road that would take us back to Newaygo.

"What's wrong?" Audrey said again. "Why are you driving so fast? What happened in there?"

And then I told her about her father finding me, how he held the pistol under my chin and threatened to shoot me, and how he finally let me leave the house. But I didn't tell her that he told me to be careful of her, because I thought that was a different subject, a private matter between me and Audrey's father. And I didn't tell her about the letter from the St. Paul Home, because that was too big a subject to be talked about when we were escaping in a car.

We were driving through Newaygo now, across the wide steel bridge with the hydroelectric dam downstream and then through the small downtown, which looked exactly like it had when we had come, only backward now, I mean the order of things, the dim lights shining feebly behind the large store windows and the civil war soldier on the pedestal in the park and the streetlights making brilliant circles on the pavement that we came and went through, and then up the high hill and past the sand mold factory to the flat ground up above, and then straight along the highway toward Grand Rapids.

"Audrey," I said, after we had gone a couple of miles. "Your father caught me. I told him you were staying at the Arlington Hotel."

"Why'd you tell him that?" There was a sudden coldness in her voice.

"He had a gun, Audrey. He held it under my chin. I thought he was going to shoot me. I was afraid."

"Well that complicates things."

"I don't think he cared about where you were staying. He acted like he didn't care."

She laughed a little, a short sarcastic laugh.

"Well, that shows how much you don't know," she said. "He'll come after me all right. He'll come after me tonight." She was quiet for a moment. "He still thinks I need to be reformed."

I glanced up into the rearview mirror, as if I might actually see the headlights of Audrey's father's car bearing down on us. But then I realized that was impossible. Before Audrey's father could leave the house he would have to tell his wife what was happening, what the disturbance had been in Audrey's bedroom, and why he was leaving. A person couldn't just leave a house abruptly in the middle of the night without an explanation, and that would take some time.

"Well, shit," Audrey said. "Shit, shit, shit."

"I'm sorry," I said, and I realized that was the second time I'd said those words. I'd said them to Audrey's father too, who was opposite to her in his intensions, having an opposite view of things I mean, and I thought that meant I was in the middle between them both.

"Is there someplace else you can go tonight?" I asked. "A friend's house. Something like that."

"I don't have many friends these days," Audrey said. "Except the men I take for walks around the city. And they don't count. They're temporary friends and they're from out of town."

"What about people you know at the Kendall School?"

"I'm the one who sits out in the hallway, remember. You don't make friends out there."

We drove on, silent now, both of us thinking about what should happen next. And then I remembered how my mother had spent a few hours sleeping in the house on Fulton Street on the night my father drove over to take her home.

"You could spend the night where I stay," I said. "There's an extra bedroom in the back. My mother stayed there once. I think it would be okay with Mr. and Mrs. Thatcher if you stayed there tonight. And even if they didn't like it, they wouldn't know until tomorrow morning and by then it would be too late to do anything about it."

Audrey didn't say anything. Out of the corner of my eyes I saw her raise her hands and rub her eyes, the way a person does when they are trying to rub tiredness away, or to blot out an ugly image that has come into their head from imagination. And then her hands went down to the christening dress and she gathered up some fabric, as if she wanted to hold as much of it as possible, and not just let her hands lay on top of it in a casual and unimportant way.

"I guess that might be okay for tonight," she said. "Though it wouldn't solve anything in the long run."

"We can think about the long run later."

Audrey was silent for a moment, and then she said, "Okay."

Chapter Sixteen

We drove back into Grand Rapids to the house on Fulton Street and I parked in the alley that ran behind the house. We walked across the back yard, dark now with no light coming through the windows or from anywhere else. Audrey was carrying the christening dress draped over one arm. I reached back and took her other hand because I knew where we were going, how you safely crossed the yard when it was dark, and she did not. And I felt a little shock at the feel of her hand, the warmth and softness of it in the damp cool night and how it closed back over mine, and it startled me, this sudden awareness, because I had just come through a hard experience when I could not feel warmth or softness, but now I could.

We walked around the side of the house and went up onto the porch and in through the front door. I led Audrey up the carpeted stairway on the right, still holding her hand, and across the small hallway and into the bedroom on the left. Some light came in through the window from a streetlamp, just enough to see your way in a room that was not familiar to you, which was the case for Audrey but not for me.

"You can stay here," I said in a whisper. I let go of her hand

and pointed toward the bed. "My mother slept here once. It'll be okay."

Audrey sat down on the side of the bed.

"What will happen in the morning when they see a strange person sleeping in their house?" she asked, whispering. And then she answered her own question: "They'll call the police, that's what they'll do."

"I don't think they will," I said, though I wasn't sure about that. "They're not that kind of people."

"I'm not sure you're the expert of that," she said. Then she spoke the word "people," just that word alone and nothing else, and she laughed as if it was a funny word, or a word that brought up funny feelings, though she stopped suddenly and lowered her head in a kind of guilty bouncing motion to show she knew she should stay quiet.

She placed her hand on the bed next to where she was sitting. "Stay with me," she said. "If they see us both together they'll know it's okay. They'll know I'm here with your permission. They won't call the police." And then she smiled at me, which made me glad, because it meant she was feeling okay about my plan and believed things would turn out all right.

"I'll stay," I said. "But I'll sit over in the armchair." I gestured toward an upholstered wing chair in the corner of the bedroom.

"Are you afraid of what will happen if we sleep together?" Audrey said with a teasing smile.

"No," I said. Though I *had* thought of that, Audrey and me together in the same bed and what could happen.

"Okay," she said. "Have it your way," and she made a face, as if she was disappointed I wouldn't sleep with her. She slipped off her tennis shoes and let them drop onto the floor. Then she took off the blue stocking cap and lay back onto the bed and drew the christening dress up under her chin. "Have sweet dreams," she said, and then she closed her eyes.

I went over and sat in the wing chair and watched Audrey

going to sleep, and I remembered how I'd watched my mother in the same bed only a few weeks earlier. And I remembered the strangeness I'd felt then—of watching over someone who is asleep and helpless, as if you were a sentinel whose job it is to keep them safe, and not let bad things happen—and I felt the strangeness again, except this time I realized I liked it.

After a few minutes Audrey's face relaxed the way a person's face changes when they drift off to sleep, losing all expression. But then her eyes came open for a moment and she smiled at me, though I think she was asleep by then and didn't know it was happening.

I waited a few more minutes to be sure Audrey was asleep and then I closed my eyes and leaned back against the wing chair and tried to go to sleep myself. But instead of finding sleep I began to think about the letter from the St. Paul Home and when I should tell Audrey about her baby. Finding out her baby was alive would be a big shock and maybe change the way she was living her life, and because of that I knew I had to tell her. But after thinking about it I decided that the best thing to do was to wait until things calmed down and we were not running away from her father, because I didn't want too many problems to get mixed up together, which can cause confusion and bring disaster.

After I had made that decision—to wait before telling Audrey about her baby—I felt calm again and went to sleep.

Chapter Seventeen

Mrs. Thatcher's voice woke me. She was standing in the doorway in a pink quilted nightrobe. Her hair was in curlers. Audrey was out of bed, standing off against the window that looked out onto Fulton Street.

Mrs. Thatcher had already said some words I'd been asleep for. The first words I heard and understood were: "You've got some nerve, young lady."

"I only slept there," Audrey said. "I slept on top of the blanket. I didn't even muss your bed. He said it'd be okay." She gestured in my direction.

Just then Mr. Thatcher showed up behind his wife. He was dressed in striped pajamas and his hair was tangled and he had beard stubble on his face.

He looked at me, sitting in the wing chair. "Maybe you need to do some explaining, Nate. Come out here and we'll talk."

I followed Mr. and Mrs. Thatcher into the bedroom in back, which was my bedroom. Mr. Thatcher closed the door and turned and looked at me. Mrs. Thatcher stood with her arms crossed and a stern look on her face. "Well," Mr. Thatcher said.

"You've got the floor, Nate," which was the way he talked sometimes, using language that didn't exactly fit the situation.

"She's a friend of mine," I said. "Her name is Audrey. She didn't have a place to stay last night. I thought she could stay here like my mother did. I thought it would be all right."

"Doesn't she have her own place?" Mrs. Thatcher said.

"She does. Yes. She does. The Arlington Hotel. She has a room there. But last night someone was after her and she was afraid to go there."

Mr. and Mrs. Thatcher traded looks as if what I'd said had some deeper meaning to them. Deeper than just the plain facts that I had spoken. "Who was after her?" Mr. Thatcher asked.

I hesitated a moment. Then I said, "Her father."

"Well, she's got to leave," Mr. Thatcher said. "She can't stay here. I think you know that."

"Yes, sir."

"And you can't either," Mrs. Thatcher said. "We can't have this sort of thing going on in our house. We have neighbors."

I understood what Mrs. Thatcher was talking about, because they were religious and cared about what other people thought. They went to the Methodist church on Sunday and said grace before their meals and had religious things around the house, a picture of Jesus praying next to a rock, and one of him being taken up to heaven in a column of bright light. People like that don't want a strange girl sleeping in their house, or anyone who helps her.

"Nothing happened," I said for the second time, because I wanted them to understand that there had been no sex. "We just came in and slept. You saw that I was in the wing chair."

Mr. Thatcher smiled, as if something I said was amusing. "I'm afraid that doesn't change anything, Nate. Can we agree that you'll leave this afternoon?"

"Okay," I said. "I'll go. I'll go right now if that's the way you feel." I wanted to say something more, something about the unfairness of making me leave when there'd been no sex but only sleeping, but before I could think of anything they turned and left and I was standing all alone.

❧

I WENT BACK into the front bedroom and told Audrey we had to leave. Then I went into my room and got my things together. There wasn't much, just a few clothes and my painting gear and the pictures I'd already finished, which numbered only three. I took all of this down to my car in the alley. When I came down with the last load Audrey was standing next to my car.

"Stay here," I said. I headed back to the house to say goodbye to Mr. and Mrs. Thatcher. I had in mind that I'd say something about the unfairness of making me leave and say again that there'd been no sex. Mr. Thatcher met me as I came up onto the porch. He was dressed in his normal clothes, khaki pants and a red and black flannel shirt. He had some bills in his hand.

"Here," he said, and he handed me the money. "That's a refund of your rent for the rest of the month. It's only fair." Then he said: "I'm sorry about this, Nate. If it were up to me you could stay, but Mrs. Thatcher is sensitive about these things. Boys and girls together in her house. We said something when you moved in, didn't we? That there couldn't be any girls."

"Yes, sir," I said. "But I thought it might be different with Audrey. Because she needed a place to stay." Then I said, because I was mad about having to leave and believed it was unfair: "We didn't fuck or do anything like that."

When he heard me say fuck Mr. Thatcher flinched, as if he'd felt a sudden stab of pain, and his expression turned angry. I knew that saying fuck would make him mad and I was glad for that.

"Just go now, Nate," he said. "Just go."

I put out my hand but he didn't take it. He closed the door and left me standing on the porch alone.

Chapter Eighteen

When I came back Audrey was inside the car. I got in and started the engine and I drove around to the front of the house and pulled in against the curb. I wanted to take one last look at the zoo and the park where the ducks and swans were. I had some nice memories about walking there at night and hearing the animals make their nighttime noises, and of meeting girls in the afternoon who would let me be a little bit affectionate, and I wanted to fix those memories in my brain. But in the cool half-light of morning the park didn't look like I remembered. Fog was rising off the water and the ducks and swans were still bedded down along the bank, with their heads tucked under their wings, looking like clumps of feathers.

"So where are we going?" Audrey said. "What's your next brilliant idea?"

"I don't know," I said. "Can you think of anything?"

"I'm out of ideas," she said. "You'll have to do the thinking for both of us." She looked at me. "That's a famous line from a movie, by the way. It was one of those old ones I watched when I was at home waiting to have my baby."

"I know," I said. "I've seen it. *Casablanca*. Humphrey Bogart and Ingmar Bergman. Rick and Ilsa."

Audrey smiled. "Maybe you can find a plane that'll fly me to a safe place. Like Rick did for Ilsa."

"Or maybe we can have breakfast at Tiffany's," I said. "A place where nothing bad can happen."

I looked at her and smiled, and she looked at me and smiled back, and then we both laughed a little. And I thought it was a good sign that we could joke together and be amusing. That we could do that after being told to leave a place where we were not wanted.

"Maybe you can check into another hotel," I said.

"They're too expensive," Audrey said. "I already checked when I first moved to town. I checked them all. The Arlington was the only one I could afford." She was silent for a moment. "Besides, now that my Dad knows I'm in Grand Rapids he'll check the other hotels if he finds out I left the Arlington."

"Well, shit," Then I said. "I'm going to be late for work. They'll dock my pay."

"Poor boy," Audrey said, and she pushed her lower lip out in an exaggerated pout. "I'm out on the street and you're going to be late for work. Isn't that just terrible?"

I looked at her. "Actually, we're both out on the street," I said. "We're partners now."

She stopped her fake pout and her expression turned serious, but then, slowly, a smile came onto her face, as if she liked the idea of us being partners together.

"I'll drop you off at the Kendall School," I said, and I put the car into gear and made a big U-turn and headed downtown. "You know that place. It'll be a comfortable place for you to be today. After work I'll come and get you. By then we'll have thought up what to do."

But even as I said those words I already had a plan in mind. But I didn't want to tell it to Audrey because I wanted more time to think it through. With a plan there is always the possibility that more thinking will find a flaw that wasn't obvious in the beginning. So I'd learned it was good to think about a plan two or three times before you commit to doing it. *Measure twice and cut once* was how the men at the factory said it.

We drove through the west-side neighborhood toward downtown. The sun was coming up but the air was cool. As we crossed the Sixth Street bridge I saw steam rising off the water.

"That's because the air is warmer than the water," I said. I pointed to the river with the steam rising off. "The moisture gets squeezed out as fog when the warm air touches the colder water."

I looked over at Audrey. She turned her head and looked back. "What did you say?" she said.

"Never mind," I said. "It's not important."

I turned onto Webster Street and went down two blocks and pulled up at the front entrance of the Kendall School. Students were starting to arrive, walking up the wide front steps carrying tubes of drawings and giant black portfolios. "Okay," I said. "This is your stop."

"Should I leave the christening dress?" Audrey motioned toward the back seat of the car.

"Of course," I said. "Where else are you going to leave it?"

I looked at Audrey. She was turned away and looking out the side window. Looking away from me and toward the world outside. And I suddenly realized that she thought I might not come back. That because I hadn't said anything about a plan it meant I didn't have one. That I just wanted to get rid of her and all her troubles.

"I'll come back," I said, and I reached out and touched her arm, just lightly on the elbow. "I won't leave you stranded." Then I said: "I've got a plan. But I want to think about it before I tell you. But even if the first plan doesn't work we'll find another one that will." And then I said again: "I won't leave you stranded."

Audrey turned and looked at me. Her eyes were watery from tears, but none had gotten on her cheeks. I moved my hand up to her shoulder and squeezed a little, like my father had done to me at Kewpee Hamburgers, which I thought would show a sense of solidarity, that we were partners in this situation and would work it out together. And then she leaned against me and put her face up next to mine. And in the moment that our cheeks touched I felt a little bit romantic and I realized that if I turned my head I could kiss her on the mouth. But then I thought that doing that would complicate things too much, complicate the moment and what it was about, mixing up romance and solidarity in a way neither one of us could understand. So I just murmured into her hair that I'd be back to get her at four. And then she leaned away and opened the door and stepped out onto the sidewalk.

Chapter Nineteen

After I dropped Audrey off at the Kendall School I drove across town to the car factory. The day shift had already started and the parking lot was full so I had to park in the weeds on the far side and make a long walk to the entrance. I showed my badge to the guard at the door and then walked to the time-clock area. The stamp on my card said 8:43; I was almost two hours late and would lose that much pay.

"Where the hell have you been?" Jimmy Palmer said when he saw me walking up to the tool crib.

"I overslept," I said. "My alarm clock didn't go off and I overslept."

"More likely you were out with some sweetie last night," he said, and he winked at me as if we shared a secret. Then: "There's some drill bits in back that need to be sharpened. You can start the day with that."

I put on safety goggles and a leather apron and heavy canvas gloves and started to sharpen the drill bits on the grinding wheel. It was easy work, all you did was hold the drill bit at a certain angle against the grinding wheel until the edge got sharp, but it took some concentration, just enough so that I couldn't think about anything else, which I was glad about. I had been thinking all morning about Audrey and her problems but now I wanted not to think about her for a while.

After I finished with the drill bits I took my morning break, which you were allowed to have under the union contract. I went to the workers' cafeteria where there were some vending machines and I got a coffee and a Pay Day candy bar. Then I stood in the hallway next to the vending machines and drank my coffee and ate my candy bar. Some workers walked past. Some were journeymen, tool-and die-mechanics and millwrights and plumbers and electricians, who I recognized from having given them tools, and when we caught each other's eye we would nod to show we had that connection. But most of the workers were unskilled labor who worked on the production lines and who I didn't know. For some reason, I started to think about how it would feel to work on the production line where all you did all day was stand next to a roaring machine and push pieces of steel into it or take them out. And I wondered what that would do to a person if they did it for a lifetime, whether it would change them in some important way, or if they could survive it and not be changed. And then I realized that there were things happening in factories that were important, because they changed the way people thought about themselves and about the world. And I realized, too, that not many artists spent time in factories, that I was unusual in that way, and I wondered if I could make factories my special subject—like Van Gogh had done with sunflowers—and call attention to my paintings in that way.

It was pleasant thinking about painting so I kept going. I thought that I was making progress and was starting to do it better, starting to paint things that meant more than what they seemed to be on the surface, things that had a deeper meaning for people who were willing to look for it. Painting was a different way of looking at the world than how I'd learned from mathematics and electricity, where everything is either right or wrong and there are no secrets. And then I wondered if I could use my new artistic thinking to analyze my plan, if I could tell whether it was a good plan or a bad plan by examining it in an artistic way, by the feelings it caused or the hidden things that it revealed. So I tried to forget the obvious things about my plan and to think about the essence of it, which is what Picasso said an artist is supposed to do. But all that was left after I had cleared away the obvious things was the feeling I had about Audrey, which was that she was in trouble and needed someone's help.

When I got back to the tool crib after finishing my break a man was standing by the counter where the tools were handed over. I recognized him as Steve Weber, who was a millwright, one of the men who moved the giant machines around the factory. "I need some batteries," he said, as I walked up. He waved a flashlight he was holding. "These ones are dead."

I went around behind the counter and asked to see the flashlight so I could check that the batteries were really dead. That was what I was supposed to do when someone wanted batteries, because sometimes they didn't really need the new batteries and would take them home in their lunch box.

"Just give me the damn batteries," Steve said.

"I need to check the flashlight," I said. "You know I do."

"Well, you're not going to check this time but you're going to give me the damn batteries."

"I can't," I said. "I'll get in trouble."

Steve stood with the flashlight in his hand and stared at me, and I stared back. And then I felt my gaze slip off, which I knew to be a sign of weakness, and I was afraid it meant that I was close to giving Steve the batteries.

But then I remembered about being in Audrey's parent's house just a few hours earlier, and having a gun barrel held beneath my chin, and being threatened with extinction. And I realized that what was happening now was small compared to what I'd gone through then.

"No," I said again, and I returned Steve's hard stare. "Not unless I see the damn flashlight."

Steve reached across the counter and grabbed the front of my shirt-and pulled me toward him. He raised the flashlight like he was going to hit me with it. But I didn't think he would, and even if he did I believed that I could stand it, just like I'd stood up to the possibility of being shot by Audrey's father.

"Fuck you," Steve said. He pushed against my chest and I stumbled back a few steps. Then he turned and walked away.

"You should've given him the batteries." I turned. Jimmy Palmer was standing behind me. "You don't have to do something if it gets you in trouble with the men. Batteries are cheap. You want the men to like you."

"Okay," I said, even though I didn't agree with what he said.

Chapter Twenty

When I arrived at the Kendall School to pick Audrey up, she was sitting on a concrete bench reading *How to Make Friends and Influence People*. I stopped and leaned across and opened the passenger door. I smiled because I wanted her to feel that I had things under control.

"I wasn't sure I'd ever see you again," she said.

"Why did you think that?"

"Maybe because I've got more troubles than you realized in the beginning and you wouldn't want to get involved."

"No," I said. "I want to."

I put the car into gear and pulled out into traffic.

"Anyway," she said, "what's this great plan of yours?"

"Wait a minute," I said. "I can't tell it while I'm driving."

We drove across the Sixth Street bridge into a part of town that was a mixture of houses and small storefronts. I saw a bank with an empty parking lot and I pulled in.

"Are we going to rob a bank?" Audrey said. "Is that your plan?"

I laughed. "No, but we might have to do that later."

Audrey smiled. "Okay, Rick," she said, "tell Ilsa what we're going to do."

I paused for a moment to get my thoughts in order. And then I started out by telling her about Gary being killed at the Army base, which was difficult because I hadn't told anyone else about it, had not yet put it into words.

"I have an older brother," I began. "I mean I had one. He was killed last April at Camp Carlisle. That's an Army camp in northern Michigan. He was killed by accident on the shooting range."

I stopped talking because of the expression that came onto Audrey's face.

"Are you all right?" I said.

She shook her head, as if she'd been dazed by what I'd said and needed to clear her mind. "I guess I'm surprised you haven't told me this before," she said. "It's kinda a big thing." She shook her head again. "Anyway, go on. Go on about your plan."

And then I told her about Gary being buried in the cemetery at Camp Carlisle, and how my mother had driven over from Detroit to ask me to go with her to bring him back, and how I'd called my father and he had driven over to take my mother home.

"It's bothered me that I didn't go with her to Camp Carlisle." I said. "That I called my father instead of going with her. It's bothered me a lot." I looked at Audrey. I could tell she was paying close attention, had gotten over being dazed. "I think a mother's got the right to have her son buried wherever she wants him," I continued. "I can see where it'd be nice for her to go out and see him once in a while. I mean go to the place where he's buried. It'd be nice to have a special place where she could remember him."

"Okay," Audrey said. "I think I understand all of that." She looked down and shook her head again, but slow this time, as if she was still amazed by what she'd heard. Then she looked back at me. "I'm sorry about your brother. I'm terribly sorry about that. And I wish you'd told me this before. But what has this got to do with us. With us right now."

And then I told Audrey about my plan, which was for us to drive to Camp Carlisle to make arrangements to bring Gary home. "It'll take five days," I said. "Maybe six. By the time we get back your father'll be tired of looking for you and he will have given up. And my mother will have Gary back where she wants him."

I smiled at Audrey, though it was just a small smile. Not a smile of being happy but a smile of having said something hard and gotten through it.

"So what do you think?" I said.

"You've forgotten one important thing," Audrey said. "Maybe more than one thing. Like where will we get the money to do this? It cost money to take a trip like that. You need gas and food and places to stay at night." She turned her head and looked at me. "How far is this Camp Carlisle anyway?"

"It's about five hundred miles," I said. "It's in the Upper Peninsula so we have to cross the bridge that goes across the Straights of Mackinaw. It'll take two days to drive there. And then a couple of days to figure out about Gary. And then another couple of days to drive back home."

Audrey looked at me with one eye squinted shut.

"What about the money?" she asked.

"I've thought of that. I've got some money back at my parent's house. I earned it doing odd jobs when I was in high school. We'll drive there first and get the money and then head north."

"What about your job at the car factory?"

"I'll call in and tell them I'm sick. I don't think they'll care if I don't show up for a few days. All I'm doing right now is handing out tools to the journeymen."

"My head is sort of spinning," Audrey said, and she put her

hands up against her forehead with the fingers spread like she was trying to stop the spinning. "I don't know what to make of all this."

"Don't make anything out of it," I said. "Just trust me. I'll take care of us both."

Audrey put her hands back down onto her lap and folded them together. She stayed like that for a minute or two. But then she smiled and said, "Okay, I'm up for it. I guess I've got nothing better on my calendar."

Chapter Twenty-One

The first thing we had to do was to get Audrey's things from her room at the Arlington Hotel. I drove to the hotel and parked in the rear alley where Audrey said there was an entrance with a stairway that wasn't used very much. We went inside and climbed up three flights to Audrey's floor. Her room was just across from the stairwell.

"Wait out in the hall for a minute," Audrey said. She was unlocking the door to her room. "I've got to change out of my burglar clothes." She was still wearing the jeans and the sweatshirt she'd worn from the night before.

"No," I said. "Stay like that. That's a good way to dress for traveling. And I like you dressed like that."

She looked at me with a disbelieving expression.

"You're fine," I said. "You look fine to me."

Audrey opened the door and we went inside. The room was shadowy and dark and the furniture and the carpeting had a worn-out look, as if they should have been replaced long ago. Pieces of clothing lay on the bed and on a bureau and a wooden chair, flimsy bright things a girl would wear. Make-up bottles were on the bureau: lipsticks in small brass cylinders and tiny cans of rouge and face creams and perfume bottles. Drawings of furniture were Scotch-taped to the wall. On the bedside table there was a lamp and some books and a condom.

"Here," Audrey said. She motioned toward the walls. "Take down my sketches. But be careful. Don't tear them." And then she saw me looking at the condom and she grabbed it and put it into the pocket of her jeans. Next she pulled an old cardboard suitcase out of the closet and began to fill it with her clothes, folding them quickly and putting them inside in no particular order. When the suitcase was full she got a cardboard box from the closet. She put her loose things in it, her lotions and lipsticks and perfumes.

As I took down the drawings I examined them. They were sketches of chairs and tables and lamps and cabinets and desks having curves and contours that seemed to defy any geometric pattern, as if they were products of the natural world and not of factories.

"I'm not a great fan of straight lines and right angles," Audrey said, when she saw me examining the sketches. "Maybe you can tell that."

After Audrey finished packing we carried the suitcase and the cardboard box down the stairway to the car. I put them into the trunk next to my things. When I turned around Audrey was heading back toward the building.

"Where are you going?" I said.

"I've got one more thing to get," she said. "It's important."

I waited at the car while Audrey went back into the hotel. After a couple of minutes she came out carrying the painting that I'd given to her.

"You didn't think I'd leave this, did you?" she said, grinning.

She put the painting into the trunk in a careful way so it wouldn't rub against something and get ruined. Then she headed back toward the hotel.

"Now where are you going?" I said.

"I've got to tell them I'm leaving. And give back the key."

"Let me do it," I said. "If they ask me any questions I'll tell them I don't know anything about it. That I'm just doing something you asked me to do."

I took the key from Audrey and walked back into the hotel and down a corridor that entered into the back of the lobby. Before going through the door I stopped and peered around the corner. The clerk was behind the counter doing some paperwork. Audrey's father was sitting in the corner of the lobby reading a newspaper. I turned and headed back toward the rear entrance.

"Your father's in there," I said to Audrey. "He's sitting in the lobby."

"Shit," she said. "Did he see you?"

"No," I said. "I was careful."

"How will I let the hotel know I'm leaving?"

"Here," I said. I reached back and threw the key into a clump of bushes at the far end of the parking lot. "There," I said. "You're checked out." I turned and looked at her. "Let's go."

Chapter Twenty-Two

We drove across the east side of town and followed the Beltline Road to where it entered onto the new interstate highway, the highway that Eisenhower was building so nuclear missiles could be moved around the country quickly. We drove along in silence. After we'd gone a few miles I said, just in a casual way: "I couldn't help but notice you had a prophylactic on the side table in your room."

"What?" Audrey said.

"A prophylactic." I looked at her. Her face was blank. "A condom," I said, "a rubber."

Audrey kept looking at me but she didn't say anything back.

"I guess I was wondering why you had one?"

I heard Audrey take a deep breath and blow it out slowly. "It's nothing amazing," she said, and she took another deep breath. "There was a boy I saw a few times last summer. I liked him but not in a serious way. He was just nice, that's all. A nice boy. But he could be quite amorous, and when he got that way I would too." She paused for a moment as if she was expecting me to say something, but I stayed quiet because I wanted her to finish her explanation. "Anyway," she continued, "I thought that something might happen in a rapturous moment and I wanted to be prepared for it." Audrey stopped talking. She was looking out the side window and I thought she must be remembering the nice boy and how he could be amorous.

"But it never did," she said, after we had driven for a while in silence. "Things never got to that extravagant place. So after we broke up I had this thing left over—whatever it was you called it—the prophy-thing—and I just put it onto the side table. Just a place for it to be before I got around to throwing it away."

Audrey looked at me. "I hope I'm not telling you anything you don't already know," she said. "You had a girlfriend. You told me that. So you must know how things go in the love department."

"Yes," I said. "I had a girlfriend for a while."

But I didn't say anything else because Diane and I had never done anything that would have needed a condom. We had kissed many times, and we had done some other things, but we had not done much.

"What happened to her?" Audrey said. "Or to you, as the case may be."

"I think I told you that already," I said. "She found a boy she liked better than me."

"Oh yes," Audrey said. "I remember now. That was why you wanted to kiss me so badly. Because of your terrible broken heart." She laughed a little and I did too. "Well, it's her loss," she said, and she looked at me and smiled.

We were getting near to where the section of the new interstate highway ended and I had to pay attention so I wouldn't miss the signs that directed us back onto the old two-lane road. But I couldn't help wondering if what Audrey said about the condom was exactly right. The story seemed odd in ways that were hard to explain, just like the story she had told about giving walking tours to businessmen and sitting in the hall outside classrooms to learn furniture design. Everything about

Audrey seemed a little off, a little different from what you would expect from a normal girl. But then I remembered that that was true of me, too, that I was living different than the normal way boys are. And then I wondered if that meant we belonged together—Audrey and I did—because we were both outsiders to normal life.

"Anyway," Audrey said, after we'd driven for a few more miles. "It's different now. They have a pill that will do it. Keep a girl from getting pregnant. It's new. So the prophy-thing is out of date. All you have to do now is take that pill."

We'd just gotten back onto a section of the new interstate and were going very fast, much faster than you can drive on a two-lane road. I thought of asking Audrey more about the pill, but then I decided I didn't want to know.

Chapter Twenty-Three

After we got on highway 42 we both got quiet. I think we realized that something different was happening, that we had set ourselves on a new mission, and we wanted to get comfortable with that, to make it feel like driving to the Army camp to get Gary's coffin was a reasonable thing to do, not unusual in any way.

I began to think about Diane, my girlfriend from last year. I think it was because Audrey had brought her up when we'd talked about the condom. I remembered the first time I kissed her, which was something I liked to think about from time to time. We had been sitting in a car in the driveway of her house after coming home from seeing the Ice Capades at Olympia Stadium. On the ride home she'd been very happy. She had done some figure skating and she talked excitedly about the skaters and their colorful costumes and the jumps they had made, which she knew the official names of. At some point she moved over to sit next to me, and she held my hand when I didn't need it to do the shifting. When we got to her house I pulled into the driveway and turned off the engine and we sat and talked for a while about the Ice Capades, and then about some other things, and then we both got quiet, just sitting in the dark together thinking our own separate thoughts, which were maybe the same thoughts. After a few minutes of sitting silently, I turned my head and she turned hers and we kissed each other, not saying a word or even planning for it to happen, probably, but just a natural thing that it was time for, placing our mouths together softly, barely touching, and not doing any of the other things that you can do when you are kissing.

"There was a song I liked to play when I got home after being with Diane," I said.

I didn't know I'd said the words out loud until Audrey spoke. "What?" she said. "What did you say? What song?"

"It was stupid," I said, because I had not meant to speak the thought out loud and was embarrassed, but after speaking it I decided I needed to say more. "It was from a music show and it was on a record at our house. It was about two people who are in love and how it felt. And it was interesting, because it didn't talk about love exactly but only about how love felt. I thought it was a nice song and I'd play it when I got home after being with Diane."

"What was the song? How did the words go?"

I laughed. "No," I said. "I'd feel foolish to say it now."

We drove on for several miles, and then I decided I wanted to say more about the song.

"One of the lines was about flower petals floating on water," I said. "And another was about how the sun looks in the morning. But like I said, the song was really about love. It was different than you'd expect because it talked about one thing but meant something else." I looked across at Audrey. She looked back with a slightly pinched expression, as if she was having trouble understanding what I was trying to say. "Then it went something, something, something," I said, and I laughed. "Anyway, those were a couple of lines that I remember."

"So you really loved the girl," Audrey said.

"I thought I did," I said. "Though maybe I loved the idea of being in love. Or maybe I loved that song about love." I laughed a little to try to show it wasn't important whether I had loved Diane or not. "Anyway," I said, "in the end it didn't matter. She found someone she liked better than me, so now it doesn't matter."

"No," Audrey said. "Don't do that. Don't spoil it by trying to be cynical and tough."

I didn't say anything.

"How you felt about the girl. Diane? Was that her name? What you said just now. Those thoughts. You should keep them. Because they don't come along that often. At least that's been my experience." After that there was a stretch of time when she was silent and then she said: "Sometimes they never come."

We rocketed along the interstate, going very fast. Then I said, "Okay," because I thought I understood what she meant, and I believed her, but I didn't want to talk about love anymore.

❦

WHEN WE GOT to the Detroit suburb where my family lived it was already dark. We drove slowly past my parents' house but I didn't stop until I'd driven a little further down the block. "We can't go there tonight," I said. "My dad'll be there."

Audrey was turned around and kneeling on the seat, looking out the rear window at my parents' house. The house had a wide lawn and a curving driveway going up to the entrance. It was like the other houses in the neighborhood.

"I guess your family must be rich," Audrey said. "That's a fact I didn't know about you."

"I don't know what being rich means, exactly," I said. "My dad has a good job but he didn't always have it. For a long time he was just a salesman and we lived in different places." I looked at her. "Anyway, right now we've got to figure out where we'll spend the night."

"Where did you think we'd spend the night?" Audrey said. "According to your famous plan."

"I don't know. I didn't think about that part."

Even though it was dark I could see Audrey smiling at me in a kind of superior way.

"I guess you didn't think this one through, Einstein," she said. "Now you've got a girl in a strange town with no place to spend the night." She smiled again in that superior way. "So I guess it's time for me to take control." She was still looking out the back window. "Drive to that church we passed back there. We'll park in the parking lot and sleep in the car. No one will see us in a church parking lot."

I drove back to the church and parked in a far corner of the parking lot where there wasn't much light. I turned off the engine and the Pontiac shuddered to a stop.

"Okay," I said. I turned in Audrey's direction. "You're in charge now. What's the next step?"

"You stay in front," she said, "and I'll get in back." She opened the door and got in back and started to arrange herself across the seat, sort of hunched down with her knees bent so she could fit across. "You have to deal with the steering wheel and the shift stick," she said. "That's your penalty for getting us into this situation."

"Okay," I said. "I guess that's fair." And I arranged myself across the seat as best I could, sort of wedged up against the passenger's door with my legs pushed under the steering wheel, and I began to try to go to sleep.

But I couldn't. And neither could Audrey. I could tell that from the sighs she made, and how she kept rearranging herself across the seat.

After a while she said: "I thought you told me your father couldn't afford to send you to college."

"I didn't say he couldn't afford it," I answered. "I said he didn't want to pay for it. Not unless I studied what he wanted me to study, which was business and economics. How you make money. I wanted to study electricity."

Audrey was silent for a while and I knew she was thinking about what I'd just said. Then she said, "Well, you're just a fool then."

"No, I'm not," I said. And I said it very strongly, because it was something I had lived myself and was the authority about, and Audrey had not. She only knew about it from the words I spoke and not from living it. "I saw it with my brother," I said. "What happens when you do things other people want you to do. He wanted to study music but my father said he had to go into the Army first. That the Army would make a better man of him. But anyone who knew Gary could've told you he didn't belong in the Army." I stopped talking and thought for a minute. "He was different from most boys. But different in a good way. He understood about music and how to play it. Not just the notes but how you're supposed to make the notes feel to other people, the sense you're supposed to give them." I stopped to think of what I wanted to say next, because I was trying to say something I barely understood. "Sometimes, when boys are good at something like music, they're different in other ways. They're different from the normal way boys are, playing sports and being outdoors and roughhousing. Gary was different like that. He was polite and he liked flowers and art and poetry. Things I never cared about." I paused for a moment and then I said: "And he paid a price for being different. Kids teased him. Some boys called him a sissy."

For a long time the car fell back into silence. But I knew Audrey wasn't sleeping. I knew she was lying in the back seat thinking about what I'd said, thinking about it very hard, so she could say something back that was worthwhile.

"And so now you want to be more like he was," she said. "With the painting, I think that's true."

"I hadn't thought about it like that. But yes, I suppose you're right."

"How did you feel when he was killed?"

I was surprised that Audrey would ask this question, because it seemed like a personal thing I shouldn't have to talk about. But I wanted to give her an honest answer so I thought about the days after we'd been given the news by the Army people. But I had a hard time coming up with any clear memory of how I felt or what had happened. My father had given us the news about Gary's death—my mother and myself—I remembered that very well—and my mother had gone silently up the staircase to her bedroom. But I couldn't remember much after that.

But then I did.

"After my mother left to go upstairs my father kept talking to me," I said. "He told me we had to be strong for the sake of my mother. He said it was a terrible thing when a mother lost a son—a sadness that a man could never understand—and we needed to be strong for her sake. So I was worried about my mother, and I tried to be the way I thought would help her most. In the way my father said. Acting strong and bearing up."

"But how did *you* feel?" Audrey said. "That was my question, if you happen to recall."

I thought for a moment. "I guess I didn't feel anything," I said. "I was trying to act brave for my mother's sake. And the best way to do it was to act like it didn't matter that much. That life would go on like before, even though Gary was dead."

There was a long silent time when neither of us spoke. Then Audrey said: "Except it didn't."

"What?"

"Your life. It didn't go on like before. You didn't go to college, and you moved to a different city, and you started to become a painter."

"I guess you're right," I said. "I never thought about it that way."

"Well, maybe you should," Audrey said.

After that she was silent, and when a certain amount of time had passed I knew it was the silence of being asleep. And then I sort of released my thoughts the way you do when you want to fall asleep yourself, or when you want to make a painting, and my undirected thoughts went toward Gary, and all the things he was missing by being dead: a wonderful career in music, and the friends he would have made from that, people who understood him and didn't think he was strange or different or a sissy. And I realized, too, that I would've liked to talk to him about my painting, I would've liked that very much, because painting was something he would've understood, in the same way he understood about playing the piano: how you strike the keys, soft or hard, slow or fast, whether to make a note end suddenly or let it linger for a while in the air, and a thousand other things. That was what you did with painting, too, although you did it with paint and not with sound. And then I pictured myself painting on a riverbank with music in the background, a piece by Brahms that Gary had played once at a school assembly, and that was the last thought I had before I fell asleep.

Chapter Twenty-Four

I was startled out of a dream. I didn't know what time it was. My heart was pounding and my hands were clenched in fists. I lay in the half-dark of the parking lot and tried to make myself relax. Somewhere off in the distance I heard the thundering of a semi-truck barreling down a highway, then the barking of a dog, and then the long lonely wail of a siren, an ambulance or a police cruiser rushing to help someone in trouble.

I had been dreaming about Gary, although I could only remember fragments of the dream, disconnected pieces that didn't fit together. But as I lay there listening, the fragments slowly came together to make a memory, a memory of something that had happened on a Friday night one year ago.

❧

I'D BEEN UPSTAIRS in my bedroom doing homework. Later, I planned to get together with Diane. It wasn't exactly a date but we had talked about getting together to have some fun.

Downstairs, my father and Gary were talking in the kitchen.

Gary was home from basic training on a five-day furlough. It was unusual to get a furlough during basic training, but Gary's sergeant said that being home for a few days would be good for Gary. Help him to relax. Get his head straight about becoming a soldier.

"You're just going to have to get through this, Gary." My father's voice carried up the curving staircase, heavy with authority and good sense. In a little while, he and my mother would be leaving to attend some glittery affair at the country club, but for now he was dispensing his wisdom to Gary. "You might as well make up your mind about having to get through it," he repeated.

"That's exactly what I'm trying to do." Gary's voice was high pitched and strained. "But I don't know whether I have what it takes to be a soldier."

"I'm sure you'll get the hang of it. Basic training's hard for everybody. That's the point of it."

I heard a chair scrape across the floor, then footsteps.

"Would you like a coffee or a soft drink?" It was my father's voice again.

"No."

"Well, I'm going to make some coffee." I heard water running. "I'll make enough so that you can have some later."

"Do whatever you want."

I closed my book and pushed back from the desk. I began to think about Diane and the night ahead. I had not slept with a girl, but I was hoping it might happen with Diane. At school dances, she held tight against me, pressed her mouth into the crook of my neck and made little murmuring sounds that I understood to be a sort of promise. The week before, parked in the driveway of her house, I had moved my hand inside her blouse and she had let it stay there for a long, suspended moment before finally pulling my hand away.

"You know, Gary, when you're all done with the Army you

can pick up with your music life again. It's just two years. After the Army you can go back to your music studies and everything will be fine. This is just an interruption of your musical career. Consider it in that light."

"I don't want everything to be the same." He was speaking in a very low voice now.

"But it's true," my father said. "I want you to think about that."

※

AFTER A WHILE I heard the front door open and close, followed by the muffled roar of my father's big El Dorado coming to life in the driveway. I was anxious to see Diane, but first I had to figure out what to do about Gary. My parents didn't want him left alone; that was something they had told me. I thought it was an odd request—Gary was my older brother, after all—but I assumed they had good reasons. Usually they had good reasons.

Suddenly I began to hear piano music: big, powerful sounds that seemed to rush up the stairwell and fill my room like a curdling fog. I left my bedroom and went downstairs. Gary was seated in his familiar spot behind the grand piano, his thin body angled forward, his eyes half closed, his large hands racing back and forth along the keyboard like frantic little animals seeking shelter.

I watched Gary from the doorway. Finally he came to a quieter passage. The little animals stopped their frightened scurrying.

"Bravo!" I shouted. I started to clap.

Gary's eyes snapped open. He stopped his song abruptly, as though I had caught him in some shameful act.

"Keep going," I said, "it sounds great."

But instead of starting to play again he reached for a cigarette burning in the notch of a crystal ashtray. "You only think it's good because you don't understand it," he said. "I haven't played for two months. To someone who knows music, it's shit."

"Well, it sounded good to me." I stepped into the room and sat down in my father's big upholstered chair. "You all right?" I asked.

"Never better." Gary took a drag on his cigarette, cupping his hand like he was standing in a strong wind.

"I heard Dad giving you a hard time."

"You know how he is. He wants everything to be perfect."

"I guess you can't blame him for that."

I half-stood and reached for Gary's cigarettes lying on the piano. I shook one out and lit it, thinking about the new Gary sitting in front of me, the one who would be going back to the Army on Sunday afternoon. My father said that Gary was a brilliant musician, but he needed seasoning in the hard facts of life. That's what the Army would do for him.

I stared at Gary, trying to figure out what was going on inside his head. I had always thought his life was pretty good. In the suburban community where we had moved the year before he was already a local celebrity. His piano playing was featured at school assemblies and civic events, like the time when Richard Nixon came to town to give a speech about the Russians. Last summer he had served as the substitute organist at the Presbyterian Church, blasting out "Rock of Ages" and "The Old Rugged Cross" with a fervor that brought tears to the eyes of old ladies in the congregation.

But I didn't want to think about those things now. I had my own problems to worry about. Like how I was going to see Diane and keep an eye on Gary at the same time.

"I'm going to get together with my girlfriend tonight," I said. I examined the tip of my cigarette, as if the burning ash might tell me something. "Maybe she can get a girl for you."

Gary looked at me from behind his giant piano. I watched his upside-down reflection in the shiny black enamel.

"You mean a blind date?" he said.

"Something like that."

He played a few odd notes. "Will it be worth my while?"

"What do you mean by that?"

"Is she blonde? Does she have big breasts?"

I laughed. "There's no guarantees," I said. "Right now, she's an unknown factor."

Gary smiled for the first time and that made me feel good. Just because he was headed for the Army didn't mean he shouldn't have some fun.

"A little romance before Gary goes back to basic training," he said, still smiling. "Sounds good to me, brother."

I stood and crushed out my cigarette in the crystal ashtray. "Well, okay," I said. "Let's go."

꙳

DIANE'S HOUSE had one of those big covered porches like they have on older houses. A light rain was falling, and as we walked up from the car I saw her standing back in the shadows. When we got close she stepped out from her hiding place and stood at the top of the steps. She was wearing a bright yellow raincoat with a hood. The porch light reflected off the raincoat in a thousand little slivers of white.

"This is my brother, Gary," I said, looking up at Diane. "He's home from basic training in the Army."

"*Bonsoir*, Gary," Diane said. Her voice from deep inside her rain hood sounded hollow and strange. "Are you as crazy as Nate?"

"Crazier," he said.

"Then I like you already," she said.

I went up the steps and gave Diane a kiss. Then, with my

hands still around her waist, I explained the idea about getting a girl for Gary. When I finished she arched her eyebrows and drew back her face. "It's kind of late," she said.

"I know," I said. I looked back at Gary. He was standing with his arms crossed, staring up at us. I turned back to Diane and made a face. "Can't you call a friend?" I asked.

Diane pursed her lips to show deep thinking. "I'd like to," she said. "But it's kind of an insult, *n'est pas?* To call a girl at the last minute."

I let go of Diane and went back down to where Gary was standing on the sidewalk. I explained to him about the friend, how it was too late to do anything. I thought he'd be mad but all he did was give Diane a sheepish grin, as though to say that it had been my idea from the start. Something out of his control.

"So what do we do now?" I asked. It seemed to me the rain was coming down harder. I felt it running out of my hair and into my eyes.

"Why don't we go for a walk in the rain?" Diane said. "All three of us."

For a minute nobody said anything. I turned toward Gary and gave him a hard stare, trying to send him a message. I wanted him to leave now, to take the car and go someplace so I could be alone with Diane. I'd done the best I could to get him a girl and it hadn't worked out. What more could he expect?

"Well, what's the verdict?" Diane said.

I kept my hard stare on Gary.

"Sounds okay to me," Gary said. He was looking up at Diane and smiling.

☙

WE WALKED for a while without saying anything, Diane and me in front, Gary coming along behind.

"I've always wanted to meet you," Diane said, looking back over her shoulder at Gary. "Nate's famous older brother."

"I'm not famous," Gary said. "Right now, I'm just a soldier."

"Well, Nate thinks you're famous. He's told me all about you." She turned around so she could face him. "I love music."

"Really?" Gary said, and he spoke as though the fact amazed him.

"Yes, really," she said, laughing. "In fact, I truly believe that music is the only hope for mankind. If it weren't for music we'd all go ka-boom in a second."

"You mean the bomb?" I said to her.

"Exactimondo, *mon a*mi." She turned around again. "Don't you think I'm right about that, Gary?"

"I don't know," Gary said from behind. "Maybe."

I looked over at Diane, but all I could see was the yellow rain hood with sparkling drops of water running down. "Well, if you've got a better idea then let's hear it," she said.

Gary was quiet for a moment. Then he said: "I don't know what the most important thing is."

"*Quel ennui*," Diane said. "You must have some opinion."

Gary was silent again. But finally he spoke. "Love," he said. "I guess I'd say that love's the most important thing."

I looked at Diane. She turned to me and smiled so that the corners of her eyes crinkled. Her face was wet and shiny from the rain. "Now we're getting some place," she said.

We walked along. Above our heads wet tree branches glistened blackly in the streetlamps. I felt the rain seeping into my clothes, damp and cold and heavy. Then Diane started to hum a tune.

"That's Tchaikovsky," Gary said.

"Exactimondo," Diane said. She started to hum again. Then she turned around and started walking backward so she could look at Gary. "Can I hear you play some time? Maybe when you're home from the Army next?"

"I don't play much these days," Gary said.

"When do you come home from the Army next? So I can hear you play."

"It'll be a while," he said. "I'm not exactly sure." And I knew from his voice that he was thinking about tomorrow night, when he would take a Greyhound bus back to Camp Carlisle, and what was going to happen after that.

"You will let me know though," she said. "Promise?"

Gary was quiet. Then he said, "Yes, I promise."

"Great," Diane said, and I could tell she meant it.

We had been circling the block and were coming back up to Diane's house. The globe on her porch light shined dimly through the rain like a ship's beacon. I decided I'd had enough of walking in the rain and all the talk about music. And I didn't like that Diane was paying so much attention to Gary. The evening was turning out like many others I'd lived through, with Gary getting all the attention and me being mostly ignored. Nothing about the night seemed right.

"I suppose we should go," I said.

"Can't you come in for a while?" Diane said.

"No," I said, and I guess the word came out stronger than I intended, because Diane looked at me with a hurt expression. "All right," she said, "if that's the way you feel." And then she came up close and I felt her cool wet hand touch the back of my neck. "Maybe this will sweeten you up," she said, and she drew in close against me.

I'd probably kissed Diane a hundred times by then, but there was something about that particular kiss that got to me. Maybe it was the warmth of Diane's mouth in the middle of that cold, clammy rain, or the odd sensation of her soft girl's body inside that stiff, crinkly raincoat. Or maybe it was Gary's strange behavior. Anyway, when Diane started to back away I sort of clutched her, as if I couldn't bear to have her leave. At first she stiffened but then she relaxed and nestled against me.

"Good night, *mon ami*," she whispered after a moment. She stepped back and began once more to turn away. "I'll see you in the funny papers."

"What about me?" Gary said.

Diane stopped. She turned back to look at Gary. She seemed to move in slow motion.

"I need to be sweetened up, too," Gary said. "I'm going into the Army, remember. In six months I'll probably be fighting Communists in Laos or Vietnam."

Diane looked over at me but I didn't know what to say or do. I thought of laughing out loud, to show that Gary was making a bad joke, or to try to turn it into one. But then I saw the expression on Gary's face and I knew I couldn't do that. It was a different expression than I'd ever seen before—sort of hopeful and alert, but frightened and defeated, too—and I knew then that whatever was happening was something that was important to him. And I wondered if Diane saw it too, saw that raw unprotected yearning, and despite what I had thought before I hoped for Gary's sake she did.

Diane took a few slow steps in Gary's direction. She put a hand on his shoulder and looked up into his face. Her rain hood fell back and I could see her gaze moving back and forth, as though she were searching Gary's expression for something.

Suddenly she smiled. "Sure," she said, "I guess I could do that." And then she put her arms around Gary's thin shoulders and rose up on her tiptoes and gave him a kiss, longer than the one she had just given me.

"Good luck, *mon ami*," she said in a whispery voice, and for the second time she turned away and walked back toward the house.

Now in the Pontiac Star Chief in the church parking lot in November of 1963, I became tired of thinking about the memory of Gary from last year. I opened the door and stepped out onto the pavement, being careful not to make a noise that would awaken Audrey. The sky was clear of clouds and black, and brilliant stars were overhead, thousands of them it seemed, more than you could ever count. I began to think about Einstein's theory of relativity, which I'd studied last year, and which in one part had dealt with stars. The night sky you saw from earth, Einstein said, was actually something that existed long ago; the starlight having to travel through space for thousands of years before finally reaching a person watching on planet earth. And it seemed to me, there in the church parking lot, that if Einstein was correct then traveling out in space would bring you closer to the truth, closer to the moment when the light had started. And then I wondered if the same applied to memories, where you are also going back in time, and if the things you thought about in memory brought you nearer to the truth.

But then my thinking began to break down, as it had with Einstein's theory, and I lost the thread of my idea. And there in the dark church parking lot, with a million dazzling untrue stars arrayed above me, I began to feel dizzy, and I had to sit down on the asphalt so I wouldn't fall.

After a few minutes, the dizziness passed. I stood and walked back to the car. And the only thought that remained in my head, of all the thinking I had done since leaving the car, was that memories might bring you closer to the truth, and with that in mind I got back into the Pontiac and continued with my thoughts about the night last year. Because now I felt it was worthwhile, would serve a purpose, would be truer than what I was feeling now.

ON THE RIDE home from Diane's house Gary sat in the passenger seat, his arms folded, staring straight ahead. He seemed to have drawn back into his own private world.

"What was that all about?" I asked. "That stuff with the kiss."

He laughed a little. "It was just something I wanted to do," he said. "Kiss a girl. Just a normal everyday thing."

"But Diane's my girlfriend," I said.

There was a long silence, and I could feel Gary watching me from across the darkened car, as if it had never occurred to him that there was anything wrong with kissing my girlfriend. As if being a great pianist gave him that right.

"Look at it this way, Nate," he said, and his voice was filled with concern now, notched down to a lower register. "It'll be a long time before I get to kiss another girl. Consider it a going-away gift for Gary."

We drove for a while in silence. I was still upset, though I didn't know exactly why. Part of me had wanted Diane to kiss Gary, but part of me hadn't. Then I noticed I was gripping the steering wheel very hard and I tried to make myself relax.

"Gary?" I said.

"What?"

"How come we never got along?"

"What are you talking about?"

"As brothers. We never got along the way brothers are supposed to. We never did things together. We never cared about what the other one was doing."

I heard him draw in a slow deep breath. When he let it out a circle of fog appeared on the windshield in front of him. Immediately it began to disappear, like a balloon losing air.

"We're different," he said. "That's the simple answer. We're put together differently. I like things that are sort of vague and mysterious. Things you need your imagination to make sense of. You like things that are real, things that you can touch, things that you can count." I felt him turn and look at me. I wanted to look back but I was driving and couldn't do it.

❧

My parents were still out when we got home. Gary headed upstairs, and I went into the den to play records on the hi-fi set —Buddy Holly and Marvin Gaye—the songs I liked to listen to after a date. I sat alone with the lights out and with the songs playing and I tried to think about Diane and feel romantic. I wanted to bring back the feeling of holding her in my arms, the feeling of being in love, but I couldn't do it. The beautiful pictures I tried to build in my mind kept fading to the image of Diane in Gary's arms.

Finally, I gave up. I just wanted to go to bed and forget about everything that had happened. I turned off the hi-fi set and headed for the stairs.

As I passed Gary's room, I noticed the crack beneath the door was dark. I stopped and listened with my ear against the door, wondering what strange things he might be up to. Then I gently pushed open the door and peered inside.

At first I couldn't see anything. But then my eyes adjusted and I saw Gary standing near the bed. In front of him were the things he'd brought home from the Army—underwear, shirts, a can of shaving cream. He was moving them one by one into a canvas gym bag.

I stepped into the room and closed the door behind me. "What's going on?" I said.

"I've decided to go back to camp early, Nate. There's a bus that leaves at midnight."

Outside, the rain had stopped and the sky was clear. Moonlight streamed in through the window, casting a pearly rectangle onto the floor.

Gary finished moving the things into his gym bag. He pulled

the zipper and I jumped at the sudden sound it made. Then he took a step in my direction, stopping in the rectangle of moonlight where I could see him better.

"I've got to go back," he said.

"But why?"

He started to answer, but before he uttered a single word he stopped and looked helplessly around the room, as if the answer to my question lay somewhere in those shadowy spaces: in the shiny music trophies arranged in perfect rows along his bookshelves, in the posters of famous dead composers adorning his four walls, in The Presbyterian Hymnal sitting open on his desktop.

He raised his eyes and met my stare. "I don't think I can stand to listen to another one of Dad's lectures," he said. He shrugged. "So I figure I might as well go back early. Get started with my transformation into a better person. Start the clock running on the new Gary." He gave a lopsided grin. "Maybe I can even find my own girl to kiss."

I looked at Gary and he looked back. And I saw the same expression I'd seen before, when he was waiting in the rain for Diane's answer, half-brazen, half-afraid, and I knew he was waiting still.

Just then I heard someone coming up the stairs. Gary heard it too. He crossed the room in two quick steps and pushed back into the closet. He pulled the door shut, although not quite all the way. Through a narrow opening I could see him standing among the hanging shirts and trousers, holding onto his gym bag, looking like a man waiting to catch a train.

The door swung open and the overhead light snapped on. "What's going on?" my father said, although he didn't say it in a mean way.

"Nothing," I said, blinking at the sudden brightness.

"Where's Gary?"

My father's hand rested on the doorknob. He was leaning

forward, as if he were about to step into the room. And I thought about my brother. How we were completely different. How we had never gotten along. Didn't understand each other. And I decided that this time I would try.

"Gary went out for a walk," I said. "He said he wanted to think about some things." Then I said: "I think he's afraid he won't make a good soldier."

My father stayed rooted in the doorway, but his expression softened and his mouth curved up into a sort of knowing smile. As if he understood everything that was happening. Understood it better than I did. Or better than Gary. And for some reason that made me mad.

"Well, don't worry," he said. "Everything will work out eventually. I'm sure it will."

"I hope so," I said. I forced myself to smile.

"Gary's got some things to learn," he continued. "It'll be hard but he'll learn them eventually."

I didn't say anything because I was still feeling that anger.

"Only I just wish he'd learn them easier." His glance moved over to a poster hanging on Gary's wall—Van Cliburn at the Russian festival in 1959—and his eyes narrowed a bit. "Like you," he added after a moment.

And again I didn't say anything because I didn't know what to say. But I realized I still had that smile spread across my face, a big stupid grin, as though I really wanted everything to turn out fine. And I couldn't tell you what I was thinking and I'm not sure I could tell you now. All I knew was that Gary was standing in the closet and my father was standing a few feet away. But they didn't know about each other, didn't know anything at all.

"Why don't you go to bed, Nate," my father said. "It's late."

I shifted my gaze and took one last quick look at Gary. From his shadowy hiding place he looked back at me and smiled. And for once I felt we were together.

"Okay," I said to my father. And I turned and followed him through the door.

❧

AFTER I LEFT Gary's bedroom, I walked down the hallway to my own room.

"Good night," my father said from the other end of the hallway.

"Good night," I said.

He disappeared through the bedroom door. I went into my own room, but I didn't bother to get undressed. I just lay down on the bed. Overhead, the tangled shadows of tree branches played across the ceiling, looking like a giant fishnet was about to drop down on me.

There were many thoughts and feelings swirling around inside my head, but I pushed them away and forced my thoughts back onto Diane. I tried to figure out what I would say when I saw her next, how I would explain Gary's strange behavior, how I would advance my campaign to sleep with her, how I would make her love me more. And then my thoughts turned back to Gary, and I suddenly wondered if Diane's kiss had been a factor in his decision to leave, whether it had tipped some strange internal forces out of balance, releasing pent-up passions or desire, and for some reason I found myself hoping that it had. And somewhere during all this thinking I heard a slight noise from out in the hallway and I pictured Gary, gym bag in hand, making his way down the curving staircase and out of our house and back to the Army camp that would turn him into a better man. And then I closed my eyes and thought harder about Diane, and I tried not to think about Gary anymore.

Chapter Twenty-Five

When I woke next it was morning. Audrey was not in the car but the word "CHURCH" had been traced in the fog on the side window. I got out of the car and stretched to loosen the muscles in my arms and legs that had gotten tight from lying in an awkward position. It was a cool morning and dew was on the car and on the grass and on the asphalt parking lot. In the distance I heard traffic but I couldn't see it.

I walked across the shiny wet asphalt to the back door of the church. It was a heavy wooden door with large brass hinges. When I opened the door and stepped inside I was in a sort of lobby. On the far side there were windows where you could see into the sanctuary. Audrey was kneeling at one of the pews in front, near where the preacher stands to give his sermon. I went through a door in that second, glassy, wall and walked up to the front. As I came close to Audrey I could see she had her head bowed and her lips were making words I could not hear.

I stopped a little way away from her. I didn't want to interrupt her when she was praying. But then her lips stopped moving and she said, still looking down, "I know you're there."

"How could you tell?" I asked.

"I heard you walking down the aisle," she said, with her head still bowed. "My hearing is very good."

"What are you doing?" I asked.

"I was saying a prayer," she said, keeping her head bowed.

"Was it a prayer for your baby?"

"It was for everybody. It was a general prayer."

"I thought you didn't believe in God."

"I didn't say I didn't believe in him. I said I wasn't sure." She opened her eyes and looked at me. "But either way it feels nice to say a prayer."

Audrey stood and we walked back up the aisle and through the glassy lobby and out through the big wooden door. It bothered me to have seen her praying, and as we walked back across the parking lot I began to think that I should tell her about the orphanage in Detroit. But then I remembered my reason for not telling her: that we were on a mission to bring Gary home, which would only take a few more days, and we needed to give that our full attention. So I stayed silent.

"Did you sleep well?" Audrey said when we reached the car.

"I slept all right," I said. "Though my shoulder hurts a little from how it was turned."

"Poor boy," she said, and she made a kind of pouting face like she was pretending to feel sorry for me. Then she asked: "Are we going to your house now to get the money?"

I looked at my watch. It said seven-thirteen. "Not yet," I said. "I want to make sure my dad's left for work."

"What about your mother?"

"She volunteers at a food charity on Thursday mornings. So she'll be gone too."

"What do we do in the meantime"

"There's a donut shop I know about. We can go there and have some coffee. And a donut if you want. I think we can afford a donut."

We got in the car and drove a few blocks to the place I had in mind.

※

AFTER WE FINISHED at the donut shop I drove to my parents' house. I knew they would both be gone so I did not have to act in a secret way. I found the spare key they kept under a flowerpot at the side door and I used it to open the door and go inside. Audrey was right behind me.

"The money's upstairs in my bedroom," I said.

"I'll come up with you," Audrey said. And I thought it was because she was curious about the house I had lived in and wanted to see more of it.

We went through the kitchen and the dining room and then to the front hallway, where a wide staircase went up to the second floor. The money was in the closet in my bedroom, in a coffee can on the shelf above the hanging clothes. I reached up and took it down and started to get the money out. While I was doing that, Audrey was looking around my old bedroom.

"This is quite a nice room," she said.

"It's just a bedroom," I said.

She was standing by the bureau holding a silver trophy.

"It's a basketball trophy," I said. "I got it in the ninth grade for shooting the most baskets in a basketball competition."

Just then I heard a noise in the hallway and I turned around. My mother was standing in the doorway.

"Oh, Nate," she said in a surprised voice. "What are you doing here?"

"This is Thursday," I said. "I thought you worked at the food bank on Thursdays."

"No," she said. "It's changed. It's Tuesdays now."

My mother looked over at Audrey. "You have a friend with you," she said, and she smiled.

"This is Audrey," I said. "The girl I told you about when you came to see me in Grand Rapids."

"Oh, yes," she said. "I remember. The girl you wanted to do a favor for." And then she smiled again at Audrey and Audrey smiled back.

"What are you doing here?" she asked again. "Aren't you missing work?"

"I am," I said. And then I explained about my plan to drive to Camp Carlisle and make arrangements to bring Gary home, and how Audrey was coming along to help. "I thought about it after you left that night with Dad," I said. "And I decided it was a good idea. Gary should be back here."

"Oh, well," my mother said. "I guess I don't think it's so important now." And she spoke in a matter-of-fact voice. There was none of the urgency she'd had when she had been on the porch in Grand Rapids, the sense that she was doing something that was important and that she cared about.

"No," I said to my mother, though I wasn't sure what I was saying no to. Disagreeing with her about what she had said, yes, but also something larger, something about the way she was or had become.

"No," I said a second time, though this time I used a louder voice. "It's a good idea to bring Gary home and I'm going to help you do it. Gary belongs here. Audrey and I are going to drive up to Camp Carlisle. That's why I need the money." I tipped the coffee can so she could see the bills inside. "We need money for gas and food and places to stay at night."

"Why don't you come with us," Audrey said, and she took a step in the direction of my mother. "Gary's your son. You should be part of bringing him home. And if you're along it might be easier to convince the Army people to let us do it. Personally, I don't know the rules about moving coffins, and I don't think Nate does either, though I could be mistaken about that." She looked at me and smiled in an apologetic way, as if

151

she felt guilty for saying that I didn't know about moving coffins.

"No," my mother said. "I'll stay here with Nate's father." She turned and looked at me. "Nate will figure out how to do it."

And then my mother did something that surprised me. She walked across the room and put her arms around Audrey and held her for a while, pulling slightly to bring her close. And Audrey's arms went up and she held my mother back, the two of them together with Audrey's face buried in my mother's shoulder and her hand still holding the basketball trophy. And it felt like an exchange was happening, from my mother to Audrey, a passing over of something important. And even though my mother wasn't going with us, and even though she'd spoken against it, I knew she was glad we were doing it. But she couldn't say it, couldn't say how she truly felt, though she wanted to do something that showed that lack.

After a moment my mother stepped away from Audrey. "Take care of Nate," she said with a smile, as if it were a little joke that I needed to be taken care of. "And take care of Gary too, when you get him."

We went down the stairs then, me first, then Audrey, and then my mother. We walked back through the house to the side door. At the side door I turned to my mother and kissed her on the cheek. "I'll let you know how things are going when we get up there," I said. "I'll call."

Audrey and I went out into the driveway. When we reached the car I looked back. My mother had her arm raised and was motioning for me to come back.

"When you get there....," she said, after I'd walked back to her. She put a hand on my forearm and leaned in close. "When you get to Camp Carlisle and talk to the people there, see if you can find out exactly how it happened. The accident with Gary on the shooting range."

"Why do you want to know that?"

"It seems strange to me how such a thing could happen. A soldier being shot on a shooting range. Teaching soldiers how to shoot a gun is such a common thing in the Army. They've been doing it for a long time and they must have rules about how you fire bullets and keep everybody safe." For a moment her gaze drifted off to the side, then it sharpened and came back. "Gary was different," she said. "You know that. You were his brother. He was different from other boys. And it was hard for him. Being different was hard." She looked at me. "It was lonely for him, too," she said.

"I didn't know that."

"Well, you never spent much time together so I guess you wouldn't have known."

"I wish we had spent more time together," I said. "I think he could have helped me with my painting. He wasn't a painter but he would've understood it and could've told me how to do it better."

My mother smiled a little, and I thought she was imagining Gary helping me with my painting and how nice that would have been.

She let go of my arm, but I could tell she wasn't finished so I didn't turn away.

"He never should have been in the Army," she said. "Your father was wrong about that. I should have stopped it. I should have stood up for him." I saw her face tighten, as if she was experiencing a sudden spasm of pain, and her chin began to tremble. But right away the trembling stopped and she looked up at me and smiled, and then she turned and went back into the house.

Chapter Twenty-Six

After we left my parents' house, Audrey and I drove north through the neighborhood. Audrey looked out the window at the houses going by. "I've never seen so many big beautiful houses all packed together in the same town," she said. "It's like Shangri La."

"It's okay," I said. Then, after a pause, I said "It's not so great," which I knew to be the truth.

When we reached the edge of town we got onto a section of the new interstate highway going north, with two large streams of traffic going in opposite directions. And for a while we didn't talk, and I thought it was because we'd started our adventure now, had come across a boundary and were setting our minds in a new direction and for a new purpose.

I was beginning to feel better. And when I thought about it I decided it was because we had a plan and were following it. Without a plan, life can be uncomfortable because you don't know where to turn or where to go or what's going to happen next. But with a plan you can relax and do the things the plan says. For a while you give yourself over to the plan so your mind can go to other places.

Next I began to think about some aspects of what we had set out to do—like what exactly we'd do when we got to the Army base, and who we would talk to, and what we would say. I assumed there would be someone on the base who was in charge of the cemetery, and I pictured Audrey and myself sitting in an office talking to a person in a uniform who was explaining what we had to do to get Gary back home. After that I pictured Gary's coffin sitting on a loading dock and a forklift truck lifting it onto a truck, and then it—the truck—driving off to southern Michigan. But I didn't know who the person behind the desk would be, or how I would find them, or what exactly I would say, and I didn't know where the truck would came from, or who would drive it, or whether you needed a special truck to move a coffin, with refrigeration maybe and special cords for lashing the coffin down so it wouldn't move around. Those were things I still had to learn.

When we got north of Pontiac the new interstate ended and we had to get on the old two-lane highway, and then we were in the country, with farmhouses and barns and crop fields and herds of grazing cattle. Audrey took the money out of the coffee can and counted it, arranging little stacks of bills across her lap.

"It's one hundred and twenty-four dollars," she said. "Is that enough to get us to Camp Carlisle and back?"

"I think so," I said. I did a little calculation in my head about how long we would be gone, which I thought would be six days, and the number of meals we'd have, and the amount of gas we'd need to buy along the way. "I think it'll be okay," I said for a second time. "But we'll have to be careful." Then I said: "Give me fifty dollars." I twisted around and got my wallet out of my back pocket and handed it to Audrey. "Put it in here. And put the rest into the glove box."

"Okay, Captain," Audrey said, and she gave a little salute like she was a soldier following an order.

Then Audrey asked: "Are you going to lose your job?"

"What?"

"You're missing work for no good reason." She looked at me. "Unless getting your brother's coffin back home is considered acceptable behavior."

"No, I don't suppose it is," I said. "When we stop for gas I'll call the factory and tell them I'm sick. They let you miss if you're sick."

"Oh, my," Audrey said. "Mr. Van Gogh is going to tell a lie."

"I guess so," I said, and I laughed a little, because I hadn't thought about it being a lie but only something I had to do.

"What about you?" I asked. "When you don't show up at the Rexall store."

"Oh, well," she said. She turned and looked out the side window. "I guess I'm not doing that anymore. Maybe I didn't tell you."

"No, you didn't," I said, and I thought she would explain more about why she left the Rexall store, because she hadn't said anything about it before. But she didn't. She just kept looking out the side window at the landscape going by.

We drove through Flint, where all the Chevrolets were made, and where the men had gone on a sit-down strike in 1936 to get the union, and then we took a long curving ramp that put us onto another section of the new interstate. It was a nice sunny day, with brightness in the sky, although there were gray clouds in the distance that looked like they held rain. When we got to Saginaw, the interstate ended and we were back on a two-lane road. Audrey fell asleep, her head against the window bouncing slightly with the motion of the car, her lips parted, and her chest moving slowly as she took in breaths and let them out. The sun coming through the side window lit her face and I thought again that she was a pretty girl, beautiful even, though her face had no particular expression, was just the natural way her face became when there was no emotion on it.

After a while Audrey woke up. "Where are we?" she said. We were passing pine forests now and not farm fields.

"We just drove through a town called Kalkaska," I said. "There was a statue in the center of town of a giant rainbow trout jumping out of the water. I almost woke you up to see it."

"I'm glad you didn't," Audrey said. "I've seen trout before."

"This one was different," I said. "It was huge."

"Well, maybe you should paint it," Audrey said. "If you liked it that much, you should paint it."

Up ahead a Sunoco gas station came into view. It sat by itself alongside the highway. I needed gas so I pulled in. While the attendant was working the pump I walked over to a phone booth at the edge of the parking lot and made a call to the factory to tell Jimmy Palmer I was sick and wasn't coming in. "You don't sound sick," he said. "More likely it's a hangover. There's too much fun in your life, young man," he said, and he laughed as if he'd made a fine joke.

"No," I said, "I'm really sick."

"Okay," he said. "Have it your way." And he hung up the phone.

When I went back to the car Audrey wasn't there. I looked around and spotted her in the office of the gas station. She was holding the coffee can and I saw her reach inside and give a bill to the attendant, a boy in greasy overalls. She said something that made the boy laugh and then he said something back and she laughed too. I headed for the office. When Audrey saw me she said, "I've paid for the gas." She waved her hand that had a bill in it. "Now I'm buying gum. Do you have any particular flavor that you're fond of."

"I guess Juicy Fruit will be all right," I said.

"Okay," Audrey said. "Juicy Fruit it is." She set the coffee can on the counter and bent down to work the gum machine. She looked back over her shoulder at me. "This is Henry," she said, and she nodded in the direction of the boy in greasy overalls.

"He and I have been getting acquainted while you made your call. He's a Christian of the Catholic persuasion."

I looked at Henry. His gaze was on Audrey where she was bent over working the candy machine. Then he turned his gaze on me and smiled as if we were together in some secret pact, the pact of being men together, I suppose. And I felt a sudden flash of anger, and I knew it was because of how he looked at Audrey —without knowing anything about her but only because she was a girl.

"Let's get out of here," I said to Audrey.

Audrey looked at me with a slightly surprised expression. "I guess I'm being summoned," she said to Henry. And then we both walked back to the car and drove away.

 ❧

WE HAD ONLY GONE a few miles along the highway when Audrey asked why we had left the gas station so suddenly. "It was kinda rude," she said. "The way we walked out on that nice boy Henry."

"I saw the way he looked at you," I said. "When you were getting the gum. It wasn't very nice."

Audrey laughed. "Well, now you know the secret weapon women have." She laughed again and looked at me. "I suppose you've never looked at a girl that way."

I didn't answer because I didn't want to say a lie.

And then I thought of something. "What about the coffee can?" I asked.

"Oh, shit," Audrey said. "I left it on the counter."

"Damn it," I said.

I slowed and made a U-turn across the highway, which was easy because there was no traffic. When we got back to the gas station we both got out of the car and headed toward the office.

Audrey had her purse tucked under her arm. When we got to the office the coffee can was not on the candy machine.

"I left a coffee can with money in it," Audrey said to Henry. "Hills Brothers. Right here on the counter."

Henry looked at her with a blank expression. "I don't know what you're talking about," he said. "I don't know anything about a coffee can."

"You're lying," Audrey said. "I left it right here on the counter and you took it. You're a god-damn thief."

"Here now," I said, because I thought Audrey was getting too excited. "We had a coffee can with money in it, Henry," I said, trying to sound reasonable. "And we're pretty sure we left it here." I pointed to the counter.

"Well, I'm sorry but you're mistaken."

"I don't think we are," Audrey said, and she spoke in a voice that made me turn in her direction. She was standing by the counter with a silver pistol in her hand and she had it pointed at Henry.

"Jesus Christ!" I said. I stepped over to grab her hand and force it down, but she stepped away and kept the pistol aimed at Henry.

"Don't shoot," Henry said, and he used a voice I instantly remembered: it was the voice I'd used with Audrey's father when he'd held the gun beneath my chin, a kind of whimpering voice that comes from knowing you might be wiped away in just an instant. "I can't defend myself," Henry said. "I'm helpless. It's not fair."

"What about the coffee can?" Audrey said, in the same hard voice she had used before. She took a step forward. The gun was just a couple of feet from Henry's face.

"I might've seen it," Henry said. "I might've seen it in the back. Don't shoot and I'll go back and look for it."

Henry turned and started back into the service bay. Audrey

stepped over to the door so she could keep the gun aimed on him.

"God damn it!" I said. I stepped over and grabbed Audrey's hand to force the gun down. But she struggled against me, twisting and turning so I couldn't keep a solid grip. And then I thought that this was how bad things happened, terrible things you thought would never touch you, things that could change your life forever.

"What the hell do you think you're doing," I said. My face was close to Audrey's. My breath was coming fast.

Finally, Audrey let me force her hand down. She nodded in the direction of Henry. He was rummaging through a storage cabinet along the wall. "That's the point, isn't it?" she said, and her voice seemed too calm in terms of what was happening. "And if you notice, it seems to be working."

I kept holding Audrey's hand down. After another minute Henry came back into the office with the coffee can in his hand. "Here," he said. He held the coffee can out to Audrey. "I don't know how it got there."

"Okay," Audrey said. "I guess it'll have to stay a mystery. Anyway, things are back to normal so I guess you can still be alive for a while."

Audrey took the can and we started walking back to the Pontiac. I thought Henry would come after us as soon as we had turned our backs—come after us with something he could attack us with—a wrench or a tire iron, something heavy—but he didn't. We got into the car and I started the engine and pulled out onto the highway. I looked for Henry in the rearview mirror but I couldn't see him.

"That was really stupid," I said, after we'd gone a little way down the highway.

"What was?" Audrey said.

"That with the gun. It could've gone off and you'd be in jail.

Or we'd both be in jail." I glanced in her direction. "Why the hell do you carry a gun in your purse, anyway?"

"For protection when I'm giving tours," she said. She spoke in a kind of stiff voice which I understood to mean that she was getting mad. "You never know when things might turn around on you."

"You said that never happened. You said that a kiss or hug was all it took."

"That's theoretical," she said. "Theoretical doesn't always work. You've got to be prepared for anything." She was quiet for a minute and then she spoke again. "And if you happen to notice I got your money back. I guess I didn't think your pleases and your thank-yous were going to do us much good." She stopped talking for a moment, and then she spoke again: "Besides, it isn't loaded. There are no bullets in it. It's just for show." She took the pistol out of her purse and pulled the trigger. I heard the hammer snap but nothing happened.

We drove along the highway. I didn't say anything else about the gun. There was no point talking about it. Audrey had made up her mind to have a gun and talking about it wouldn't help. But it reminded me there was a part of Audrey I didn't understand, a part that she kept hidden, just like her father said. And then I wondered what else was in that part of Audrey I didn't see.

Chapter Twenty-Seven

We drove north all afternoon, mostly on country roads but sometimes on stretches of the new interstate highway. We passed through Saginaw and West Branch and Grayling and some smaller towns that didn't even bother to put up a sign telling you what they were called. I was slowly getting less mad with Audrey about the gun. I realized she was right about the money, that we probably wouldn't have gotten it back just by talking.

For a while Audrey read from the Dale Carnegie book, and occasionally she'd read a passage out loud that she thought was particularly good. One was about how a shy person would become an eloquent speaker if you walked up and punched him in the face. "He means that when a person gets mad he'll find the words to say what he feels," Audrey said. "That you need to have passion behind what you say." Another passage was about how you could become a great conversationalist by letting people talk about themselves. "Dale Carnegie says it's backward from what most people think," Audrey said. "Most people think you've got to tell everybody how great you are. But people don't care about you. They only care about themselves."

"That's not exactly true," I said. "I care about other people. I care about my family. And I care about you."

"It's sweet of you to say that," Audrey said, "but unfortunately you're not a regular person. You're a special case, so you don't count. We have to throw you out of the sample."

Audrey laughed a little and I did too. Then I said: "Please don't throw me out. I want to be counted too."

"Sorry," Audrey said. "Come back when you're normal and maybe we'll reconsider."

Up ahead a red neon sign came into view. It said "The Dew Drop Inn," which sounded like the name of a place where you could spend the night. It was getting close to five o'clock and I was starting to feel tired. I hadn't slept much the night before and Audrey hadn't either.

I pulled off the highway so we could take a closer look. A group of small log cabins were arranged around the property. One had a sign in the window that said OFFICE.

"What do you think?" I said to Audrey.

"It looks okay to me." She was looking out at the log cabins. "We can pretend we're pioneers."

I turned off the car and started to get out. But then I thought of something and I stopped and turned back. "How are we going to do this?" I said.

"What are you talking about?"

"We can only rent one cabin. That's all we can afford."

"So what?"

"How're we going to do it when we're in the room?"

Audrey laughed.

"I saw this movie," she said, after she had stopped laughing. "It was one of those old black-and-white ones I watched when I was waiting at my parents' house to have my baby. A man and a woman were traveling together and they weren't married. Clark Gable was the man; I don't remember who the woman was. Anyway, when they stayed in a motel they strung a rope across the room and hung a blanket from it. They called it the Wall of Jericho, which I didn't understand and still do not. But with the blanket they each had their own private space." She looked at me. "Do you see what I'm saying? About the rope and the blanket?"

"Yes," I said. "We'll try that." And then I thought of something else. "When I check us in I'll have to say we're married. Otherwise they might not let us stay together in one cabin."

Audrey looked at me and laughed again. "You're crazy," she said.

Chapter Twenty-Eight

I checked us into the Dew Drop Inn as Mr. and Mrs. Nathan Walker. And then I knew why Audrey had laughed, because it was obvious the woman who checked us in didn't care if we were married or not. I guess what happened in her cabins didn't matter as long as you paid the bill upfront.

We got settled in our cabin, and then I walked back down to the office to ask for a rope.

"You're not going to hang yourself, are you?" the woman asked. "I don't want any suicides in my motel."

"I guess we won't do it tonight, then," I said. "We'll save it for another time." I smiled and the woman smiled too. "But I do need some rope. The bumper on my car is loose and I need to tie it down. Otherwise, I'm afraid it'll fall off."

I knew that what I'd said wasn't a very good lie. But I thought the woman wouldn't care enough to ask me to explain and she didn't. Most people, if they don't understand you, won't ask you to explain. That's something I'd learned from trying to talk to people about electricity.

The woman went through a curtained door into the back of

the office and returned with a length of clothesline. "Remember what I said about no suicides," she said with a fake stern look, and she handed me the rope.

When I got back to our cabin I set up the blanket in the way Audrey had described, but it was not perfect. It sagged in the middle so you could see across if you were standing, and there were big gaps between the blanket and the walls.

"I guess it's supposed to be a symbol," I said to Audrey. I was standing on my side looking over at hers. Audrey was sitting on her bed. "It's a symbol more than it's practical."

"Just don't get any ideas," Audrey said, and she looked up at me with a kind of scowl, her eyes squinted down to slits and her lips pressed together and furrows on her brow. "I still have my gun," she said, and then she smiled. I couldn't keep from smiling too.

We were both tired from sleeping in the car the night before, so we decided to skip dinner and go right to bed. I got ready on my side and then Audrey got ready on hers. Because of the problem with the hanging blanket, I could've seen Audrey in her underwear if I had wanted to, but I kept my head turned toward the wall, because that was the deal we had made and I thought that I should keep it.

But even though I was tired, I couldn't sleep. My mind had too many thoughts in it. And I guess it was the same for Audrey, because every few minutes I could hear her changing her position in the bed.

"Claudette Colbert," she said, all of a sudden.

"What?"

"Claudette Colbert. She was the actress in the movie with Clark Gable. I just remembered."

"So that's who you are."

"Except maybe not as pretty."

"You are, though," I said.

"Why thank you."

We were quiet. And then I said: "Except you're already Audrey Hepburn. You can't be two people at the same time."

I thought Audrey would laugh at this, even though it wasn't much of a joke, but she didn't. She was quiet and then, after a few more minutes passed, her breathing slowed and steadied and I knew she was asleep.

I CAME AWAKE SUDDENLY in the darkness. I had been dreaming about Audrey and in my dream she held a baby in her arms, and then, suddenly, the baby was gone and she was searching frantically through her parents' house and crying. And I knew that it —the dream—was about the lie Audrey's parents told her. The lie that Audrey didn't know about but that I did.

I lay awake wondering if I'd made the right decision to not tell Audrey until after we were done with our mission to Camp Carlisle. And the more I thought about it—all alone in the dark and with the dream still strong in my mind—the more I began to think I was making a mistake.

I threw back the blanket and got up out of bed and looked across the Wall of Jericho. Audrey was lying on her side. One hand was wrapped in a fist and tucked up under her chin. I thought about going over and waking her and telling her the truth about her baby. It seemed to me in that moment that she should know the truth, that the truth was all that mattered. But then I began to think about it in a different way—a logical mathematical way. And I thought about my plan, which was to wait to tell her until after we'd made the arrangements for getting Gary home, and I thought about the amount of time left for doing that—which I figured to be about four days—and I compared that to the amount of time Audrey had already lived with her parent's lie, which I knew to be a year or more. And I saw that the time for staying silent was very small compared to the time that had already passed. And so keeping the secret for a few more days—the pain it might cause to Audrey—was small compared to the pain she'd already lived through. And knowing that—knowing the strict logic of it—I felt calm again, justified in my decision, and I went back to bed and soon I was asleep.

Chapter Twenty-Nine

Next morning we got some coffee and cinnamon rolls from a little country store next to the motel and then we got back onto the highway, eating the cinnamon rolls and drinking the coffee as we rocketed along. We crossed the Mackinaw Bridge at about noon. Audrey was asleep so I woke her up so she could see the bridge.

"It's the longest suspension bridge in the world," I said. "Five miles. Longer than the Golden Gate."

Audrey looked out the passenger window at the cables going by and at the water down below. A strong wind was blowing. You could feel it push against the car. Whitecaps were on the water.

"We're crossing the Straights of Mackinaw," I said. "Over there's Lake Huron." I pointed off to the right. "And over there's Lake Michigan." I pointed off to the left.

I thought Audrey would say something but she didn't. She just kept staring out the window.

"The bridge is supported by two towers through a network of cables," I said. "The forces get distributed through the cables so each cable only holds a small part of the total weight." I glanced over in Audrey's direction. "That's why they call it a suspension bridge. It's suspended from the cables."

Audrey kept looking out the side window.

"Okay," she said, after we had reached the other side. "That's pretty cool. But I guess you like bridges a little more than me."

After that she settled herself and closed her eyes and went back to sleep.

᛫

WE WERE in the Upper Peninsula of Michigan now, the far north, and there was not much traffic or much of anything else, just dense forests of pine trees and cedars and hemlocks and occasionally a run-down house or cabin with cast-off things scattered around the property: broken pieces of furniture, rusted farm machinery, stacks of lumber, a pile of tires, a baby's crib.

Audrey was working in her sketchbook, making a drawing of a chair that was shaped something like a clam shell. But evidently she wasn't happy with her design because suddenly she wadded the paper into a ball and threw in on the floor.

"Let's talk," she said. "I'm bored by all these pine trees."

"What do you want to talk about?"

"Tell me why you want to learn to paint?" she said. "I don't exactly understand that, since you're so good at other things like mathematics and electricity. And bridges; you're good at bridges too." She looked at me. "It seems like you're going in the wrong direction."

"You asked me that question already," I said. "The day we met. I told you it's about understanding life."

"That's just a concept," she said. "I want to know the particular reason."

I thought about Audrey's question. I had never actually considered it before, not in a particular way, and I was surprised that I hadn't, because I'd always thought that things you do should have a reason.

"I guess I don't have a good reason," I said to Audrey.

"You must have a reason," she said. "Otherwise you're crazy."

I thought back to when I'd started to paint. It was a few weeks after Gary had been killed and after I'd had the arguments with my father and had moved to Grand Rapids to take the job in the car factory. I'd found the Time-Life series on the great painters of Europe in a used bookstore on Campau Square where I had gone one Sunday afternoon to kill some time, and I bought the books and found them interesting. I particularly liked the ones about the Impressionists—Monet and Renoir and Degas and Pisarro—the artists who had found a different way of looking at the world. But I couldn't tell Audrey that my interest in painting was because of books. That didn't seem like a proper answer to her question. So I stopped thinking and I sort of relaxed my brain so it could go in whatever direction it wanted to. And then I said the first thing that came into my mind.

"It's a way of learning about the world," I said. "But indirectly. It's like the biggest secrets can only be approached from an angle."

"I don't follow you."

"An angle," I said. "Like you can't come at some things head on. Big things like loneliness and courage and beauty." I looked at her. "And love. Love too. That's another."

I paused a moment to let Audrey say something back but she didn't, so I said some more. "When you paint you have to sort of sneak up on your subject from the side. You're painting something—a scene—but you want it to be more than just what it looks like. You want it to carry some meaning. But you don't really know the meaning like you know a date in history or the name of a place on a map, but you feel the truth of it anyway."

Audrey looked at me. Her brow had little furrows. "You're a very unusual young man, Nathan Walker," she said.

Just then I heard a siren. I looked up at the rear-view mirror. A sheriff's car was bearing down on us with its red-light flashing.

"Shit," I said.

Audrey saw it, too. She was turned around and looking out the rear window. "Just be quiet," she said. "Let me do the talking. I've had experience with police."

I pulled over onto the shoulder of the road and the sheriff's car pulled up behind. I watched in the sideview mirror as the officer got out of his car and walked up alongside us, just walking slowly like he was in no particular hurry. I rolled down the window.

"You were going a little fast back there, son," the officer said. "Do you have any idea how fast you were going?"

"No, sir," I said.

"I clocked you at sixty-seven. Fifty-five's the limit here."

I started to say something, but Audrey touched my arm and leaned across so she could see the officer. "It was my fault, sir," she said. "He's taking me to the doctor and I told him to hurry. I encouraged him to go fast." She smiled at the officer. "I'm pregnant," she said, "and I've been having terrible morning sickness." She smiled at the officer in a kind of apologetic way, like she was sorry to have to speak about such awful things as morning sickness and being pregnant. "I've had sickness real bad and this morning there was some blood and it scared me." She put her hand up to her mouth like she was feeling a wave of sickness at that very moment. "This boy—Nate— is visiting our neighbors —they're the Richardson's—and he was the only one around, so I asked him to drive me to the doctor. He's doing me a favor."

The officer looked from Audrey to me and then back again to Audrey. I could tell he was wondering whether to believe her. I had already gotten out my license and had handed it to him.

"Never mind, son," the officer said, and he gave my license

back. "Go ahead and get the young lady to a doctor. Just watch your speed."

"Yes, sir," I said. "I will. I certainly will."

"Thank you, sir," Audrey said, still leaning across. "I'll make sure he does."

I put the Pontiac in gear and released the clutch and pulled out onto the highway. After we'd gone a little way Audrey laughed. "How'd I do?" she asked me.

"You lied," I said.

She laughed again. "All you have to do is start talking about being pregnant and men get uncomfortable. I learned that when I was. And if you throw in being sick, it really mixes them up. They just want you to go away and not come back until you have a baby in your arms. They don't want to think about how it got there."

"What did you mean about having experience with the police?" I asked.

"Oh, you know. How the police sometimes ask you what you're doing."

"That's never happened to me."

"Well, it probably will when you start to do things that are more interesting."

"Like what? What kind of things?"

"If I told you you'd know too much about me," Audrey said. "I'd rather remain a mystery." She put her hands up to her face like she was hiding. And then she laughed. And I laughed too, though I wasn't sure what I was laughing about.

Chapter Thirty

We reached the town of Carlisle in the late afternoon. It was a small north-Michigan town pretty much like all the others we had passed through, with four or five blocks of turn-of-the-century storefronts and small wood-framed houses scattered on the streets behind. The only difference was that it had more bars.

"I suppose the bars are for the soldiers," I said. "Something for them to do on their days off."

"I suppose," Audrey said.

"What's Linda's?" I asked. We were passing a big Victorian house that had a red light bulb shining over the front door, even though it was not dark. A hand-painted sign in front said "Welcome to Linda's."

"That's something else for the soldiers to do on their time off," Audrey said, and she gave a quick unfunny laugh.

"Okay," I said back, and that was all I said. I thought she meant it was a brothel, but I wasn't completely sure. Not sure enough to answer in that way.

Then I said: "It's too late to go to the Army base today, so we might as well find a place to stay tonight."

"I saw a motel when we came into town," Audrey said. "It looked pretty awful but it'll probably fit our budget."

I turned the car around and drove back through town. The motel that Audrey had seen was a low cement-block building painted white. There were spaces for cars to park right next to the doors that opened into the rooms. A blue neon sign said "Sandi's Motel."

In the office an older woman with short red hair sat on a stool behind a counter. A cigarette was hanging from her lips. She smiled when I came in.

"Are you Sandi?" I asked, smiling back at her.

"No," the woman said. "Sandi was the one before. I'm Barbara. Barbara Cook." She smiled. "People call me Babs."

"Well, we'd like a room, Babs," I said.

"You're lucky then because we've got a few of those."

"We'd like two beds," I said.

Babs raised her eyebrows. "That doesn't sound like its going to be any fun." She was looking out through the window at the Pontiac with Audrey inside.

I smiled to show her that I understood her joke. Babs pushed a card across the counter and I began to fill it out.

"Are you two running away to get married?" she asked. "We get a lot of runaways here."

"No," I said. "We're married. Just two lost souls looking for a place to lay our weary heads."

Babs looked at me with a funny expression, as if what I'd said was stupid. Which of course it was. Most people, if you say something stupid, will stop asking questions. That's something I had learned.

I paid for one night and we carried our bags to the room Babs gave us, which was room fifteen. I'd saved the rope from the night before and I was going to set up the Wall of Jericho but Audrey said she was hungry so we left the room and walked back into town. The weather had turned cold and snow was in the air, just small pieces of ice that drifted down with no direction.

"I feel like we've landed in a different world," Audrey said. She hugged herself against the cold.

"We have," I said. "We're near the top of the Upper Peninsula of Michigan. The Arctic isn't too far away. Russia's close if you go over the north pole. That's why the Army base is here."

"So they can fight back against the Russians?"

"It's to protect the airport near Marquette where they have the B-52 bombers that are loaded with atom bombs. The planes can get to Russia faster because they won't have so far to go."

"So if Russia bombs us we'll be able to bomb them back," Audrey said through her shivering. "We'll have the satisfaction of knowing they're all dead, even though by then we'll all be dead too."

"That's right. We'll all be turned to dust. Both sides will."

"It's hard to feel satisfaction when you're dead. Has anyone thought of that?"

"I guess not," I said. Then I said: "Kennedy's trying to get the Russians to agree to stop testing new atomic bombs."

"That doesn't sound like such a great improvement."

"At least it's a start."

Up ahead a neon sign said "Big Buck Grill." It blinked on and off in an erratic way, like it was close to burning out. "Let's try this one," I said, because I wanted to get Audrey in from the cold.

Inside, a long mahogany bar went down one side of the room with a mirror behind and sparkling liquor bottles lined up on shelves. Two soldiers were drinking whisky at the bar. They looked up when we came in, but only for a moment. Other soldiers were in back where I could hear the click of billiard balls. A small band played loud rock music. At the far end of the room a woman was dancing on a little platform and she was naked.

Audrey and I both sort of froze when we saw the naked dancing woman. I mean we came to a sudden stop. It was unexpected.

"I guess this isn't such a good place," I said. "Let's leave."

"Are you folks looking for something to eat?" the man behind the bar said. He wore a white apron and was swabbing down the bar with a towel.

"Yes," Audrey said.

"Well, you've come to the right place. We've got some nice dinners and a special on fried onion rings. Take any table."

"Let's leave," I said a second time to Audrey. I took a step in the direction of the door but Audrey didn't follow.

"I don't mind," Audrey said. She nodded toward the dancing woman. "I've seen naked women before, haven't you?"

"Sure," I said. "I've seen a lot," though that was not exactly true. I'd actually seen only one. It was in a Ypsilanti strip club where I'd gone one day with two other boys. And that time might not have even counted, because the stage was lit with strobe lights which made it hard to see. Hard to see much detail.

"Then what's the problem?" Audrey said.

"There's no problem," I said. "It just seems strange to be eating dinner while a naked woman is dancing just a little way away."

Audrey looked up at the woman. The woman saw her looking and smiled back.

"She's not completely naked," Audrey said. "She's wearing high heel shoes."

That made us laugh and the laughter sort of changed the mood, made the situation funny instead of awkward.

"Okay," I said. "You win. Let's eat here."

We took a table near the dance floor. After a minute or two a waitress came up. She wasn't naked but she had on skimpy clothes, shorts that hugged her body and a cut-off tee shirt that showed the bottom of her breasts.

Audrey ordered a rum and soda and I ordered a neat bourbon, which was the drink I'd learned about from Mr. Smollett. I was pretty sure I wouldn't like it, since I hadn't liked it before, but it seemed to be a drink you'd order if you were old enough to be drinking in a bar, which is what I wanted the waitress to believe.

Our drinks came and we sat and drank them without talking. The dancing woman was behind my back. I kept trying to find ways of looking at her—just casual movements of my head that happened to send my gaze in her direction. After a few minutes, Audrey noticed what I was doing.

"Do you want to change seats?" she said.

"No, I'm fine."

"Do you like the way she looks?" She nodded toward the dancer.

"She's nice," I said, looking.

"But do you like the way she looks?"

I looked again.

"Not as much as I thought I would. I guess being naked is better in the abstract." Just then the dancer caught my eye and smiled. And it felt like an electric shock had entered my body. I could feel my face go red. "It's too extreme," I said to Audrey, though I'm not sure what I meant by that.

"Well, now you've learned a good lesson," Audrey said. "Sometimes your imagination is better than real life. And sometimes less is more. That's two lessons, I guess." She raised her glass but stopped before it reached her lips. "I mean less nakedness, by the way," she said, "Less nakedness would be more clothes, wouldn't it?" She looked off to the side and scrunched up her face like she wasn't sure she understood what she'd just said.

Just then one of the soldiers who'd been playing pool walked over to our table. He was tall and thin and wore a little brass nametag that said Pvt. Riley. He walked up to Audrey with a big grin on his face. "Would you like to dance, miss?" he said.

"Not now," Audrey said. "I'm trying to get warm with this drink." She raised her glass a little.

"I know a better way to get you warm," the soldier said, still grinning.

"Maybe later," Audrey said.

"I don't have much of that later stuff," the soldier said. "I've got to be back on the base by nine." He reached down and took one of Audrey's hands and began to pull her up.

"Hey," Audrey said. "Stop it."

"Just one dance," the soldier said, and he kept pulling.

"She doesn't want to dance," I said to the soldier. But he didn't stop.

And then I thought of something. Audrey's purse was on the floor. I reached in and felt around until I found the silver pistol. I brought it up and lay it on the table. That's all I did: I laid the pistol on the table with my hand on top.

"Christ Almighty," the soldier said when he saw the pistol.

I looked up at him. I didn't say anything. I thought of different things to say, but saying nothing seemed to be the best.

"Jesus," the soldier said. He let go of Audrey and started to back away.

"Stop now," Audrey said, "let's not get extreme." She reached and covered my hand that was lying on the pistol.

"I guess one dance won't hurt," she said. She smiled at the soldier, then she looked in my direction and frowned. "Let's stop now," she said. "Let's all be friends."

Audrey took the soldier's hand and they walked out onto the dance floor. At first a rock-and-roll song was playing and they danced apart, but then a slow song came and the soldier took Audrey in his arms and held her close against him, closer than he needed to, I thought, and closer than she'd want. Then another slow song started and a different soldier danced with her, and after that there was a third.

I was beginning to feel a little jealous. I had never held Audrey in my arms like that, close up against me, even though I knew her better than the soldiers. And for a while I thought of going up and cutting in, which I'd seen done in movies, where a man taps another man on the shoulder and the girl comes over to him. But I thought it might be something you only saw in movies and not something that would work in real life, so I stayed seated.

The slow song ended and the saxophone player said the band would take a twenty-minute break. I sensed some movement behind me and turned around. The bartender was helping the dancer climb down from her platform. He held her hand to steady her while she stepped onto the bar and then to a chair and then to the floor. And it was an odd sight: a naked woman stepping down from a dancing platform in a sort of dainty way, like a queen descending from a carriage with a footman to assist her. And for a moment I wondered if that could be a painting, like one I'd seen in the Time-Life series, Manet's *Olympia*, which had shown a prostitute being attended by a servant while lying naked on a bed. The prostitute was looking out of the canvas toward the viewer, showing no sign of embarrassment or shame. The painting had caused a scandal when it was shown at the Paris Salon in 1865, the Time-Life series said, because it carried a message that a woman is important and deserves respect, even if she's a prostitute—or, by extension, a naked dancer in a bar.

The bartender passed the dancer a white terrycloth robe and she put it on and cinched it at the waist. Out on the dance floor, Audrey spoke a few words to the last soldier she was dancing with, then she came back to our table. She was slightly out of breath and color was on her face.

"Did you like that?" I asked, which was the same question she'd asked me about the dancing woman.

Just then the dancer started to pass our table on her way to the dressing room in back. But one of the soldiers had come over to talk to Audrey and he blocked her path so she had to stop beside our table. I looked up and she smiled down at me, and then she made a face, as if she was embarrassed to be standing there beside me, naked beneath her robe, and she wanted me to know it, wanted me to know that standing there was not her choice.

"You're a very good dancer," I said, because I thought a little conversation would make her feel more comfortable, give her a reason to be standing there.

"Thank you," she said back.

"Did you take dancing lessons? Is that how you got to be so good?"

"No. It's just natural. I was born with a natural talent."

"Well, however it happened, you're very good."

I kept trying to keep my gaze fixed on the dancer's face but it slipped a couple of times and went to where the robe was slightly parted down below. Then I thought about what else I could say, because the soldier still blocked her path.

"Did you grow up in the Upper Peninsula?" I asked.

"No. I'm from Minnesota. In the north part. Almost to the Canadian border."

"I've heard Minnesota's a nice place. Lots of lakes."

"It's okay," she said. "It's a lot like here except it's Minnesota."

Finally, the soldier moved and the dancer began to walk away. But before she'd gone too far she turned back to me and smiled. And I was pleased to see her smile at me, and I think it was because she was a person to me now, someone with a natural talent for dancing who came from Minnesota, and not just a naked woman dancing in a bar.

"It looks like you've made a conquest," Audrey said. She was looking back and forth between me and the dancer.

"I guess we both have," I said, thinking about the soldier. Then I said, "She's nice," which I believed to be the truth.

The waitress brought our food and we ate without saying much. Between Audrey dancing with the soldiers and the naked woman walking past our table, I felt a little flustered. All the words I thought of to start a conversation seemed wrong.

"I'll put up the Wall of Jericho when we get back," I said. We were walking along the shoulder of the highway on our way back to the motel.

"It doesn't matter," Audrey said. "It's just a symbol. If you're going to ravish me, I don't think a hanging blanket will make much difference."

"Well then I won't hang it up," I said. "And I promise I won't ravish you."

❧

LATER THAT NIGHT, when I was in bed and trying to fall asleep, I couldn't stop thinking about the dancer. And she seemed better in my memory than she had been in real life, more appealing and attractive, and I wondered if there was a message there that I should know about. Something about your memory not always being true, which was opposite to what I'd thought two days earlier in the church parking lot, when I'd thought about memory and space. And then without wanting to I thought of Audrey, lying close by, and even though I tried not to think of it I could not stop. And then, a few minutes later, when I was on the edge of sleep, I had a half-dream about going over and lying down and putting my arms around Audrey and going to sleep like that, not making love but just holding her against me like the soldiers held her on the dance floor, with her long smooth body touching mine and all of that. But then, suddenly, I came out of my dream and my heart was thudding in my chest and my breath was coming fast. And after that I was awake for another long amount of time, and during that time I forced myself to think about Clark Gable and Claudette Colbert, and the blanket and the Wall of Jericho, and I decided finally that we should use the blanket after all, and I got up and hung it between our beds. And even though it was just a symbol it seemed to work. Because soon I fell asleep.

Chapter Thirty-One

The next morning we had breakfast in a downtown restaurant called Northern Lights Cafe. Just before we went through the door Audrey stopped and asked if I thought they had a naked dancing woman there too, that maybe all the restaurants in Carlisle had naked dancing women, that maybe it was a feature of the town, a military town with thousands of young men nearby who liked to look at naked women. It was a stupid thing to say but it made me laugh and Audrey did too, and the laughter sort of broke the awkward spell that had carried over from the night before and made the day feel normal.

After breakfast we drove north on highway 27 in the direction of Camp Carlisle. A few miles out of town a sign directed us down a side road, and after another mile or two we came up to a guard shack with a red-and-white hinged pole blocking the road. Two soldiers were in the guard shack; as we approached, one of them stepped out and raised a hand. He had a revolver in a holster at his waist. I stopped behind the red-and-white pole and he walked over.

"We're looking for the cemetery," I said. "Can you direct us to the person who's in charge of that aspect of the Army base?"

The soldier looked at me in an odd way and some wrinkles came around his eyes. "What business do you have at the cemetery?" he asked.

"My brother's there, sir. He was killed last April and that's where they buried him. In the cemetery here. But my mother wants to bring him home." I looked at the soldier. "His coffin, I mean. She wants to bring his coffin home."

"Your brother's Gary Walker?"

"Yes, sir," I said. "How does it happen that you know his name?"

"We all do," he said. "We know about the accident. They worked it into some training because they don't want it to happen again."

"I understand," I said. Then I said: "It was a terrible tragedy for my family. My mother especially. She still hasn't gotten over it." I thought that saying this would make him want to help us more.

The soldier turned and looked back at his partner, who was still inside the shack, and then he turned back to me.

"Pull over there," he said. He pointed to a gravel parking space at the side of the road. "I'll make a call."

I pulled over and turned off the engine, because I thought it would take a little time for the soldier to find out where to send us. Going to see the person who ran the cemetery was probably not something very many people asked about, so I could understand that it'd take some time to find out where to send us.

Through the window of the guard shack I watched the soldier make a call. Then he dialed a second number, and then a third. I could tell from his expression that he was getting frustrated and I was beginning to be afraid he might take his frustration out on us by sending us away. While he was talking on the telephone, the other soldier came out of the guard shack and walked over to us.

"How's it going?" he said, which surprised me because it didn't seem to be a thing a soldier would say when he was guarding an Army base.

"Okay," I said. "It's going good." I nodded my head to emphasize that everything was good. Then I said, "Your partner's trying to find out where to send us. We have some business at the cemetery."

"Okay," the soldier said, which made me think he didn't understand me and just wanted to say a word. Then he said, "Why aren't you in the service? You look like you're about the right age."

"I injured my foot, sir," I said, which was the quickest lie I could think of. "I broke a toe and now I can't march very well. I wanted to sign up but they wouldn't let me." I made a kind of punching motion in the air to make it look like I was upset about not being able to be a soldier.

"That's too bad," the guard said. "The Army's okay." He looked off into the distance and rocked back and forth at his waist, like he was loosening the muscles in his back. "I'm getting shipped out next month to Vietnam. Have you heard about Vietnam?"

"I've heard a little, sir. I know the Communists are trying to take it over."

"That's right," he said. "But it's not going to happen. We're going to kick their butts back to China. And it won't take very long."

"That's good," I said.

He looked at me. "Why'n't you go to a doctor and see if you can have your toe fixed."

"That's a good idea. I'll look into it."

"Do it soon and maybe you can get to Vietnam before the fighting's all over."

"Yes, sir. That'd be nice. I'd like that."

The soldier stared off into the distance with a pleasant expression on his face, as if he could picture himself killing Communists in Vietnam. Then he looked back at me.

"So have a nice day," he said. He leaned down and looked across at Audrey. "And you have a nice day, too, miss." I turned to Audrey just as she was giving a smile back to the soldier. It was a quick smile, fast, as if she didn't really mean it.

"You're such a fraud," Audrey said, after the guard had walked away.

"What are you talking about?"

"How you're so sweet and polite when you're talking to someone who has power over you. Those soldiers. And the cop who stopped us. And the mechanic who stole our money." She looked at me. "It's kind of sickening," she said, and then she said in a sing-song voice. *"Yes, sir, it'd be really nice to be killing Communists. I just hope I can get to Vietnam in time; Yes, Mr. Sheriff, I certainly will drive within the speed limit; Please give us back the money you stole from us, Mr. Mechanic."*

"I don't want to cause any trouble, that's all."

"Well, you won't get any, that's for sure. But you won't get anything else either."

"Maybe I should let you do the talking."

"Maybe you should."

I wanted to say something back to Audrey, to defend myself against being called a fraud. But I didn't want to start an argument while we were waiting for the soldier to come back. So I thought I'd try to calm her down by being funny.

"I'll try to do better," I said. "How's this: *Fuck you, officer, I wasn't driving that fast and you can just go to hell if you think different.* And maybe this: *We've got no right to be fighting in someone else's country, Mr. Soldier, and you're an idiot if you think we should.*" I looked at her. "Is that better?"

Audrey was laughing. "Yes," she said. "Just try to keep it up."

We sat for a longer time at the side of the road. Probably fifteen or twenty minutes. I began to get nervous. I thought I might've asked my question about the cemetery in the wrong way or done something else that raised suspicion. Finally, the first solder came back.

"You'll have to go to the Commander's office," he said. "He's the one you want to talk to." He handed me a slip of paper. "This pass will let you be on the base." He handed me another paper. "This is a map of the base. The Commander's office is here." He pointed to a little square on the far side of the map.

"Is he the one in charge of the cemetery?" I asked.

"He's in charge of everything on the base. You're going to start at the top."

"I hope we won't be inconveniencing him," I said, because I thought the Commander probably had a lot to do besides talking to people about the cemetery.

The soldier looked at me as if he didn't have an answer to that question and didn't really care that he didn't. Then he slapped the roof of the car twice to show that it was time for us to leave. I started the car and put it into gear and pulled out onto the road.

Chapter Thirty-Two

Audrey opened the map across her lap and told me where to make the turns. We drove past several rows of wooden barracks, and then an open field where a squad of soldiers was marching in formation while another soldier called out instructions. Next we went by a large parking lot filled with tanks and Jeeps, and then an obstacle course where men were running over fences and climbing walls and crawling through the mud.

After the obstacle course we entered a neighborhood of yellow brick houses that all looked the same. At the edge of the neighborhood there was a building bigger than the others, with a parking lot in front. The number 337 was stenciled in big white letters on the side, which was the number of the building the soldier had circled on the map.

"This is it," Audrey said, and I pulled in.

Inside the building there was a small lobby where a woman soldier sat at a desk. Behind her was a door. She wore a regular Army uniform except she had on a skirt instead of pants. We told her we were there to see the Commander.

"Are you the ones about getting the dead body?" she asked.

"Yes."

The woman soldier picked up the telephone and told the Commander we were there. Then she said for us to go right in, but before we'd taken any steps she said "Wait" and we stopped. "When you talk to the Commander be respectful. He likes to be called sir even if you're a civilian. And don't sit down until he tells you to. When he stands up that means the meeting's over and it's time for you to leave.

"You don't need to worry," Audrey said, and she smiled at me while she spoke. "He's a very polite boy."

"You can knock it off about the politeness," I said, when we'd stepped away from the desk. "I got your message before."

Audrey smiled but said nothing.

The Commander was sitting behind a big wooden desk with an American flag pinned to the wall behind him. He was a heavy man with glasses having thick lenses that made his eyes look big and kind of watery. They didn't seem to be the kind of glasses an Army Commander would wear. What I mean is that it was difficult to imagine him on a battlefield with those glasses. Above his right breast pocket were rows of colored ribbons.

"I understand you're here about Private Walker," he said, smiling.

"Yes, sir," I said. "He's my brother. I mean he was my brother."

"My sincere condolences for your loss," he said. "Private Walker was a fine soldier. We all felt terrible about what happened."

"Thank you, sir," I said, though I was pretty sure he didn't know if Gary was a fine soldier or not. "I'll pass that along to my parents. I'm sure it'll mean a lot to them."

I stopped talking then because I thought the Commander would already know why we were there from the conversation he had with the guard at the gate. I thought he'd just begin to tell us what we should do to get Gary's coffin.

"So what's the problem?" he asked instead.

"There's no problem, sir," I said. "It's just that we want to take my brother Gary back home. My parents do. So they sent me here to make arrangements."

The Commander sat back in his leather chair and looked at me. He brought one hand up and began to rub his cheek.

"That's all been taken care of," he said. "He's in the cemetery here. Your brother is. It's unusual to put a Private in a military cemetery. Generally, it's an honor reserved for the higher ranks. But we made an exception in your brother's case."

"Yes, sir," I said. "And we appreciate that. But my mother, and my father, would like to have him repose in a cemetery nearer to our home. So he'd be closer and my parents could go out to see his grave from time to time." I looked at the Commander. His head was tilted to one side and he frowned like I was saying something that was hard to understand.

"We'd pay," I said, because I thought that might be the thing that was troubling him. "We'd pay for digging up the coffin and sending it back to Detroit. We understand there'll be expenses and we'd be happy to absorb them."

The Commander kept looking at me. He looked like he was troubled by something. Then he said: "Do you know how we bury our soldiers, son?"

"No, sir, I don't."

"We use a simple coffin made from pine boards. It's a military tradition going back to the Civil War. Even Generals are buried that way."

I looked at the Commander. I didn't think his statement needed a response. I thought he was just telling me something interesting that I would like to know about. Just a plain fact that didn't mean anything more than what it was. But then he spoke again and I realized I was wrong.

"It's probably started to deteriorate," he said. "The pine boards have probably started to rot. And the body too. So it's not a pretty picture."

There was silence in the room. An image of a rotting coffin with Gary's decomposing body inside came into my head but I pushed it back because it was too awful. Then Audrey cleared her throat in a noisy way and we turned in her direction. "That's not exactly right," she said. "Maybe you use a wood coffin but the coffin goes inside a concrete box. It's the health law. I know about that." Audrey looked at me: "What he's saying isn't true," she said.

The Commander looked at Audrey as if he was seeing her for the first time. "And who are you, miss?" he said.

"I'm a family friend. I'm a close family friend. I know his mother. I know her really well."

"Well, I'll thank you to keep a civil tongue in your mouth."

"I'll thank you to tell the truth."

The Commander looked across the desk at Audrey. I thought he'd be mad because of what she'd said but he just looked at her with a calm expression, as if what she'd said didn't matter too much, one way or the other. Then he looked back at me. "I think we've finished our business here, son," he said, and he stood up. "I've told you how things stand. I'm not going to get into an argument about it." He pointed to the door.

I stood up but Audrey didn't. She stayed sitting in her chair.

"We're not done yet," she said. She nodded in my direction. "He's come here to make arrangements for his brother's body."

The Commander stayed standing. He didn't look at Audrey when she spoke. He looked at me.

"I've told you how things stand, son. You can tell that to your family. I'm sure they'll understand. Your mother and your father."

The Commander reached across the desk and I reached out and we shook hands. That seemed to be the right way to bring things to an end. Then I turned to Audrey. "Let's go," I said. I made a motion with my head in the direction of the door.

"Don't leave," she said. "Not until he tells you how to make arrangements. He doesn't own your brother's body."

I felt awkward and a little bit afraid, caught in the middle between Audrey and the Commander. But Audrey was just a civilian and the Commander was the one in charge of things. So I reached down and took Audrey's arm and lifted slightly, like my father had done to my mother when he was getting her out of bed that night in Grand Rapids.

Audrey jerked her arm away. "Let go of me," she said. "Don't touch me."

"Come on," I said. "Let's go."

Audrey looked up at me with an angry stare. But then it changed to something else. And I recognized it as the expression I'd seen on my mother's face that night in Grand Rapids, that expression of betrayal.

Audrey opened her mouth and started to say something but then she stopped. I glanced at the Commander; he had a small smile on his face, like he was enjoying Audrey's anger. Then Audrey stood and started toward the door. I followed along behind.

❧

I DROVE BACK across the Army base and out past the gate where the two soldiers were standing guard, and then back into the little downtown of Carlisle. Audrey didn't speak and I didn't either. I was afraid to say anything because I knew she was mad. I drove through town and then out in in the direction of the highway. And then I realized I didn't really know where I was going. I was just driving to get away from the Army base but not driving *toward* anything.

I let up on the accelerator and coasted over onto the shoulder of the highway. Then I turned and looked at Audrey.

Her arms were crossed and she was staring straight ahead. A pinched expression was on her face.

"There's a little café I saw back in town," I said. "We could get some lunch and then head back home."

Audrey kept staring out through the windshield as if she hadn't heard me.

"It's not the Big Buck Grill," I said. "It's another place. They probably won't have any naked dancers," and I forced out a little laugh because I wanted to change Audrey's mood from being angry.

She turned and looked at me. "That was bullshit," she said. "What he said to you about the coffin was bullshit. That's not the way they do it when they bury somebody."

"I believe you," I said.

"Then why'd you leave? Why'd you let him get away with that? What he told you was a lie."

I tried to think but I didn't really have an answer. I didn't know anything that would explain what I had done.

"I told you he was lying and you acted like it didn't matter," Audrey said. "You acted like you'd do whatever he told you to do and then smile and say thank you and shake his hand. It was just like I said this morning when we were waiting at the gate: you're a fraud."

"It was because he was the Commander," I said. "He's the one in charge. You're supposed to do what he says."

"Like hell you are," Audrey said. "Not if he's telling you lies."

I was silent for a while, trying to think how I could explain how I had acted. It was partly because he was the Commander, but it was partly something else.

"What he said about the coffin," I said. I spoke the words without looking at Audrey because I could think better that way. "I hadn't really thought about it before, about the coffin being underground with Gary all alone inside. And I could picture it in my head and it upset me. It upset me a lot."

Just then I realized some tears were starting on my face. I reached up and wiped them off so Audrey wouldn't see them.

But I was pretty sure she saw. Because when I looked at her there was some sympathy in her expression; it wasn't total anger now.

She reached out and put her hand on my shoulder and let it rest there for a moment, just in a casual way, like she was done being angry and wanted me to know it. Then her hand moved back behind my neck and that felt nice, too. As if she was saying it was all right. That what I'd done hadn't been so bad.

"Let's go and have lunch," she said, and she finished by giving me a little smile. "At that place you said. The one without the naked dancer. Then we'll regroup. We'll regroup and figure out what comes next."

Chapter Thirty-Three

I drove back into town and parked in the gravel parking lot next to the place I had seen, which was called the Northern Lights Cafe. Inside, an older woman in a pink dress took our order. I ordered a grilled cheese sandwich and Audrey ordered a tuna fish salad sandwich with lettuce but no tomato. While we ate we talked about what we should do next. I was ready to drive back to Grand Rapids but Audrey had a different thought.

"I think we should go back tonight and do it ourselves," she said.

"Do what ourselves?"

"Get your brother's coffin. Dig it up and take it back to Detroit." She looked at me. "You kept that slip of paper, didn't you? The pass the guard gave you."

"Yes."

"It's got today's date on it. That means we can go back. We can use it to get back into the base tonight."

My first thought was that Audrey's idea was completely crazy. Digging up Gary's coffin and driving away with it sounded like something you'd see in a movie but not anything that would happen in real life. But I didn't want to say that to

Audrey—that her plan was crazy—because I knew it'd make her mad again. So I decided to complain about the practical aspects of it, and not the plan itself.

"How're we going to get it up from underground?" I said first. "Even if we dig down that far and open up the concrete box, how're we going to lift the coffin up?"

"They throw the ropes in," Audrey said. "They lower the coffin into the concrete box with ropes and after it's down they throw the ropes in on top. They don't bother to get the ropes because it'd be too much trouble. So we can use the ropes to lift it."

"How do you know so much about it?"

"I had a friend who died when I was twelve. Gloria Metzner. She had diphtheria and they couldn't stop it. So she died and they had a funeral and I saw it. And I remember about the ropes."

I took a bite of my grilled cheese sandwich; while I chewed I thought of another practical objection.

"Two of us can't lift the coffin," I said. "You'd need four. Because you've got to go hand-over-hand with the ropes and there's a rope at each corner."

Audrey looked off to one side. Her gaze went to a table where four soldiers were drinking coffee. They looked like regular soldiers, just privates and corporals, the lower ranks. She smiled.

"I could get some people to help us," she said. She nodded in the direction of the soldiers. "Like those. I could use my wiles to get them to help us."

I didn't know what she meant by *wiles* and I told her that.

"Feminine wiles," she said, grinning "The magic spell a woman can cast."

I looked at the soldiers.

"Not those," Audrey said. "They're just an example." She

looked over at the soldiers and in just that moment one of them turned and smiled and Audrey smiled back.

"Okay," I said, and I thought of another practical objection. "So let's say we get some soldiers to help us get the coffin up. Two soldiers plus you and plus me. Then what? We've got Gary's coffin sitting on the ground. What happens next?"

"Have you ever heard about trailers?" Audrey said. "We'll get a U-Haul trailer to carry the coffin back to Detroit."

"How will we get it off the base?" I said. "The guards will see the coffin on the trailer and not let us leave."

Audrey smiled like she knew a secret that she was going to share with me. "There's a back road," she said. "I saw it on the map. It looked like an old logging road because it goes through the forest. But it'll get us from the cemetery to the main road without having to go back through the main gate."

I took the last bite of my grilled-cheese sandwich and then pushed the plate away. Part of me saw that Audrey's answers made sense, but another part still thought her plan was crazy. I knew that a person can get carried away by their own thinking, as if their thoughts had momentum that drew them irresistibly forward. And I believed that might be happening with Audrey.

"It seems unusual," I said to Audrey. "Not a normal thing to do."

"What's wrong with unusual?" she said. "Does everything have to be exactly normal? Like you can't do something unless everybody else would do it too."

I couldn't think fast enough to have an answer. But it still seemed like a bad idea: digging up a coffin and carrying it away on a rented trailer.

But I'd run out of practical objections.

"I'm still not sure it's a good idea," I said.

Audrey sat back in her chair and folded her arms and looked down at the floor. I could tell she was thinking again. And I remembered the time when she'd been ready to smash my toe after getting me drunk. This—digging up Gary's coffin—felt like that. Extreme and full of unknown dangers. And then I saw her smile.

"Think of it like when you paint," she said. "You don't exactly know what you're trying to do but you do it anyway. You do it by instinct. You have faith in your instincts. You do what feels right."

And for that I didn't have an answer. Because what Audrey said was true. There are things you do you can't explain, but you still know they're right. And maybe those were the most important things. Painting was one of them: the colors you choose, the kind of strokes you made, what objects go in front and which ones go behind. Getting Gary's coffin might be another.

"Okay," I said. "You've convinced me."

※

WE PAID the bill and left the café. As we were walking across the parking lot a police cruiser pulled off the street and rolled up next to us. The officer rolled down the window.

"Let's see," he said. He took a little black notebook out of his shirt pocket and began reading from it. "Are you Nate Walker?"

"Yes, sir."

"And you, miss." He looked at Audrey. "You're Audrey. Audrey something. I don't have your last name."

Audrey took a half step backward. For a moment I thought she was going to run away. "What business is that of yours?" she said.

The officer stared at Audrey. His glance went up and down her body. His eyes narrowed into a little frown.

"Take it easy, miss," he said. "I'm not here to give you any trouble. Though if you want me to I can."

Audrey stared at the officer for another moment. Then she said, "Yes, I'm Audrey."

"Okay," the officer said. "That's better." He looked back at me. "Your mother called us this morning, Nate. She called the Carlisle Police Department. She thought you might be in town and she asked if we could find you and give you a message. She described your car...." He nodded in the direction of the green Pontiac "....and what you look like. That's how I could tell it was you." He smiled as if he was proud that he was able to find us. Then he looked back down at his notebook. "Let's see. I want to get it right." He studied the notebook for a moment. "She said she was coming up here and for you to wait for her. She's coming up on a Greyhound bus that arrives tonight at seven o'clock."

"She's coming up from Detroit?" I said.

The officer looked back down at his notebook. "I don't have that information," he said. "I'm not privy to where she's coming from. All I have is what I told you." He closed his notebook with a snap and put it back into his shirt pocket. He looked again at Audrey and then he looked at me. He had a kind of smirking smile. "Are you two on your way to getting married?" he asked.

"No, sir," I said. "We have some business at the Army base. It's a family matter we were sent to look into."

"Well, whatever you're doing your mother wants you to wait for her before you do it." He started to roll up the window but then he stopped. "And if you run into any trouble our office is just over there in City Hall." He turned and looked back over his shoulder toward where there was a yellow brick building with an Army tank and an American flag in front. "They know about you there. In the sheriff's office. Because your mother called."

"Thank you, sir," I said. "We'll keep that in mind."

Chapter Thirty-Four

After the sheriff drove off, Audrey and I stood in the parking lot and talked about what we should do next. "I guess we've got an empty afternoon to fill," Audrey said. "How're we going to spend it."

"We should get a room back at Sandi's Motel," I said. "That's one thing we need to do. We'll need a place to spend the night."

"And your mom will need a room, too," Audrey said.

"Right," I said. "Two rooms." I thought of something. "You should probably stay in my mother's room. Not mine."

Audrey laughed. "No more Wall of Jericho?"

"I guess not."

We were standing side by side, leaning back against the fender of the Pontiac. The sun had come out and it cast our shadows out across the gravel parking lot.

"After we rent the rooms we could just drive around," I said. "Drive out into the country and see what things look like here. What the countryside is like."

Audrey looked at me again. I could tell she had a different idea. "I think we should go ahead with what we said before," she said. "For me to find some people to help us with the coffin. I think your mom will agree with what we've planned." She looked at me. "You go back and rent two motel rooms. I'll stay in town for a while and find some people who'll help us raise the coffin."

"What'll I do while you're in town?"

"Maybe you could find a place and do some painting. There was an old wooden railroad bridge we passed when we came into town. That might be a good subject." She looked at me. "Bridges have a lot of meaning, if you stop to think about it. Other than just for people to get across. Maybe you can show that other meaning in your painting." Audrey was leaning back against the fender of the Pontiac and she sort of bumped out with her backside to push herself away. "I'll go into some of the stores and talk to people," she said. "Maybe I can learn something that'll help us with the coffin. Then, after, I'll walk out to the bridge and meet you. It's not too far as I recall. Not a bad walk to make on a nice sunny day."

I thought about Audrey's plan, although 'plan' didn't seem to be the right word for it. It seemed more like a way to use up time until my mother arrived. But I liked the idea of doing some painting because it'd been a couple of days since I had done any, and I was afraid I might get rusty. But it seemed like I was leaving Audrey to do all the hard work, and I told her that.

"No," she said, and she spoke as if the decision had already been made. "Don't think of it that way. It's something I enjoy: going around and talking to people." She put her hand out. "Give me a little money," she said. "I may need some money."

I took out my wallet and gave her twenty dollars. Then I got into the Pontiac and drove off in the direction of Sandi's Motel. As I pulled away, I looked at Audrey in the rearview mirror. She was standing in the parking lot, holding the money in her hand.

Chapter Thirty-Five

When I got to Sandi's Motel I told Babs that we liked the town of Carlisle and had decided to stay over for another day, and that another person would be joining us. The part about liking the town wasn't entirely the truth but it seemed to work all right for an explanation, which was all I wanted it to do.

"Where's your pretty wife?" Babs said as I was leaving the office.

I turned back and looked at her. It took me a moment to realize she was talking about Audrey.

"She's shopping," I said. "You know how women are about shopping," which seemed like something a man would say about his wife.

"Isn't that the God's honest truth," Babs said, and she laughed out loud.

❧

THE WOODEN RAILROAD bridge was about a mile outside of town, a little way off the highway in an area of shrubs and grasses, and it spanned across a river that was not wide. I pulled the Pontiac off onto the side of the road and got my painting gear and walked across a field to where the bridge was. I walked up and down the riverbank, trying to find a good angle to paint from. I had learned that finding the right way to look at something was important. Things can have a different meaning depending on how you look at them. Then I had an idea and I walked out onto the bridge itself, stepping awkwardly between the cross ties. When I got to the center I looked down into the water. I could see the gravelly bottom through the bright clear water and I could see the water grasses swaying in the current. Some trout were holding steady against the current, just dark shadows in the water. I stood and watched, paying particular attention to the trout. They held steady in one position for a while, then switched over to another spot, so fast you barely knew it happened.

And then in my imagination I blocked out part of what I was looking at, the unimportant parts, like Picasso says you're supposed to do, and the picture I had left had the steel rails in the foreground, shiny from train wheels grinding over them, and the darkly oiled wooden cross ties, and in the background the flowing water with the ripples and the gravelly bottom and the moving water grasses and the dark mysterious shadows of the trout. And then I decided that was the angle I would paint from, looking down into the water from the bridge. And for a few minutes I tried to find words that would express why that particular scene appealed to me, because I thought it needed words to make it be worth painting. But I couldn't think of any words that seemed to capture it, and so I decided that I would simply paint it as I saw it and as I felt it, and that the meaning would come out while I was painting, or maybe after.

I walked back to the bank and got my gear and set up my easel on the bridge and started to paint. And it felt good to be making something on a canvas that hadn't been there before, something I was in control of and could decide about, and I realized how much I'd missed it over the last few days—painting—when my attention had been on other things.

I worked for a couple of hours, lost in the images that were emerging on the canvas, and then I felt a change, like the way the air feels just before the sun goes down, when there is only a sliver of light above the horizon and you know that in another moment night will come and everything will change. I turned around. An old man was standing on the riverbank. He was dressed like a farmer or a manual laborer, with canvas jeans and a faded flannel shirt. The sleeves of his shirt were rolled up high on his arms, like he was ready to put his hands down into an engine that needed fixing, or to pitch hay bales up onto a wagon. He was chewing something that I thought was probably tobacco. When he saw me watching he walked out onto the bridge, stepping between the alternate ties with little jumps.

"You might want to know that there's a train that will come by here at about three o'clock," he said. "You might not want to be standing here when that happens." He smiled as if he was telling me something I should have known myself.

"Okay," I said, "I'll keep an eye on the time."

The man came around behind me and looked at my painting. "That's an odd way to paint a bridge," he said. "Why don't you get back on the bank so you can paint the whole thing." He pointed upstream to a place along the riverbank.

"I want it to be more than just a bridge," I said. "I want to get the water and the fish in it. They seem important, too."

He stood behind me and studied my painting.

"Okay," he said. "I guess I see what you're up to. But you've made it harder. A harder thing to paint. That's all I have to say about it." He turned in my direction. "Anyway," he said, "you're on my land. That's what I came out here to tell you. Not the bridge—that belongs to the railroad company—but the field you walked across to get here. It's mine." He made a gesture in the direction of the riverbank. "You should ask permission before you walk on someone else's property."

I set my brush on the little shelf at the front of the easel. I wanted to give my full attention to the man and I wanted him to know it.

"I'm sorry," I said. "I didn't know it was your land."

"Now you're stuck," the man said, grinning. "You've got yourself on the bridge but you can't get back. Not without getting my permission to walk across my field."

"Then I guess I'll have to die here," I said. "If I'm stuck and can't get out."

"I guess you will," he said. "Too bad for you." He turned his head and spit a glob of brown tobacco juice into the river. It floated on the surface for a moment, then thinned out and floated away.

"I suppose I should try to save myself," I said. I looked at the man and I arranged my face in a serious expression. "Can I have permission to cross your land, sir?"

The man looked at me, cocking his head and squinting his eyes like he was studying whether I was an acceptable person to walk across his land.

"You look reliable," he said. "So the answer's yes."

"Thank you," I said, though I thought the joke was getting a little stale. It hadn't been much of a joke to begin with, in my opinion, and stretching it out seemed to make it even less funny.

"So what are you doing here?" the man said next. "I don't mean the painting. I mean in a general sense." He swung his arm around to show that he meant the whole space. "Up here in northern Michigan."

"I've got some business at the Army base," I said. "Some family business."

"Are you a soldier there?"

"No, but my brother was." I stopped talking. The man

continued to look at me, as if he was expecting more. More words. But I tried to stay silent, because I thought my reason for being there was not his business. But then, after a long moment had passed, with him staring at me like that, my will broke down.

"He got killed," I said. "My brother got killed on the shooting range. And my family wants to get his body back to southern Michigan where we live. That's why I'm here."

"You're Gary Walker's brother."

"Yes, sir. How'd you know his name?"

"It's not that often a soldier gets killed on the Army base. It made the local paper." He turned his head and spit another brown glob into the river. "There was a stink about it at the Army base. Him getting killed on a shooting range like that. It shouldn't have happened."

I didn't say anything.

"Your brother was a pianist, as I recall."

"Yes, sir. How'd you know that?"

"That was in the paper too. That he was a special sort of person. Different from what you'd expect a soldier to be."

"Did the paper say anything else?" I asked. "About how the accident happened?"

"Let's see," the man said. He narrowed his eyes and looked up toward the sky as if he would find an answer there. "Your brother was in charge of the targets. That's another thing the paper said. He was the one who changed the paper targets after they got shot up. And he was supposed to stay crouched down behind a concrete wall when the shooting was going on. And something happened, or there was some confusion, because he stood up from behind the concrete wall just when they started shooting and he was hit." The man looked at me. "Maybe I shouldn't be telling you this, son. It's probably painful for you to hear the details."

"Yes, sir," I said. "It is. But I'd like to know what happened."

"There was an investigation," the man continued. "About how such a thing could happen. They sent some officials out from Washington, and the people who run the Army base came in for some criticism. Quite a lot of criticism. That was in the paper, too. But I don't recall what came out of the investigation. I don't think the paper followed the story that far."

The man turned his head and spit another brown glob into the river. This time he watched it float away. "Anyway, that's pretty much all I can remember. If you want to know more, I suppose the Army people can tell you."

"I was there this morning and talked to the Commander. He said he wouldn't help us take my brother's body back to where my parents live."

"I'm not surprised. They don't want anything to happen that would draw attention back to the accident. Like I said, there was some criticism about the way the Camp was run."

I had another question but I didn't know if I wanted to ask it. But then I did.

"Did the paper say where he was hit? Where the bullet went."

The man looked at me for a moment before he answered.

"It was his head," he said. "I'm sorry to have to tell you that. But the good news is that it happened very fast. It was over for him in just an instant. That's the good part."

"Yes, sir," I said, though the thought of Gary being shot in the head made me feel a little sick.

Just then I heard some footsteps on the bridge behind me; when I turned I saw Audrey coming toward us along the rails.

"This is the man who owns the land here," I said, when she got close.

Audrey looked at him and smiled, and he looked at her and smiled back.

"I should be leaving," the man said. "You two have got better things to do than talk to an old man."

"It's all right," I said, because I wanted him to stay so I could ask more questions about Gary. But before I could think of another question he spoke again.

"So have a nice day," he said," and he looked at me. "And remember what I said about the land." He blinked one eye to show it was still a joke.

"Yes, sir," I said. "I will. I certainly will. Thank you."

"What'd he mean about the land?" Audrey asked, after the man had gone away.

"It was a sort of joke he was making. That he owns the land and we needed his permission to walk across it."

Audrey looked at the man walking away. "Well, fuck him," she said.

I hadn't heard Audrey say fuck in that way—just casually in a normal conversation—and it surprised me. And I guess she could tell that from the expression on my face.

"Excuse my language," she said. "I forgot that you're a nice boy who doesn't know such awful words."

"I know them," I said. "I use them sometimes."

"Well, good," she said, smiling in a teasing way. "Maybe there's hope for you yet."

Audrey stepped closer and looked at my painting. Then she turned and looked at some logs that were piled up along the riverbank. Three painted turtles were sunning themselves on the logs.

'Your painting's nice," she said, "but if it was up to me, I'd paint the turtles. They're more interesting because they're alive."

"I have trout in mine," I said. "They're alive too." I pointed to the trout. "They're alive and they're trying to hold themselves against the river current that's trying to carry them away." I looked at Audrey who was still examining my painting.

"So it's a painting about struggle," she said. "Trying to hold your place when something's trying to take you somewhere else."

"I guess so," I said, though I hadn't really thought about it in that way until she'd said it. "I guess it's a subtle message."

Audrey studied my painting for a moment longer, then she turned to me. "I don't suppose it's subtle to the trout though, is it?" she said, and she laughed.

"Anyway," she said, a few moments later, after I'd packed up my painting gear and we were walking back to the car. "I got some boys who'll help us get the coffin up. It's two of those who were in the restaurant. I went back to have another cup of coffee and they were still there—two were—and I got to talking to them. Rusty and Jack. They're nice boys, and they'll meet us at the cemetery tonight at ten o'clock. "They'll even bring some shovels to do the digging."

"That's great," I said, though my heart was not behind the words.

We walked back to the car. I started to unload my painting gear into the trunk.

"Oh, wait!" Audrey said. "I haven't told you the best part. Rusty and Jack will have a truck. So we'll have something to carry the coffin off the base. They work in something called the motor pool where they keep the trucks and they can get one."

"Terrific," I said.

"We'll still need a trailer. Tomorrow we will. But we won't need to bring it on the base. We can transfer the coffin after."

I slammed down the trunk lid, sending a cloud of road dust up into the air.

"Maybe we should go out to the cemetery now," I said. "See what it looks like and get ready for tonight."

"Good thinking," Audrey said.

She was leaning back against the fender of the Pontiac with her face up toward the sun, which had come out strong that day. She hadn't turned away when she spoke to me, so it looked like she was talking to the sky.

Chapter Thirty-Six

There were different guards at the gate when we got back to the Army base but the pass the guard had given me that morning got us through. We followed the map to the cemetery. It was on the far side of the base and down a long dirt road that wound through a forest and then up a high hill where it ended in a little clearing surrounded by a white-picket fence. It was a small cemetery, only about fifty graves. A sign at the entrance said "U.S. Government Military Cemetery."

"This is different than I expected," I said. "Small. And out in the middle of nowhere."

Audrey and I walked up and down the rows until we found Gary's grave. A brass plaque on the ground said he'd been a Private in the United States Army and he'd lived from 1944 to 1963.

"I wish it said he was a pianist," I said. "Because that was the most important thing for people to know about him."

"Your mother can change that when we get him home."

Audrey walked over to the edge of the cemetery and looked out at the countryside.

"It's nice here," she said. "You can see miles and miles of forest. And beyond the forest you can see Lake Superior." She pointed to a blue stretch of water above the treetops. She turned and looked at me. "It's not exactly what you expect to see in a cemetery."

I stood and looked at Gary's grave. And then I noticed that the grass above his grave was different from the rest, greener and more lush, and I realized it was because it was newly planted after they'd filled the hole with dirt. And then I thought about Gary being down there in his pine-board coffin, beneath the earth and the lush new grass. And the thought disturbed me very deeply, as it had before, and my heart began to pound a little faster and my hands began to shake. And I think it was because my memories of Gary were completely different from what I was seeing in the graveyard, memories of him alive and doing things he loved to do. And I felt the unfairness of what had happened to him, but I felt it in a different and a stronger way than I ever had before, I mean all that he had lost and would never have, his piano playing but also all the other things, the acts and thoughts and feelings that would have made his life.

"Are you all right?" Audrey asked.

I didn't answer because I was not all right. But I didn't want to say it. I wanted to bear up against the feeling like I'd done so far, the way my father told me.

"I'm all right," I said, after a moment. "I just noticed that the grass is different where they dug the hole."

Audrey looked at me with a curious expression, as if what I'd said was strange, which of course it was. But I didn't want to tell her that the real reason was about Gary being dead.

We stayed there for a moment longer. Overhead, a breeze moved through the trees, rustling the leaves and making a sound like a thousand whispering ghosts. And suddenly I felt that I was on the edge of something large and powerful, some insight or understanding completely new, and I stiffened the muscles in my arms and legs and I tried to slow my breathing, and after a while I was able to make my mind go blank, to erase the thought of Gary being underground and all alone, and that was how I felt as we walked back to the car.

Chapter Thirty-Seven

When we drove back into town there was some commotion going on. A small crowd was gathered in front of an appliance store where a TV set was playing in the window. Other people were in groups along the sidewalk, talking excitedly to each other. We drove down to Sandi's Motel and pulled into the parking space next to the office. Babs saw us and came running out.

"Have you heard the news?" she asked. She was quite excited.

"What news?"

"The President's been shot. He's dead now."

"What are you talking about?"

"It's on TV. He was shot in Dallas. He was in a car on his way to give a speech and someone shot him."

"That can't be right."

"It is, though. It's on TV."

Audrey and I went to our room and turned on the TV. All the stations had the same news. The President had been shot and it had killed him. Jackie was all right but there were pictures of her with blood on her dress from where the President had bled on her while they were going to the hospital. We sat and watched the news reports all afternoon, even though they had no new information to report. And we didn't talk much, we just sat looking dumbly at the flickering images on the black-and-white TV. At five o'clock we decided we didn't want to leave our room to get dinner in a restaurant, and I went out to get some candy bars from the vending machine in the lobby. Babs was standing behind the desk watching a tiny TV that sat on the counter. "It's terrible," she said, as I came in. I could tell she had been crying. "Don't you think it's terrible?"

"Yes," I said, but I didn't say anything else because I didn't want to start a conversation.

"Poor Jackie," she said. "And Caroline and that little John-John. Their daddy's gone now."

"Yes," I said.

I went back to our room with the candy bars. We kept watching the news reports. I was sitting on the bed and Audrey was lying on her stomach. "It makes everything else seem small," she said. "Everything about your life that worried you. It doesn't seem to matter that much now."

She rolled onto her side and looked at me. "Do you think those two soldiers will be there tonight. Rusty and Jack. After this, I mean." She gestured toward the TV.

"I don't know. I suppose we should be there in case they show up."

"And your mom. She's coming on the bus at seven. We need to meet her."

"Yes."

Audrey rolled back onto her stomach so she could see the TV screen. They were playing a speech the President had made yesterday, where he had talked about getting rid of missiles and atomic bombs.

"You memorized his speeches," Audrey said.

"Some of them. The parts I liked." I thought for a moment. "It's funny," I said. "I mean what you just said about nothing being important. Because for me the speeches seemed to do the opposite, make things seem important that I had never thought about before. At least I hadn't thought about them in the way he explained them. Like helping people in poor countries, and being fair with Negroes, and not letting big corporations get away with things."

Audrey was lying on the bed looking at the TV screen; she rolled onto her back so she was looking up at the ceiling. "I feel kinda funny," she said. "Like things are out of control. Like anything can happen. Like there are no limits."

We were silent for a while, listening to the voices on TV.

"I didn't know you cared about him so much," I said.

"I didn't. Not exactly. But he was younger than the other ones. The other Presidents, I mean. So you could understand him better. You could understand when he explained things because it wasn't so different from your own thoughts. Except you didn't know you had those thoughts until he explained them to you. Until he gave you the right words to use. About Negroes and about the Russians and about going to the moon. And he had a family, a wife and two little kids." She paused for a moment before continuing. "He was kind of like an older brother. The same as you only smarter and stronger. So you knew if you needed something he'd be there to help you out."

Then Audrey started to cry. It was not a strong cry because there was no sound but only tears. Tears rolling slowly down her face. After a minute I went over and took her into my arms to comfort her—it seemed like the right thing to do—and she rested her head against my shoulder. And the tears were still happening because I felt the wetness of them on my neck. And then I started to feel a little bit romantic. In spite of everything that had happened that day and all of the sadness, I began to feel a little bit romantic. And at first it seemed wrong, with the President being shot, but then it seemed to be all right, to be a kind of victory, that romance could happen in the middle of all the sadness, and I lay back onto the bed and brought Audrey down beside me, and she did not resist, because she felt it too, I think, the strange and unexpected victory, and then I kissed her and she kissed me back, and then I moved my hand along her body and underneath, where the warmth and softness of her skin was, and eventually we made love, and it was slow and it was with affection and with the TV set playing in the background.

❧

AFTERWARD WE LAY in bed together. Night was starting and the room was getting dark. The TV set played in the corner with the sound turned low.

"Now you know the great secret," Audrey said.

"How do you know I didn't know it already?"

"Just a guess." She was lying on her back staring up at the ceiling. But then she rolled onto her side and looked at me.

"Was it worth the wait?"

"It was nice," I said. "I'm glad it was with you."

"I am too. Does it change anything? Anything about how you feel about me?"

"No. I liked you before. I still do."

"What about love? You're supposed to be in love for that to happen."

I thought for a moment about Audrey's question, then I said: "I had a girlfriend and I thought she loved me but then she left me for someone else. So I guess I don't know what love is."

"I understand. It's complicated."

We were silent then for a long time together, listening to the voices on TV. They were saying something about the man who did the shooting. That he'd lived in Russia for a while and supported the communists in Cuba.

"We should go to meet your mother's bus." Audrey said.

"Yes."

"You first or me?" She gestured toward the bathroom.

"You," I said.

Audrey threw back the sheet and got out of bed. I watched her gather up her clothes and walk with them into the bathroom. And it was nice to see her walking away like that, and I tried to make a strong memory of it, to fix it strongly in my brain, because I didn't think I would ever see her that way again.

Chapter Thirty-Eight

The bus station was a small cement-block building near the center of town. Floodlights beamed down into the parking lot where the buses came and went. I went inside to ask about the bus from Detroit. There was a blackboard on the wall that listed all the buses and their arriving and departing times. It said the bus from Detroit would be on time.

There were only a few people in the lobby and they were clustered around a TV set that hung from a metal rack beneath the ceiling. It was tuned to the same channel Audrey and I had been watching in the motel room. Some of the women were crying, holding handkerchiefs in their hands to wipe the tears away.

"Is the bus from Detroit going to be on time?" I asked the man behind the counter.

"What?" he said. He had been looking across the lobby at the TV set hanging from the ceiling.

"The bus from Detroit. Is it going to be on time?"

He looked at me and his face showed irritation. "It's right there on the blackboard."

"I wanted to be sure."

"You can trust the blackboard." Then he said: "Have you heard the news?"

"Yes."

"I mean about the man who shot him. They caught him. He was in a movie theater."

"I heard that, too."

He seemed disappointed that I already knew about the assassin being caught, and he turned his attention back to the TV.

I went out to the car and sat with Audrey. After a few minutes of sitting quietly she said: "That thing that happened back there at the motel."

"What thing?"

"You know."

"Yes," I said.

"I think it was just a one-time thing. Is that what you think, too?"

"Yes."

"I think it was because of the sadness. After a while you do something to fight back. To show it's not permanent."

"That's what I think, too."

A black Chevy pick-up pulled into the parking lot and nosed into the space next to us. A man got out. When he spotted us sitting in the darkness of the Pontiac he jumped a little, as if he was surprised to see people there. Then he smiled and waved to let us know that everything was all right, and I waved back.

We sat for a while in silence, just thinking our own separate thoughts. "But it was more than just the sadness," I said. "It was because of how I feel about you."

"Yes, of course. It was because of how we feel about each other."

Just then a bus pulled in and came to a stop beneath the floodlights. The folding door came open and people began coming out. My mother was the last. She stood at the edge of the parking lot and looked around, blinking from the glare of the floodlights beaming down. She was dressed in a blue cloth coat that was unbuttoned. Beneath the coat she wore the blue jeans and the gray sweater and the tennis shoes I'd seen her in that night in Grand Rapids.

"Hi, Mom," I said. I had gotten out of the car and was standing in the parking lot.

My mother turned around and squinted through the brightness. It took her a moment to see me through the glare. "Oh, there you are," she said, and she smiled.

She stepped over and we hugged. She held me for a long time, as if the hug meant more than just a greeting. Audrey had gotten out of the car and was standing behind me. My mother went over and hugged Audrey for a long time, too.

"The world's gone mad," my mother said. "I mean the news about the President."

"I wasn't sure you'd know," I said.

"A man on the bus had a transistor radio," she said. "He turned up the volume so everyone could hear. But the reception wasn't good after we got away from the cities, and the batteries died for the last half-hour. Has anything happened?"

"They caught the man who did it," I said. "But that's all I know."

Just then the bus driver opened the storage compartment underneath, where the luggage was carried. He reached in and placed the luggage on the pavement, lining up the pieces in a nice straight row. I recognized my mother's leather suitcase and I went over and picked it up.

"Okay," I said. "The car's over here."

Chapter Thirty-Nine

"We have a motel room for you," I said to my mother as we were pulling away from the bus station. "You and Audrey will stay together. Is that all right?"

"Yes, it'll be fine. I like Audrey," my mother said, though I didn't know how that could be true since she had barely met her.

"Shall I take you there now?" I asked.

"I'd like something to eat first," my mother said. "I haven't had anything since breakfast."

I drove to the Northern Lights Cafe. It was almost empty. The only customers were four men who sat at a table in the corner; they wore heavy red and black Mackinaw jackets with hunting licenses pinned to the center of their backs and they had on leather boots caked with mud. They were talking very loud and laughing.

We found a table away from the hunters and a waitress came and took our order. My mother wanted an egg salad sandwich and some tea and Audrey ordered a bowl of cottage cheese with pineapple. I ordered just a coffee. I was hungry but I didn't want to be eating while I told my mother about our new plan.

The waitress left. My mother rubbed her hands together, as if she was trying to get them warm. Then she folded them and placed them on the table.

"After you left the other day I got to thinking," she said, "and I decided I should be here when you make the arrangements about Gary. I thought it wasn't fair to leave it all up to you and Audrey." She picked up a spoon and began to examine it, turning it over and looking up close so she could see who made it. Then she set it down. "Your father didn't think that I should come," she said. "We argued about it some. So I decided to take a bus. Somehow taking a bus made it seem more like my own idea."

I learned forward and put my forearms on the table. I thought that leaning forward would be a signal to my mother that I had something important to say. My mother looked at me.

"Our plan has changed a little," I said. "About bringing Gary home."

"Oh," my mother said.

"Yes. We talked to the camp Commander this morning, but the Army won't help us. He said it was a closed subject as far as the Army was concerned and Gary should stay in their cemetery."

My mother looked at me.

"So we decided we'd do it ourselves," I said, "and we've made arrangements for that."

My mother's eyes widened. "What arrangements?" she said.

"To get Gary's coffin. We've got some people to help us. Two soldiers who'll do the digging and help with the lifting. Audrey found them. They'll meet us at the cemetery tonight at nine o'clock."

Just then the waitress brought my mother's tea. I leaned back to give her room to put it on the table.

"This is different than what I thought," my mother said after the waitress had left. And I sensed that her feelings were

223

stronger than the words she spoke; that she was trying to spare me from what she really thought about the plan. How terrible it was. "I thought the Army would do it for us." she said. "Or else we'd hire an undertaker. A professional."

"It's because the Commander won't help us," I said.

My mother started to dunk the teabag into the hot water, using little plunging motions. I could tell she didn't like our plan, and I was beginning to think differently about it too. Explaining it in words felt different than thinking about it in my mind.

"I'm not sure that doing it ourselves is the right way to do it," my mother said, and she spoke slowly, as if she were choosing her words carefully. "I appreciate your...." she paused to search for a word "....your enthusiasm....but I believe it's more complicated than you think." She stopped dunking her teabag and set it on the table where it made a little pool of water. Then she looked at me. "There are rules about...." she paused again, and I sensed that she was hardening her thoughts so she could say the next words. "There are rules about moving the deceased." She winced as if it was difficult for her to use that word for Gary.

"It's because the Commander won't help us," I said again. "That leaves us no other way."

My mother took a sip of tea. She set the cup down carefully as if it might break if she handled it too roughly. "Let's go out to the cemetery," she said. "Then we'll talk about it some more." She leaned back and looked across the restaurant at the table with the hunters. "I think Bobby needs some training," one of the men said in a loud voice, and they all laughed. "I'm not sure he knows which end of the gun the bullets come out of." And then they all laughed again, and one of them turned and looked at us and winked.

My mother turned back to me. She smiled in an encouraging way. "Let's go out to the cemetery," she said for a second time.

"Maybe I'm wrong about moving Gary. Amazing things have happened today. Things I never would've thought possible. So it's hard to know what to think anymore."

Chapter Forty

We left the Northern Lights Cafe and drove out highway 38 to where the road to Camp Carlisle branched off. No one talked. I could feel some tension in the car on account of the doubts my mother had expressed about our plan.

There were more soldiers at the entrance to the Camp than there had been in the afternoon. Besides the two guards in the guard shack there were eight or ten soldiers carrying rifles standing off to one side of the road. They were not in any formation but they held the rifles as if they were ready to use them at any moment. A little further away I saw a machine gun with a soldier seated on a stool behind it.

"What's going on?" I asked the soldier who came up to our car to check us out.

"They're reinforcements," he said. "Because of the President being shot. The Camp Commander thinks it might be the beginning of a Communist attack. So he ordered reinforcements." He nodded in the direction of the soldiers.

"Well, we're not going to attack you," I said, grinning. "I promise." I raised my right hand like I was taking an oath.

"It's not funny," the soldier said, and he gave me a stern look.

"You shouldn't make jokes on the day when the President's been killed."

"You're right," I said. "I'm sorry." Then I said: "We're going to the cemetery. My mother wants to see my brother's grave. He's Gary Walker."

I handed the pass to the guard and he tipped it toward a streetlamp so he could read it.

"Okay," he said. He handed the pass back to me. Then he leaned down so he could look across to my mother in the passenger seat. "My condolences for your loss, Mrs. Walker," he said.

"Thank you," my mother said, although she did not look back at him.

The soldier motioned to the other one to raise the gate. I drove past the reinforcing soldiers with their rifles and the machine gunner seated on his stool. I followed the road across the camp and down the dirt side road that went through the forest and then up the hill to the little cemetery. As we reached the crest of the hill, I saw an Army truck parked at the edge of the clearing. Two soldiers were standing next to the truck smoking cigarettes. I recognized them from the group we'd seen in the Northern Lights Cafe.

"This is Rusty and Jack," Audrey said, after we got out of the car. She gestured toward the soldiers who were walking over. She looked at them and smiled.

"It's very nice of you to help us," I said. I stepped forward and shook their hands and told them I was Gary's brother. "We've got shovels in the truck," Rusty said, and they started back to get them.

"Wait a minute," I said. While we had been talking my mother had walked over to the graves. She walked slowly down the rows of headstones, pausing at each one to read the inscription. When she got to Gary's grave she stopped.

"Let my mother have a few minutes alone," I said.

Rusty and Jack went back to where they had been standing and they lit up new cigarettes. Audrey and I stayed standing by the car. After a minute I walked over to where Rusty and Jack were.

"Can I have one of those cigarettes?" I said to the one called Jack.

He took a pack of Chesterfields from his breast pocket and shook it so some cigarettes poked out. I took one and leaned in his direction so he could light it with his Zippo. After the cigarette got going he snapped the lighter shut.

I breathed in some smoke and blew it out, sending a white stream out into the moonlight.

"Did you know my brother?" I asked the one called Jack.

"No. I don't think anybody did."

"What do you mean?"

"He kept to himself. He was different from the rest of us."

"What do you mean? Different."

"Just different. Like he wasn't too happy to be here. To be a soldier."

I took another puff on my cigarette. Then I held it up and looked at the burning tip, as if I was looking for something in the ash.

"Did you know he played the piano?" I said, still looking at my cigarette.

"No. I didn't know that."

"He was very talented. Like Liberace or Van Cliburn. Just as good as they are. If he'd lived he would have become a famous pianist."

"That's interesting," the soldier said.

I let some time pass before I spoke again.

"Do you know anything about the accident?" I asked. "The accident that killed my brother."

Jack inhaled some smoke and turned his head and blew it out. "What do you want to know?" he said.

"Just what happened. How the accident happened."

Jack looked at me. "There's nothing much to tell. He just stood up when he shouldn't have. The ones who saw it said he just stood up from behind the concrete barrier. He stood up when the soldiers started shooting." Jack looked at me for an instant and then he looked away. "It was almost like he wanted something to happen," he said. "Or that he didn't care if it did." He paused for a moment, holding the cigarette up near his mouth. "That's what the ones who saw it said."

"That doesn't make any sense."

"I'm just telling you what the others told me," he said. "The ones who saw it. I don't care if you believe me but that's what they said." He put the cigarette up to his mouth and drew in some smoke. Then he threw the cigarette down and ground it into the dirt with the toe of his shoe.

"I believe you," I said. "I wasn't trying to argue. I'm just surprised that that's how it happened."

I walked back to Audrey and thought about what Jack had told me. It made no sense that Gary stood up when the shooting started. There was only one way it made sense and I didn't want to think about that way.

Several minutes passed, ten or fifteen, and my mother stayed standing by Gary's grave. The soldiers came over to where Audrey and I were.

"So what's going on?" the one called Rusty said. "We can't stay out here all night."

"Okay," I said. "Let me talk to my mother."

I walked up to where my mother was standing. Her head was bowed and her eyes were closed. I tried to think of what I should say to her, what words I should use to explain that we needed to start digging up Gary's coffin, but they—the only words I could think of—all seemed too harsh. Too harsh in terms of what we planned to do with Gary.

"Have you ever taken a long bus ride, Nate?" my mother said

before I had a chance to find the right words. "I can't remember if you have. Or a train? A long train ride?"

"No, I haven't."

"It's an interesting experience. You have a long time to think while the world is passing by outside your window. Passing quickly, as if your life has speeded up." She turned and looked at me with a calm expression. "And today, being on the bus on the day the President was killed, it moved my thinking in a different direction."

I took a step forward so I could hear her better. She was speaking very softly.

There was a long pause while she said nothing, and then she said: "We can leave now." She raised her eyes and looked at me, though her face was hidden by a shadow.

"But we're going to get Gary's coffin," I said. "The soldiers are here to help us."

"No," she said. "I've changed my mind about moving him."

I waited for her to explain what was happening. Off in the distance, I heard the yip-yip-yip of a coyote, and then I heard the rustle of some small animal scrambling through the underbrush.

"This is nice," my mother said. She made a gesture toward the forest of pine trees and out to Lake Superior where you could see the moon's reflection riding on the endless stretch of water. "It's different than I thought it would be. I imagined that cemetery in France, or the one in Arlington, where they have rows and rows of white crosses and all of them are soldiers. I wouldn't want that for Gary. But this one is small...." She made a gesture toward the graves. "....and comfortable. Just a little clearing in the woods with a view out toward the water. And these...." she motioned to the other graves "....some of them are regular people. Wives and sons and daughters. Maybe someone's girlfriend. I don't know, they could be anyone. But I like that Gary's here with regular people and not just soldiers."

"But what about going out to see him," I said. "You won't be able to do that if he's up here in northern Michigan."

"That's not important. That's what I decided on the bus. He's in my mind. That's where he is now." She made another gesture toward the grave. "This is just the shell of him."

I didn't say anything because I didn't understand what she was saying. I mean I understood what she was saying but I couldn't follow the thoughts that were behind the words. When I realized she was not going to speak again, that her decision was final, I walked over to Rusty and Jack and told them we would not be doing any digging. I took out two ten-dollar bills from my wallet and handed one to each of them. "This is for your trouble," I said. "We appreciate it, even though it didn't turn out the way we thought it would."

"What about her?" Rusty said. He looked at Audrey who was standing talking with my mother. "She said she'd come out with us."

"I don't know what you're talking about."

"She said she'd come out and we'd have some fun together. There's a bar we know about that has music. She said she'd dance with us. And, you know, give us the company of a woman."

"I think there's been a misunderstanding," I said.

"I don't think so," Rusty said. "Audrey!" he shouted. She heard him and came over.

"Audrey, we're ready to have some fun now." He grinned and rubbed his hands together like he was ready for something to start. "Like we talked about at the cafe. Drinking and dancing. We're ready to do that now."

Audrey looked at me and then she looked back at Rusty. "Not now," she said. "Things have changed from when we talked. The President's been shot. I don't think we should drink and dance on a day like this."

"We kept our side of the bargain," Rusty said, and I heard

some meanness in his voice. "If you folks changed your mind it doesn't change the deal we made." He reached out and took Audrey by the arm and pulled her toward him. She pulled back.

"Hey," she said. "Stop. You're hurting me."

Rusty kept holding Audrey and she kept trying to pull away. He smiled a little, as if they were playing some strange game.

I reached out and grabbed hard on Rusty's wrist, but it made no difference; he kept holding Audrey's arm and she kept struggling to get away. So I made a fist and hit him in the face. That was all I could think of to do in the immediate moment, though it was a feeling and not a thought, to hit him with my fist and hurt him.

Rusty let go of Audrey's arm and he stumbled back but did not fall. I got ready to hit him again but Jack stepped up and grabbed my arms and held them back. Then Rusty hit me in the face and I felt an explosion of pain, more pain than I had ever felt before. And then he hit me in the stomach and I felt another explosion, and then he hit me in the face again and my legs went wobbly and I slumped down to the ground. And just before the blackness came, I remember thinking that this was how it felt to hit a man and to have him hit you back, which was something I hadn't known about before.

Chapter Forty-One

I woke up hearing my mother's voice and seeing her face above me. She was speaking my name and slapping my face lightly with her fingertips. It took me a moment to remember where I was.

"There you are," my mother said, when she saw I had come awake. "How do you feel?"

"I feel all right. My head hurts a little."

"Why don't you lie there for a moment?"

"I'm okay."

I sat up and looked around. Rusty and Jack and the truck were gone. So was Audrey. It was just my mother and myself alone in the cemetery now.

"Where'd they go?" I asked my mother.

"They left in the truck with Audrey. They said they were going to a bar. Some bar that had music."

"Did they force her to go with them?" I asked.

"No," she said. "She went with them. She wasn't happy but she wasn't upset. She didn't seem too upset."

I stood up. My mother held my arm to steady me.

"Did they say where the bar was, or what it was called?"

"No," my mother said. "It was just a bar with music."

I stood for a moment until my head cleared and I felt steady. I had the sensation of being in a forest with my mother on a hill overlooking a beautiful moonlit countryside and the endless stretch of Lake Superior, and, of course, that's exactly where I was. But there were graves. The graves made it different, but not in a particularly awful way. It was just another part of the beautiful landscape.

"I guess we should go now," I said. "There's nothing else to do here."

"I'll meet you at the car. I'll be along in just a moment."

My mother walked back to Gary's grave and stood for several minutes. I could see her lips moving and I thought she was probably saying something to Gary, even though it was just the shell of him, perhaps explaining why we were going to leave him there. Then she came over to the car and got inside and we drove back down the hill and through the forest and across the Army base and out past the guard shack.

At the motel, I carried my mother's suitcase into the room that she was going to share with Audrey, and I handed her the key.

"Okay," I said. "I guess Audrey won't be back for a while." Then I said: "I'm a little worried about her."

"Don't be," my mother said. "Audrey's a girl who can take care of herself."

I kissed my mother on the cheek and we said goodnight and I went back to my room and got undressed and into bed. But I couldn't sleep. Each time a car came into the parking lot I got up to see if it was Audrey. Finally, at about two o'clock, I heard the rumble of a truck and I went over to the window and lifted a corner of the shade. The Army truck was standing just outside my door, sending a stream of white exhaust out into the frigid air. Audrey and one of the soldiers got out. I think it was Rusty, the one who had hit me, but I could not be sure. Audrey stumbled a little stepping down from the truck and the soldier caught her so she didn't fall.

"I guess this is good-bye," the soldier said.

"I guess so," Audrey said. "Two ships passing in the night and all that. Have a good life. And your buddy, too." She waved into the truck where Jack was.

Rusty got back into the truck and it pulled away. Audrey walked unsteadily toward her room. I thought about going out and saying something to her but I didn't know what that would be. After she went into her room, I kept staring out into the empty parking lot. I don't know what I expected to see, because everything I cared about that night was over. Finally, I stopped looking and went back to bed.

Chapter Forty-Two

The next morning I woke early. The room was still in darkness. I lay in bed, watching the brightness come and thinking about the President being shot and trying to decide if it was real or something I had only dreamed about. It seemed to be the kind of thing that you would make a dream about, something that would only happen in an imaginary world, but then I remembered other details of the day and things began to fall in place and I realized that it was true.

I got up and dressed and went to the coffee shop next door and sat drinking coffee while I waited for Audrey and my mother. The sound of a radio came from back in the kitchen. A voice said that the President's body was back in Washington now and his coffin would be on display in the Capitol building and that people were already lining up to see it. I thought about Gary being in a little cemetery in a forest in northern Michigan, and I tried to decide if that was better or worse than being on display in the Capitol, and I decided that for Gary it was better, and that my mother was right to leave him there.

When my mother arrived we ordered breakfast. She was dressed in the same clothes she had worn the day before.

"Do you still feel the way you did last night?" I asked. "About Gary staying here?"

"Yes." She unfolded a napkin and placed it on her lap. "There's something special about that cemetery, even though it's very small." She took a sip of her coffee. "Gary was a special person," she said, "and it's nice that he's in a special place." She paused for a moment to stir some sugar into her coffee. "And he liked beautiful things and that's a beautiful place," she said, still stirring.

We sat for several minutes without talking. The waitress brought our food and we began to eat.

"I guess we should start driving back after breakfast," I said.

"I won't be going back right away," my mother said. "I'm going to stay here for a while."

"Stay here in Carlisle? What for?"

"I want to be alone and do some thinking. I've got to do some thinking and I've decided this is a good place to do it. There are places here where you can walk in the woods or sit on the bank of a river. Being here would help me think."

"Think about what?"

"About what comes next. What comes next for me." She paused for a moment to take a sip of coffee. "I wanted to be an architect once," she said next. "Isn't that crazy? Your mother designing buildings. I don't think I can do that now but maybe there's some other way I can help." She stopped talking and looked around the room, as if she expected to see someone that she knew. Then she turned back to me. "Maybe I can build the models that architects use to show their ideas. I used to build models when I was a girl. Airplanes and cars. Other girls didn't do that but I did and I liked it. Or maybe I can work in a hardware store where people come to get their tools. I'd like that too. Explain to people about tools. But I have to think about it."

"That's what I've been doing at the car factory," I said. "Giving out special tools to the journeymen."

237

"Is it?" she said. "That's interesting. I'd be following in your footsteps."

She looked across the restaurant to where an elderly couple was eating breakfast. The man wore faded overalls and the woman had on a flower-patterned dress. When my mother spoke again it was like she was talking to them. "Maybe it's because of what happened yesterday in Dallas. Suddenly you see how things can turn upside down in just a moment. You think your life is solid and can never change but then something happens and you realize it isn't that way at all. Everything is balanced on a narrow edge. Things can change at any time. Your life can change. Or you can change it." She reached out for her cup and took a sip of coffee.

"I think I understand," I said, because I remembered what had happened in the motel room with Audrey and how that was because of Dallas, too.

"Are you going to leave Dad?" I asked next, because I thought that was what she was going to do.

She smiled in a quiet way, as if the idea amused her. Or as if she was pleased that I could think that such a thing could actually happen.

"No. I don't think so. There's still a lot between us. A lot that holds us together. It's different than it was. It's been changed by things that have happened, but it's still there. The holding is."

Just then I saw Audrey come into the restaurant. She stood by the entrance and looked around until she spotted us and started to come over.

"I should go now," my mother said to me. "You and Audrey have to plan your trip back home."

My mother stood and began to walk away. She met Audrey coming in and they stopped for a few minutes and exchanged some words.

"What's happening?" Audrey asked as she sat down. Her face was puffy and her eyes were bloodshot.

"My mother's going to stay here for a while. And you and I are driving back to Grand Rapids."

"Your mother's staying here? Why?"

"She wants to do some thinking about how to live her life."

Audrey turned in her chair and watched my mother pass out the cafe door. "She's got a lot to learn," Audrey said. "I hope she's ready for it."

"I think she is."

Audrey picked up the menu and began to study it.

"You had quite a night," I said to her.

Audrey made a face and lowered her head like a child who expects to be scolded for bad behavior.

"Those poor boys," she said. "Those poor lonely soldier boys. They almost never get to have fun but last night they did. They took me to a bar that had music. It was only jukebox music but it was music and it was loud. And we danced. They took turns dancing with me." She smiled at the remembrance. "At first I didn't want to go, but then I decided it would be all right. Because you need to have some fun in life," she said. "You need it, don't you think? Fun. So for a while you can forget about the things that hurt you. The things you carry around that hurt." She paused for a moment, looking off to the side. Then she added: "Like the President being murdered, and....other things." She looked at me and then she looked away. "They took some liberties," she said. "The soldiers did. But it didn't amount to much."

"The magic spell a woman can cast," I said, and I tried to say it in a sarcastic way so she'd understand it was not a compliment.

"I guess so," she said, and she laughed a little. "Something like that." But then she looked at me and her face became hard. "Though I can see you don't approve. I can see it in your face. *You* took some liberties," she said, and her voice was sharp now.

239

Sharp with anger. "If you happen to recall. You took some liberties in the afternoon."

I said nothing because I didn't want to speak so close to Audrey's anger. I wanted to let a moment pass so things could settle down. And then I said: "That was different than being in a bar with music."

Just then the waitress came to take Audrey's order. She was a young woman about Audrey's age, and she wore her blond hair in a thick braid that swayed when she moved her head. Audrey forced a smile at her. "I'm afraid I'm still making up my mind," she said, and the waitress went away.

We sat without talking. Audrey was still studying the menu. After a while the anger seemed to have drained from her face. She set the menu down and looked at me.

"It was," she said. "I mean what you said about it being different in the afternoon. It was different than being in a bar with music playing." She reached across the table and touched my hand. But then her gaze drifted off to the side and I could tell that some new thought had come to her. And I believed it was about losing her baby—that that was one of the hurts she had just spoken about. And I remembered that I had to tell her the truth about that, and I needed to do it soon.

The waitress came back and Audrey and I ordered and the orders came and we ate our breakfast in silence, listening to the news reports on the radio playing in the kitchen. It seems there were rules about how you buried a President and they were going to follow the rules exactly right. There would be a procession through Washington with the casket on a special wagon pulled by six white horses and Jackie and a few distinguished people would walk behind the wagon. And there would be soldiers marching with the wagon and another horse with an empty saddle and someone would be beating a drum, but only very slowly.

AFTER BREAKFAST we went back to our rooms and packed our bags and put our things into the trunk of the Pontiac. My mother sat in a rust-spotted metal lawn chair just outside the door to her room and watched as we packed the car. The air was cold but there was no wind; little bits of snow floated down with no direction. When I finished loading my things my mother walked out to where I was standing.

"Does Dad know you're staying?" I asked her. I reached out and brushed some flakes of rust that had gotten on her arm.

"Not yet. I'll call him in a little while."

"What will he think about it?"

"I don't know."

"How long will you stay?"

"I don't know. Maybe just a day or two. Maybe a month. Maybe forever."

"It's going to get cold soon. Winter's coming." I pointed toward the gray sky where the icy snowflakes were floating down."

"I've thought of that."

"Are you afraid."

"No. Well, yes. A little maybe. But no."

Audrey finished putting her things into the trunk and my mother walked up and hugged her. She held her for a long time, and I had the same feeling I'd had when she'd hugged her in my bedroom four days earlier, of something being passed, though this time I couldn't tell which way the passing went.

Audrey and I got into the Pontiac and I started to pull away. But before I'd left the parking lot my mother called out and I stopped. She ran up to the car and leaned down. We looked at each other through the open window.

"Did you ask about how it happened?" she said. "How Gary happened to be shot on a shooting range."

I was silent for a moment. And I knew the next words I spoke would be important and I wanted to make them right. Right in terms of what was needed and not in terms of how it really was. There is truth and there is what is needed and sometimes they are not the same.

"It was an accident," I said. "Everybody said that. A soldier's gun went off by accident while Gary was changing the targets."

"Are they sure about that?" my mother asked. "That he didn't do anything himself that might've caused it to happen. A mistake he made. Or...." She paused for a moment, and when she spoke again I heard tightness in her voice. "....or even deliberate. That maybe for a moment he did something that was dangerous."

"No," I said. "That's not what they told me. It was an accident."

"Okay," my mother said. Then she said: "I'm glad it wasn't anything he did himself."

She stood up, but I sensed she wasn't finished so I didn't pull away. She looked calm and that surprised me since only a few minutes earlier she'd said she was afraid. And then I had another feeling, and I realized it was the same feeling I'd had when my father walked out of Kewpee Hamburgers, about something changing that I would never get back.

"I should have taken better care of him," my mother said.

"What?" I said. Because I was still thinking about the night at Kewpee Hamburgers.

"I should have looked out for him more. Your brother. I didn't protect him. Not enough."

I didn't say anything.

Chapter Forty-Three

I had one more thing to do—tell Audrey what really happened to her baby—and I knew it would be hard and I did not want to do it. I had decided I would do it before we got to the Mackinaw bridge. There was no particular reason I had to do it by then, but I thought a deadline would help, even if it was just a made-up deadline.

Audrey and I had been on the road for a couple of hours and we were on the highway that took you to the bridge. The highway ran close beside the shore of Lake Michigan. Between the birch and hemlock trees I caught glimpses of big waves crashing against the rocky shore.

Audrey was listening to the radio, tuning to different stations in the hope of hearing something different about the President. Suddenly there was an interruption and the announcer said the man who'd shot the President had been shot himself. He was being walked from the police station to a van that would take him to another jail and someone stepped out from the crowd and shot him. We listened to the announcement, but we didn't say anything. It seemed like just another crazy thing that had happened along with all the rest.

I waited a few minutes after the announcement ended. I wanted the craziness to subside a little.

"Audrey," I said. "There's something I need to tell you."

She turned off the radio and turned and looked at me.

"That night when I went into your parent's house to get the christening dress."

"Yes."

"There were some papers on the refrigerator door. They were held up with magnets. You know how people use those little magnets to hold papers on a refrigerator door. Photographs and bills and grocery lists. Papers like that."

I stopped talking for a moment to change my thinking, because I knew the magnets were not important and I was only using them to take up time.

"Well, one of the papers was a letter from a place called the St. Paul Home. It was in Detroit." I stopped talking for a moment to gather more courage. "And it said that everything about the baby was fine and they were going to place him with a nice family."

I glanced over at Audrey. She was staring straight ahead.

"It's an orphanage, Audrey," I said. "The St. Paul Home is. Your baby didn't die. Your parents lied to you about that. They gave the baby to an orphanage." I looked at Audrey. Her hands were on her lap and clasped together, the knuckles white.

"Stop the car," she said in a quiet voice.

"What?"

"Please stop the car."

I slowed the Pontiac and pulled off onto the shoulder of the road. I turned off the engine because I thought we would be stopped there for a while.

"We can go there," I said. "Go to Detroit. Now. Instead of going right back to Grand Rapids. We can go there and get your baby."

A semi-truck passed and the air blast rocked the car a little.

"Are you the devil?" Audrey said, in a voice that seemed too quiet.

"What?"

"Are you the devil who's been sent to torture me?"

"I don't know what you're talking about."

Audrey looked down at her tightly clasped hands. She sat like that for a while. And then she suddenly turned and lunged at me, slapping me and hitting me with her fists. I tried to protect myself but she kept hitting. And then I put my arms around her so her arms were pinned against her sides. Inside my strange embrace I felt her body heaving and her heart pounding strongly in her chest. Finally, she stopped struggling. I still held her.

"Okay," she said, after a quiet moment had passed. "You can let me go. I'm all right now. I'm back to normal."

I opened my arms. Audrey pushed away and moved back over to the passenger's side. She sat for a while, looking out at the water being thrown against the rocks.

"I know it," she said.

"What?"

"I know where my baby is. At that place in Detroit. We sent him there."

I didn't say anything.

"What else could I do?" she said, still looking out at the crashing water. "I didn't have any money and I didn't have a husband and my parents said they wouldn't help."

I didn't speak.

"I hate myself for doing it. For giving away my baby. Don't you think I hate myself? I hate myself for that. That's why I ran away. I wanted to live in a new place where I could be a different person and do things better. Start over. Like Audrey Hepburn started over in the movie."

"Maybe you can change your mind," I said. "The baby's still at the St. Paul Home. According to the letter he's still there.

We can go there and you can get him back. We can do it today."

Audrey looked at me. There was no expression on her face. With no expression her face looked different.

A long time passed while neither of us spoke. Finally, I started the engine and pulled back out onto the highway. A minute later we were on the bridge and we began the long gentle climb to the center. The tires hummed against the steel grating, and the suspension cables flashed by, a blur of thick black stranded steel. Up ahead we could see the northern tip of the giant peninsula that was the lower half of Michigan.

"When we get to the other side, I'll need to know which way to go," I said. "Two highways branch off; the right one goes to Grand Rapids and the left one goes to Detroit. I need to know which one to take."

Audrey stayed quiet, just looking out at the cables flashing by. Down below, Lake Michigan looked cold and threatening. An iron ore carrier was struggling to make it through the passage. It was November, the most dangerous time for storms out on the lakes.

"Audrey," I said. We were almost across the bridge.

She stayed quiet.

"Audrey, you need to tell me which way to turn."

"You decide," she said in a voice that had no life behind it. "You do the thinking for me. Like Ilsa said to Rick in *Casablanca*."

I swung right, though I couldn't tell you why. It was just an instinct, like how you make a painting.

I glanced over at Audrey. She was staring out the passenger's window. I don't think she even knew which way I'd turned.

CHAPTER FORTY-FOUR

We drove all day, only stopping for gas, and made it to Grand Rapids at midnight. During the first part of the trip we had listened to the radio and the news reports about the President. Important people were saying how sad it was that he'd been murdered and what a wonderful President he'd been and how much he would be missed. At some point, a voice broke in to say that the man who had shot him was dead now, too. He had died from the bullet wound from the man who had shot him in the police garage. When the announcement was finished, Audrey and I looked at each other as if we were trying to decide whether the news was worth talking about, but then we both looked away. Everything about the assassination seemed crazy and tragic and sad. There was nothing to be gained from talking about it further, no insight or understanding, nothing you could say to make sense of it or to make it fit into a larger pattern of how life should be.

As we came into Grand Rapids, I suddenly remembered we had no place to stay. I had been kicked out of the house on Fulton Street and Audrey had checked out of the Arlington Hotel and I had thrown away the key.

"What do you think we should do?" I asked Audrey.

"Let's sleep in the car like we did before?" she said. "Then we can figure out something tomorrow."

I thought about everything that had happened on our trip to northern Michigan. Sleeping in the car didn't seem like the right way to end it.

"No," I said. "We still have money. We didn't spend that much. Let's go to a hotel. A nice one."

I drove downtown to the Pantlind Hotel, because that was the one my father had wanted to have dinner in, in the Timber Barons' Room, on the night he came to talk to me about college. When I drove up under the portico a man wearing a red uniform with gold braids and a shiny visored cap came out to take my duffle bag and Audrey's cardboard box. He looked at us, at the clothes we were wearing and at the mud-splattered Pontiac Star Chief. As we walked up to the front desk he came along behind us. The man at the front desk looked at me and then at Audrey. I was wearing the rumpled khaki clothes I wore at the factory, and Audrey was wearing the blue jeans and sweatshirt she'd started out in four days earlier.

"Are you sure you're in the right place, buddy?" the man said with a smirk. And I knew we'd been insulted. Even though we were only looking for a place to spend the night, which we had every right to do, we'd been insulted, and I felt a flash of anger, and for a moment I wanted to hit the man, just like I'd hit Rusty in the cemetery the night before, because now I knew I could do it. But as quickly as the feeling came it went away; I already knew it was impossible to act on every outrage. There would always be too many.

"Yes," I said to him. "I'm certain."

"Okay. It's your money, bud." He looked down at a piece of paper. "We've got one room left. With a double bed."

I looked at Audrey and she shrugged.

"Okay," I said. "That's fine."

I signed us in as Nathan Walker and Audrey Brubaker, because now I knew we did not have to hide who we really were.

"Should we look at the news on TV?" I asked Audrey, after the bellhop had taken us to our room and we had given him a dollar and he had gone away. "Maybe something else has happened about the President."

"No," Audrey said. "I've heard enough."

"I guess I have, too."

I was very tired and so I got undressed and into bed. Audrey did the same. And then we lay there, side by side, both awake, looking up at the high ceiling which had angels and storm clouds painted on the plaster.

Audrey moved a little on her side of the bed. And then, after a little more time had passed, she said, "I lied to you. I lied to you about my baby and I lied about a lot of other things. I'm sorry."

"It's okay. It's fine."

"I lied to myself too. Maybe that's the worst part." Her voice wavered as she spoke, then she took a deep breath and continued. "After I gave my baby away it was like something broke inside me. Maybe it's still broken. That might be true."

Again we lay in silence. I thought of different things to say but nothing seemed exactly right. Not right for what was needed in that particular moment.

Finally, I said the only thing I was certain about.

"But not the painting," I said. "You didn't lie to me about my painting. The advice you gave. How I could do it better. How I could think like an artist. That was true."

"Yes," she said. "That was true."

Out in the hallway, an elevator door opened and then came together with a soft pneumatic sigh. Traffic noises rose from the streets below, a faint muffled roar. And then without speaking we moved together to the center of the bed so that our bodies touched, but only slightly. I did not feel romantic, but I wanted to feel the nearness of someone I cared about and who cared for me. And I believe Audrey felt the same.

Chapter Forty-Five

The next morning I dropped Audrey off at the Arlington Hotel with her suitcase and her cardboard box and my painting of the abandoned furniture factories. She was convinced she could get her room back, could use her feminine wiles to persuade the hotel manager to forget she had left without giving notice.

Next, I drove to the house on Fulton Street and I apologized with great sincerity to Mr. and Mrs. Thatcher for all that I'd done wrong, and in the end they said I could have my room back, as long as I promised to obey all the rules this time.

❦

IN THE FOLLOWING days I got back into my old routine—going to work at the car factory and painting in the afternoons and sometimes walking in the zoo at night. But I didn't go to the zoo in the afternoons to meet girls who would let me hold their hand and sometimes be affectionate. That was over, though I didn't know exactly why. But later, after I had thought about it, I decided it had something to do with the lesson I'd learned the year before from Diane, but had not learned completely: that girls are just another type of human being—another type from men—and deserve the same regard.

My mother stayed at Sandi's Motel in Carlisle for about three weeks. During that time she became good friends with Babs and even helped out at the registration desk on some afternoons. I received several letters from her, and once a phone call. She said in different ways what she had told me in the cemetery: that things were looking better for her, becoming clearer, and that soon she would figure out a new plan for her life. And then during the middle days of December she returned to my father and the house in the Detroit suburb. When the new year began she enrolled in a course in architectural drafting at the community college. She believed that would bring her close —close enough—to the work she had wanted to do ever since she'd been a girl.

Audrey said I would see her at my painting spot by the river but she did not come by, and I was not surprised by that. Too much had happened on our trip to Camp Carlisle for our friendship to continue in the easy way it had before. Occasionally, I would see her at a distance on a downtown street, walking with a man who wore a suit and a tie and shiny leather shoes, making gestures toward the buildings and the statues and the street signs.

In the meantime, I kept painting, though now I did it in a practiced and deliberate way, not changing the color or the shape of things to make a message, but only trying to paint a scene exactly as I saw it and exactly as it was. I knew now that I'd never find Van Gogh's passion, but it—that failure—didn't seem to matter. The world as it existed was enough. For me and for that time it was enough. I didn't need to change it to make it interesting or to find out what was true.

Chapter Forty-Six

But I had one more thing to learn.
A few days after Christmas, I was awakened in the night by Mr. Thatcher. He was standing in the doorway of my room in his pajamas.

"There's a phone call for you, Nate," he said.

I looked at the alarm clock on the bedside table. It said 12:37.

"Who is it?"

"It's a girl. She didn't give her name."

I went and took the phone from Mr. Thatcher. I could tell he was upset for being awakened in the middle of the night, and I knew in the morning I would need to have a good explanation. I waited until he was back in his room and the door was closed before I spoke into the phone.

"Yes," I said. "Hello."

I heard a kind of sob. Then Audrey's voice.

"Can you come and get me?" she said. "Can you do that now?"

"Audrey, where are you? What's going on?"

"I had an accident. I don't think I can make it home by myself."

"What kind of accident?"

"It doesn't matter. It was just something that happened."

"Where are you?"

"I'm in the lobby of the Saxony Hotel. Please come."

"Of course. Of course I'll come to help you. But should I bring someone? A doctor or the police?"

"No," she said. "It's not like that. Just get here quickly."

I went back into my room and got dressed. When I came out into the hallway Mr. Thatcher was standing there.

"We can't have this sort of thing, Nate. Girls calling in the middle of the night. We've talked about this before."

"The girl is a friend of mine," I said. "She's in trouble and needs help." I looked at him, and for a moment I felt the same flash of anger I'd felt when checking in at the Pantlind Hotel, because I was not meaning to trouble him in any way but only trying to help a friend.

"It won't happen again," I said.

"It better not," Mr. Thatcher said, and he went back into his bedroom.

When I got to the Saxony Hotel, the man behind the desk called out as I was walking across the lobby. "Hold on, young man," he said. "Where do you think you're going?"

"I'm meeting someone."

"Are you here about the girl?" He looked down at a piece of paper on the counter. "Audrey? Is that the girl you're here about?"

"Yes."

"She's over there." He pointed to a shadowy corner of the lobby where there were three big upholstered chairs. "She walked in from the street about an hour ago," he said, "pretty badly beat up. We told her to call someone to pick her up and to wait over there in the corner where our guests wouldn't see her."

"I'll take care of her now," I said. I started to turn away.

"Wait a minute," the man said. He came around from behind the counter and walked up close to me. "We've seen her here before," he said. "That girl. In the lobby in the afternoon. But she's not been registered. She's never been a guest here." He looked at me as if he'd said enough for me to understand.

"Isn't that all right?" I said. "If she's in the lobby."

"If she's not a guest that needs to stop."

"But isn't the lobby a public place? Where people are allowed to come and go?"

"Don't argue with me, son. We know what she's up to. If we see her here again we'll call the police."

"But I don't see how it could hurt anybody. She runs a kind of guide service. She's just looking for customers who want to take a walking tour of the city."

The man pulled his head back sharply, as if recoiling from the nonsense he'd just heard. "Well, if you believe that then I've got a bridge in Brooklyn I want to sell you," he said with a smirk.

I looked at him, and at first I thought he meant the walking tours, how improbable that was as a business enterprise, but then I realized he meant something else. And suddenly I felt nervous, because I knew I had to make a choice. Between what Audrey had told me in the Starlight Lounge and what the desk clerk said. And what I decided in that moment is that sometimes truth is not as important as what it does to people, the consequences it leaves behind. And I realized, too, that I'd grown to love Audrey in a peculiar way, not a boyfriend's love but something simpler and more direct, a love without adornment, stripped down to the essentials.

I looked at the desk clerk. He still had that simpering smile on his face.

"You're wrong about that," I said to him, and I turned and walked away.

I went over to the corner of the lobby. Audrey was asleep in one of the big upholstered chairs. Her dress was torn around the buttonholes and bruises were on both arms.

I knelt and placed my hand on her arm. Her eyes flashed open and she tried to pull away.

"Oh, Nate," she said, when she saw it was me. Slowly her expression changed into a kind of drowsy smile.

"Audrey, what happened?"

She raised herself in the chair, slowly, as if it took great effort. Then she looked off toward the ceiling and squinted. "Mr. Sheldon," she said. "That was the gentleman's name. Charlie Sheldon. Except he wasn't much of a gentleman. He was a lawyer from Lansing who'd finished a big case and he wanted to celebrate."

"Did he get fresh with you?" I said, and I tried to say it with conviction. "Is that what happened?"

Audrey looked at me. Across the lobby the bellhop and the night manager were watching us. The manager leaned in close and said something to the bellhop that made him laugh.

"Yes," Audrey said. "That's what happened. It was like you warned me about. He tried to get fresh."

"You've got to be more careful about choosing your customers."

"Yes. I know. I'll try."

She stood up, pushing hard against the chair. I held her arm to steady her and we walked across the lobby and out through the big brass doors to the Pontiac I had left parked under the overhang. I helped Audrey into the car and then I drove through the dark empty streets to the Arlington Hotel. Audrey was angled in the corner, her head resting against the side window. Her eyes were closed. I thought she had gone to sleep but when we got to the Arlington Hotel she roused herself and sat up.

"I'm better now," she said. "I believe I can make it to my room without assistance."

"I'm worried about you. Are you going to be all right?"

"Of course. Why wouldn't I be?"

"I don't know. I guess it was a stupid question. Of course you'll be all right."

We sat together for a while. Outside the car, an old man in a trench coat came walking down the sidewalk leading a large black dog. When they came alongside us the big dog began to bark ferociously, lunging at the car. The old man held him back. Then he yanked viciously on the leash and the dog whimpered and came back along beside him and they passed on.

"I'm going to the university in Ann Arbor," I said. "They told me I could start in January. I've saved enough to get through the first semester. After that, there are jobs I can do to earn money. Washing dishes in the Union is one they mentioned. There are others, too."

"I'm glad. That's where you should be."

"Come with me," I said, and I reached across and took her hand. "They have an art school there. You can learn about furniture design." I smiled. "Maybe we can wash dishes together."

"That would be nice, wouldn't it?" Audrey said. "But no. I'll stay here and keep working on my plan. Giving tours and learning things in hallways and reading Dale Carnegie." She paused, staring off to the side. "I think it's working," she said, "My plan is." She nodded slowly. "One of my designs won a prize at the Kendell school. I guess I forgot to tell you that. They didn't find out I wasn't a registered student until after they'd done the judging and by then it was too late to take it back."

"That's great. I know you'll be a great success."

Again we fell back into silence. I think we both knew this might be the last time we saw each other, and we didn't quite know how to end it. Finally, Audrey reached out and grasped the door handle. She opened the door and put one foot down onto the pavement.

"Audrey," I said. She turned back, half inside the car and half outside. I tried to think of something to say that would make the moment feel special but no special words came to mind. Finally, I said the only thing I could think of.

"Thank you for teaching me about painting."

"I didn't teach you very much."

"You taught me a lot."

She looked at me. Her face had no expression. But then she smiled. But only slightly.

"Okay," she said. "Thank you. I'm glad."

She turned away and stepped down onto the pavement. I watched until she was through the hotel door and then I drove away.

Chapter Forty-Seven

I cruised around the city for a while. The streets were empty, like in the movie about atomic war. I drove to the house on Fulton Street, but I wasn't ready to go back to bed so I walked over to the zoo and squeezed in through the opening in the chain-link fence behind the Monkey Island. And as I walked among the sleeping animals I remembered the photograph of a girl with a radiant smile and a yellow dress and a beloved boyfriend holding tight against her side. And then I thought of later, after she'd been betrayed by the boy and was waiting in her parents' house to have her baby, watching old black-and-white movies on TV while her parents hid her from the town and made her feel ashamed. And I thought about how she'd made a plan that would take her to a better life, and how she'd improbably built that plan around a character in a movie, and a self-improvement guidebook, and lessons learned by listening through doors that were closed to her. And in spite of everything she still pressed on, convinced that a better life was waiting out there for her, if she could just keep going.

A movement in a nearby cage caught my eye. I walked over

and peered through the steel bars. A Bengal tiger, barely visible in the gloom, paced nervously back and forth. When he saw me, he stopped pacing and stared back, not with menace but with curiosity.

I began to walk again. And now my thoughts broadened and went further: to my brother, a pianist who'd been sent off to be a soldier, abiding in a pine-board casket in the far north woods of Michigan; and to my mother, sitting on a riverbank trying to recapture the person she'd longed to be as a girl; and to my father, a man who gave up things he loved for the sake of his career.

In the distance a light appeared, faint and moving closer. A watchman with a flashlight was walking over.

"What are you doing here?" He shined the flashlight onto my face so I had to squint against the glare.

"Nothing. Just out for a walk."

"The zoo is closed. You're not supposed to be here."

"I thought it would be all right. If I wasn't causing any trouble, I thought it would be all right."

"Well, it's not. It's against the rules. You have to leave."

"But I'm not causing any harm. I just like to walk among the animals at night."

The watchman pointed outside the fence.

"Get out," he said.

I began to walk away. But then I stopped and turned around.

"No," I said.

"What?"

"I'm going to stay a while longer."

"I'll call the police."

"Do whatever you have to do."

I watched him walk away. And then I headed toward the field where the giraffes were kept. Sometimes they would come out at night and it was nice to see their peculiar shapes moving gracefully in the moonlight. It was a scene that would make a great painting. I knew that now. If someone could do it right, it would make a great painting.

About the Author

Donald Lystra is an engineer and writer whose work has been praised for the strong emotions captured in its quiet understated prose. His debut novel, *Season of Water and Ice,* was selected for a gold medal in the Midwest Book Awards competition and named a Michigan Notable Book by the Library of Michigan. His second book, a short story collection entitled *Something That Feels Like Truth,* was also selected for a gold medal in the Midwest Book Awards and named a Michigan Notable Book.

Lystra has received creative writing fellowships from the National Endowment for the Arts and the MacDowell Colony, where he was honored with the Gerald Freund award for emerging writers. He and his wife divide their time between a farm in northern Michigan and a small town on the Atlantic coast of Florida. He has two adult children.

facebook.com/donaldlystraauthor
amazon.com/author/donaldlystra

Also by Donald Lystra

Season of Water and Ice
Something That Feels Like Truth

Made in the USA
Columbia, SC
28 March 2025